Island No. 6

Ty Roth

Author of the acclaimed novel, *Goodness Falls*

First Edition Design Publishing
Sarasota, Florida USA

Island No. 6
Copyright ©2020 Ty Roth

ISBN 978-1506-909-31-8 PBK
ISBN 978-1506-909-32-5 EBK

LCCN 2020909676

June 2020

Published and Distributed by
First Edition Design Publishing, Inc.
P.O. Box 17646, Sarasota, FL 34276-3217
www.firsteditiondesignpublishing.com

"We are all innocent."
Our Lady Peace

The Lake Erie Islands and Ohio Coast

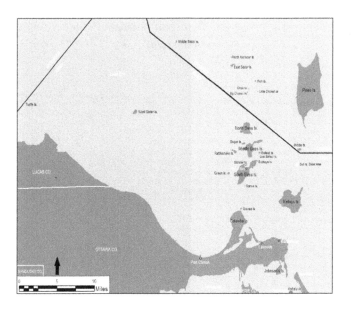

Kelleys Island

Foreword

A WARNING

"This is not hyperbole. In 1997 the world came perilously close to another global epidemic of the 'flu.' If this particular virus had attained the ability to spread from person to person, the pandemic might have taken the lives of a third of the human population. As it was, only six people died – and all of them had contracted the virus from chickens sold in Honk Kong poultry markets. The only thing that saved us was the quick thinking of scientists who convinced health authorities to slaughter more than a million domesticated fowl in the city's markets. The avian virus turned out to be a new strain – one that the human population had never seen before. These deadly new strains arise a few times every century, and the next one may arrive any day now."

Robert G. Webster and Elizabeth Jane Walker
from the article "Influenza" as it appeared in the
American Scientist, vol. 91, 2004.

Prologue

*May 30, 209_*

Tomorrow will be my one hundredth birthday. There was a time when that would have been worthy of a celebration, but with the average life expectancy fast approaching, it's nothing special. In fact, there are nearly as many centenarians today as there are teenagers and even a few among the One Percenters who claim to be immortal.

We'll see.

It's quite sad really.

What does make me special is what happened the week of my eighteenth birthday. A girl I knew then described me as "the kind that lives to tell the story." I didn't much care for her characterization at the time, but it turns out she was right. Frankly, it has taken me this long because I've been afraid. I saw some things that week that I didn't care to remember, and I did some things that I'm not proud to admit. But please, do not think me courageous in my telling. Old men lose the privilege of doing the right thing and calling it courageous.

You may not think so at eighteen or twenty-eight or thirty-eight or forty-eight, but even at one hundred, life remains precious, and you don't want to forfeit a day of it if you don't have to. Even now, after all these years, if they discover that I'm alive and that I intend to tell my story, I have no doubt that they will take all measures to silence me. If believed, what I am about to reveal will require a reexamination of a portion of American history and the vilification of those who conspired to erase and rewrite it. An already black eye will be made much blacker.

The reality is that my story will most likely never be read. Even if it is, it will be thought fiction, or I will be accused of misremembering or be thought mad. With no other witness or a single shred of physical evidence to corroborate my version of events, I can't blame my doubters.

At least I will have tried.

After my eighteenth birthday, I spent fifty-two years working the decks of Great Lakes freighters, moving coal, iron ore, grain, and salt. In my free time, I regularly read from a chest of books I'd accumulated and stowed on board every ship I worked and which served as a sort of ship's library until they stopped printing books sometime around the mid-century. Those books have been my most prized possessions.

When my hands could no longer pull their weight on deck, I spent fifteen more shipping seasons cooking in galleys. In all those years, I had no family, few friends, no driver's license, and no permanent address. None of my shipmates even knew my real name. They all just called me Fluke; although, after the first few years, none of them knew why.

Since they declared Island No. 6 safe once more for habitation just fifteen years ago and reopened it for settlement under its former name of Kelleys Island, I've lived here under the phony name I've used for eighty-two years. I keep to myself like the native born Kelleys Islander I am and of which I am the last, but every day of these past fifteen years spent on this limestone rock in Lake Erie, I've retraced again and again the paths I traveled during that week that wasn't. In my imagination, I've repeatedly relived every moment and conjured reluctant memories and images – some pleasant, most not – which I'd recorded and preserved in my mind for this day, the day on which I will finally tell that one week's story I promised that girl I'd someday share all those years ago.

My real name is Danny Foe, and this is the story of Island No.6.

Chapter One

*Day 1 – Friday, May 24, 201_*

"If you hurry, you might make the two o'clock," the matronly attendant inside the ticket booth said as she handed me an assortment of grimy coins in change.

"Thanks. I think I will."

I pulled the straps of my backpack tight, picked up my black canvas sea bag, threw it over my shoulder, and took off in a lopsided sprint toward the opened maw of the large passenger, car, and freight ferry bound for Kelleys Island, the largest of the Lake Erie islands in American and Ohio waters. The sea bag was a high school graduation gift from my sister-in-law. She said it would make a perfect laundry bag. I took her observation as a less-than-subtle hint that it was time for me to move out of the smallish house I'd shared with her and my brother for the past ten years and their twin daughters for the past five.

It was a downhill run to the loading platform over the crunch and through the nauseating stench of rotting mayflies or what my grandfather called Canadian soldiers. The water-born insects infested the islands and the nearby Ohio shore every spring. That May the swarms had been particularly thick.

During their pathetic twenty-four hours or so of life, they bred, rose, formed thick clouds, and rode lake breezes toward the nearest street, storefront, and/or parking lot lights. There they died in the gazillions.

Beneath a sunny and mostly cloudless sky, the Lake's waters dampened the light northwesterly wind. The winter had been mild. The Lake had remained unfrozen from Detroit in the west to Buffalo in the east so that the water was unusually warm for late May, and it already felt like summer all along America's North Coast.

Impatient to begin the bounce-back trip from the mainland, the ferry's engines rumbled inside its steel hull and commanded me to hurry if I hoped to make that 2 o'clock crossing.

I recognized the old salt of a deckhand who reached for the lever to raise the ramp. "Cleats!" I called. "Cleats, wait!"

He stood facing me with his back to the island and to the South Passage, the three mile wide strait of fast current that separated Kelleys Island from the ferry's mainland dock on the Marblehead Peninsula and also from the normalcy of mainland living. Cleats raised his hand to the frayed bill of his faded green ball cap in a sort of salute, which blocked out the sun still high to his right.

"Who's that?" Cleats asked through a piercing, blue-eyed squint that forced the creases and cracks on his weather-beaten face to reveal themselves dark and deep.

"It's me. Danny Foe."

"Who?"

"Danny Foe. You remember me. Jimmy and Alison Foe were my parents. I used to ride with you in the engine room."

The captain's blast of the ferry's horn prompted the old man to signal a thumbs up towards the wheelhouse and to raise the south-facing loading ramp. With ramps on both ends, the ferry had been christened *Janus* for the two-faced Roman God of portals and, therefore, of both beginnings and ends. The horn blast seemed to jar Cleats's memory, for when he returned from a slow inspection tour to ensure all was ship-shape on deck, he said, "Why, I haven't seen ya in," he paused to do the math.

"Ten years," I interrupted his calculations.

"Ten years," he repeated. "Not since that fire killed your folks." In his gruff and tactless old age, Cleats would have made a terrible Wal-Mart greeter. "Where've ya been, kid?"

"On the mainland. Living with my brother's family in Port Clinton."

"What brings ya home?"

"I graduated from high school last night and I start college in the fall. Until then, I'm working and living on the island."

"Do ya want to ride in the engine room like ya used ta?"

"No thanks," I said. "I'm going to stay here on deck and take in the air. I think I may have lost my sea legs and stomach. That engine room might be more than I'm ready to handle."

"Ahhh," Cleats said with a wave of both of his hands. "You're a born islander. It's in your blood. We never lose our sea legs."

"Still. I think I'll ride this one from the rail."

"Suit yourself. You know where ya can find me if ya change your mind."

"I do. It's good to see you again, Cleats."

He leaned in close and lowered his voice. "Ya might want to keep your eye on that one." He nodded towards a young man positioned beneath the starboard side gunwale who was either doing yoga or praying to Allah. Facing east toward Cleveland in a bent knee position with his arms slightly before him, palms pressed to the rug lying beneath him, and apparently kissing the deck, the dark-haired, olive-skinned young man chanted. I'm sure, however, that it sounded more like demonic gibberish to his Midwestern shipmates, whose provincial eardrums it stabbed like an ice pick.

Cleats harrumphed, turned around, tucked his chin against

his chest, and leaned forward on his bowlegs in order to balance himself against the slight pitch and roll of the ferry, then he disappeared inside the engine room at mid-ship.

A ring of the curious and the xenophobic gathered around the young man of clear Middle Eastern descent. The crowd was a mixed mob of islanders returning from errands on the mainland, day trippers, a few pre-season weekend partiers, and a large group of mostly middle-aged birders identifiable by their bush hats, the high-powered binoculars draped around their necks, and the field notebooks nosing out of various pockets. The smattering of islands in Erie's Western Basin were then popular stopovers for many species of migratory birds and for the human flocks of birdwatchers from around the world who ogled them. May was the peak season when nearly every restaurant, bar, and hotel along the western Lake Erie shoreline declared "Welcome Birders!" on their signage. This disparate group of ferry passengers, temporarily united in their suspicions and fears of what they did not understand, were slowly tightening the circle around the young man, who, at least to all appearances, remained oblivious or indifferent to their menace.

I scanned the deck for someone in authority to intervene, but Cleats's two crewmates had apparently joined him in the engine room, and I could see the captain's back, inside the wheel- house on the bridge, turned to the rising hostility on deck.

A small fraternity of college-aged boys in tight-fitting t-shirts, baggy and frayed cargo shorts, flip-flops, and all holding cans of opened beers climbed out of a silver Range Rover Sport, packed with camping and partying supplies, and infiltrated the circle.

"Hey, Mohammed," one of them said, "why don't you take that mumbo-jumbo back to Iraq?"

"Yeah, Aladdin," another said. "Do us all a favor and fly away on that magic carpet." His witticism sparked a round of fist bumps from his friends.

"Let's throw the goat-fucker overboard," a third, sporting a crew cut and with biceps the size of my thighs, said in a tone empty of even the slightest hint of humor or facetiousness.

The devotee remained oblivious to the insults and continued to pray.

I watched a mother cover her child's ears and remove her from the mob, but she made no show of going for help.

Having finished his prayer, the young man rose, jutted his bearded jaw directly into the face of the crew cut, and stared him in the eyes. "Try it," he said.

In the very instant that the crew cut initiated his move, a simultaneous blast from the ferry's horn froze his fist.

All eyes turned to the bridge, where behind the rising steam from his coffee cup, the captain stood glaring authoritatively at the unseemly proceedings until all dispersed like chastised children on a playground. For a long moment, the young man stood alone on his rug locked in a visual embrace with the captain. No show of appreciation was sought; none was given.

After rolling up his prayer rug and securing it under his arm, he threw a book bag over his shoulder, extracted the retractable handle from his suitcase, wheeled it in my direction, and passed me before leaning his arms on top of the portside rail and staring off towards the west.

I slid out of my backpack and set it next to my duffel bag on the grey steel deck. Dozens of expectant gulls flew circles over and occasionally dive bombed into the ferry's wake in which a feast of bait fish were being churned up for the obnoxious birds' easy-pickings.

On an elevated deck beneath the pilot house, a single bench for passengers bisected the ferry and ran nearly its entire length. Near the top of the stairs, a dark-haired girl sat alone. Her ponytail spilled through the adjustable opening in the back of a baseball hat, and her button nose was deep inside a book. I recognized her immediately.

"No way," I said to myself.

I'd been in love with Daphne Moyer since the first day of the fourth grade. However, no matter how many different ways I tried, I could never convince her to think of me as more than a friend. I joked with her a lot about going on a date, but Daphne never seemed to sense the seriousness behind my teasing.

Her mother was one-half of the formerly husband-and-wife co-owners of the Moyer Real Estate Agency. Mrs. Moyer's big hair, high-arched eyebrows, and heavily made-up face graced for sale signs and billboards all over the coastline of north central Ohio and its islands. For years, the Moyers had ruled over Port Clinton's social elite and lived in its largest and one of its oldest homes: a majestic stone mansion along the shore of Lake Erie on Perry Street. Despite its grand façade, the interior of the house was a constant fixer-upper. As it turned out, so was the Moyers' marriage. After their divorce just prior to my and Daphne's senior year, the former Mr. and Mrs. Moyer divvied up of their personal assets and their only daughter. Mrs. Moyer received full-time custody of Daphne but barely enough money to pay the mortgage and nowhere near enough to complete the almost-constant upkeep the house required. Her father liquidated as many of his belongings as he could, moved to Key West, and hadn't been home since.

Neither of her parents much cared for me or my humble island origins. Once, when I was on the phone with Daphne, I overheard Mrs. Moyer refer to me as "that orphaned island boy."

That afternoon, when the shuttle bus had driven east on Perry Street on the way to the Kelleys Island ferry, Mrs. Moyer's face smiled at me from one of her for sale signs, and for the first time, I had smiled back without making plans to return with a Sharpie to take out a tooth, to blacken an eye, or to doodle a dick on top of her head.

I pulled myself up to the passenger deck using both hand rails and climbed the metal stairs, where Daphne sat cross-legged and lightly bouncing her foot from which a pink flip flop hung precariously between pink toenails. She was either so engrossed in her novel that she didn't see me coming, or she saw me coming and pretended to be engrossed in her novel.

"*The Last Man,*" I read the title of her book out loud.

Daphne didn't even bother to look up. "As in, I would go out with you only if you were the 'last man' on Earth, Danny Foe."

"I can live with those odds," I said.

She dropped her hands to her lap. "You are such a dork."

"Who wrote it?"

"Mary Shelley."

"Like, Mary Shelley *Frankenstein*?" I said, lifting my arms and wobbling back and forth from foot to foot in imitation of the monster.

"Yes," she said brusquely, but my impersonation had managed to pry loose a tiny smile. "Sit down, stupid. It's for my first semester lit course on apocalyptic fiction." Daphne was a decidedly-declared English major.

"That sounds cheery," I said.

"Don't be sarcastic, Danny," she chastised me. "It doesn't flatter you. Anyway, I can't wait for college. I emailed my professor for the syllabus. I'm going to read every book on the reading list this summer. I picked up the first three at the library on my way to the ferry."

"Only you would do that, Daph. What's it about?"

"It's a plague story and a mash up of socio-political allegory and a medieval romance."

"All in one book? Sounds interesting!" I said with the sarcasm dripping.

"It is," Daphne insisted. "It makes you wonder how you would live in this moment if you knew your next healthy breath may be your last one."

"Tell me more."

"Okay. But, remember. You asked."

"I accept full responsibility," I said with mock seriousness.

"It's about freedom."

"What kind of freedom?"

"I don't know," she said a little exasperated. "Freedom, freedom. Like being able to make your own choices." She looked out from beneath the bill of the ball cap that shaded her sea-green eyes and impossibly-high, crabapple-shaped cheeks. The breeze caused her to continually corral and brush back wisps of her long, brown hair that the hat couldn't contain.

"Like freedom from dictators and shit?" I asked.

"Is this going to be another joke about the president?" she asked. Daphne's mother was the chairperson of the Ottawa County Republican Party.

"No.   I   promise." "Then, yeah. Dictators or governments in general. But also from the rules and demands of parents and society. Even from regular people who try to control your life, you know? Like bullies or boyfriends."

"Speaking of assholes, how is Derek?"

"Stop. Derek's not an asshole."

"He hit you!"

"He didn't hit me. He grabbed me. There's a difference. He didn't even mean to hurt me."

"Tell that to the bruises."

Daphne crossed her arms and covered the ghosts. "That was weeks ago. Besides, it doesn't matter. We broke up."

Over the top of my imitation Ray-Bans, I gave her a look of disbelief.

"What? Don't look at me like that. We have. Once I start

college, neither one of us wants to be tied down. Long distance relationships never work out anyway, so it was better to just end it now."

"Maybe if he'd spent less time in the weight room and had done his own homework, he could have scored higher on his A-C-T and gone to college himself."

"He could have gotten into plenty of colleges. Derek's just not the college type. You know his family," she said. "They're very close, very blue collar, and very Port Clinton." I'd never understood Daphne's attraction to him. He was everything she was not. Maybe that was it.

"Hey, whatever. If it caused you two to break up, I'm glad you did his homework for him."

"Sometimes, Danny, I don't like you."

"Sometimes, Daphne, I don't like me either. Look, forget about it. Tell me more about . . ." I bent over to read the book's cover and remind myself of its title, ". . . *The Last Man.*"

"It's about how nothing stays the same and how all things, especially good things, come to an end."

"Like what?"

"Innocence, relationships, lives, governments, species, entire worlds."

"It sounds perfect for you," I said, referring to the end of her relationship with Derek and her newfound freedom.

"What do you mean by that?"

"Nothing." Over the years I'd grown somewhat tired of having to explain the obvious to Daphne. For someone so head smart, she could be heart stupid. I looked away from her and squinted into the sun. "When I was a kid," I said seemingly apropos to nothing, "my dad told me that was a Cloudmaker."

"What are you talking about?"

I pointed towards a mushroom cloud of steam rising from the hourglass-figured, concrete cooling tower of a Toledo Energy nuclear power plant, maybe twenty-five miles distant.

"He said that all the clouds in the sky were made right here in Ohio. They puff out of the Cloudmaker then drift all around the world."

"Wow. That might be the most nefarious euphemism I've ever heard. It's like naming a nuclear warhead the 'Peacemaker.'"

"Whoa! First off, my dad was trying not to scare me with the truth. Secondly, 'nefarious?' I mean, it is officially summer. Let's keep the big words to a minimum."

"First off," she mocked me, "excuse *me* for having a twelfth grade vocabulary, and secondly, I'm sorry that I don't believe parents should lie to their children. When I was a child, my mom and dad always told me the truth."

"They told you there was no Santa Claus?"

Daphne nodded her head, "Yes."

"Or Tooth Fairy?"

"Yes."

"They refuted the efficacy of supply-side economics during a recessive economy?"

Daphne smirked and rolled her eyes.

"Sorry," I said. "Anyway, I have to admit that there's something about a nuclear power plant in the foreground that takes the aesthetic edge off of a lake view."

"Efficacy,' 'recessive,' and now 'aesthetic?' I thought you swore off big words."

"You better me," I said only half-jokingly.

"Did anyone ever tell you that you talk too much?" She asked.

"Yeah. You did in Mr. Daniels' class right before he gave us both detentions for disturbance, but if I remember correctly, somehow you got out of it and I spent the entire two hours watching Mr. Daniels pluck hairs from his nose and ears."

She rolled her eyes once more. "What are you going to Kelleys for anyway?" she asked.

"I'm working at Island Adventures and staying in the dorm for the summer."

Before she could give a snarky response or I could ask her the same question, Daphne's phone buzzed with an incoming text just as the ferry snuggled up against the dock at Seaway Marina on the island's southeast coast. She read her message and stood up. Distracted by the text, she gathered her carry-on bag and proceeded toward the stairs and ramp at what was now the bow of the ferry without saying goodbye. If not impulsive and dramatic, Daphne was nothing. She'd always had a way of blowing me off as soon as things got too comfortable. It was as if, although she enjoyed my company, as long as she had more interesting friends waiting for her someplace else or at least the potential for those friends, Daphne was afraid that if she settled for me, she'd never meet them. I consoled myself with the news that, at least for now, she was broken up with Derek.

I returned to retrieve my backpack and bag on deck in the former stern while the vehicles were directed off the ferry and onto the island. By the time I weaved my way through my fellow passengers to the front of the ferry, I'd already lost her, so I waited and allowed the others to exit before I made my way onto the island. Descending the ramp, I nodded a goodbye to Cleats, who gave me a wave and immediately began to direct the mainland bound vehicles and passengers on board the *Janus*.

On the landing, several former passengers loaded themselves into the vehicles of welcoming friends and family. Others hailed island taxis or rented golf carts or bicycles for the short trip into Kelley's Island Village. I took a seat on a bench beneath the awning of the marina store, watched the flurry of activity subside, and recalibrated myself to island time before plunging into its un-reality and the five-minute trek into town.

I took my time as I walked and absorbed the familiar sights of my boyhood: Inscription Rock, a flat, limestone boulder covered in ancient Indian petroglyphs; Sunrise Marina, where

I'd fish off the dock with the Masur twins; the haunted Kelleys Mansion; Memorial Park at the heart of downtown on the corner of Division Street and Lakeshore Drive, which every July was turned into an amusement park for Islandfest and in August hosted a traveling circus. I turned right onto Division Street. Across the street on the corner was Saturday's, a popular dance bar. A general store sat next to it amongst a row of seasonal clothing and jewelry boutiques, all wood buildings at least a century old. Beyond those to the north loomed Island Adventures and the Village Dorm, respectively, my workplace and home for the summer. A laundromat, a hardware store, and the limestone police station were on the right past the northern end of the park. I was surprised by how everything looked much smaller than I remembered.

Over two hundred years since its first settlers arrived, three-fourths of Kelleys was still uninhabited forest, meadow, and dormant rock quarries. Fewer than a hundred residents lived on the island year-round, and that number had been decreasing yearly. Of those, no more than two or three were young adults of a working age; therefore, a number of workers ferried back and forth from the mainland each day during the summer tourist season, like Daphne. In addition, the island's chamber of commerce hired a recruitment company each summer to provide foreign workers for the remainder of the island's seasonal employment needs. The off-island but non-commuter workers, like me and the foreign employees, were housed in the Village Dorm where I was headed for check-in.

Chapter Two

I entered the dorm through a set of glass doors facing Division Street. Behind a reception counter sat the dorm matron with a roster, a list of dormitory rules, and room keys at the ready. I recognized her as my former elementary school teacher.

"Mrs. Barnes!" I said. "Do you remember me? Danny Foe."

"I most certainly do. I saw your name on the list. How could I forget the only second-grader I ever had who, one day, successfully drove himself to school."

"Yeah, well, the school was less than a quarter mile from my house, and I would have been late if I hadn't."

"Come here, Danny." Mrs. Barnes came out from behind the counter to hug me. "You poor boy. It's just awful what happened to your parents, and you left us without a real goodbye. It's so good to see you." She hugged me again.

"It's good to see you too, Mrs. Barnes."

She continued to stare as if she were taking some kind of measure of me. It was awkward and I wasn't quite sure where to direct my eyes. "So you said I'm on your list?"

"What list?"

"A room. I'm living here this summer."

"Oh, yes. Oh, Danny, I'm sorry about this, but I have to warn you. Your roommate. He's a . . . well . . . he's . . . one of those."

"Those what, Mrs. Barnes?"

"It was purely alphabetical. Had I known, I wouldn't have placed you with him, but these foreign names sound so strange. I couldn't tell he was one of *them* until he came in carrying his little rug. He's from Detroit, not actually one of the foreign workers at all. He came over on his own. I'm so sorry, Danny," she continued to ramble. "We're full now, but sometimes, kids decide the work and the island aren't for them and they leave, then a room assignment opens up and we can transfer you."

"Mrs. Barnes."

She continued, "I've already warned the Chief, and he promised to keep an eye on him."

"Mrs. Barnes, I'm sure it will be fine," I said, still with little clue of what "one of those" could mean.

"Well, all right." She returned to her position behind the counter, checked my name off the list. "The two of you are the first to arrive," she said. "The recruitment company will be bringing over the rest of the international kids later tonight. Your key also works on the outside door, which is always locked, so have it with you at all times. Starting Monday, the cafeteria serves three meals a day. Hours are posted on the door. There are no laundry facilities, but there is a laundromat right down the street. Each room has a refrigerator and microwave. The communal men's and ladies' room with showers are located on opposite ends of each floor. This is the only entry into the building, but there are additional emergency exits on both floors. Your meal and room fees will be deducted directly from your paychecks. Are there any questions?"

"No, Mrs. Barnes. Thank you."

She handed me a small brown envelope labeled "Rm. 205."

"Thanks again, Mrs. Barnes. It's good to see you again."

"You too, Danny."

The sound of thumping bass and super-fast, freestyle riffing over a hip-hop beat called me towards what had to be my room. The door was open and my new roommate was throwing down slides, turns, pops, and locks with his back to me all the while putting his things into his desk and dresser drawers.

"Hello," I said from the doorway, but he completely ignored my greeting and continued unpacking. I was forced to enter and to tap him on the shoulder just to get his attention.

He stopped dancing, turned around, and stared.

It was the Muslim kid from the ferry.

"It looks like we're roommates," I said.

He stared.

On the door, I noticed our names written on a green cut-out in the veal cutlet shape of the island. "You must be," I read, "Jalil Ajami from Detroit, Michigan." It turned out that Mrs. Barnes's "one of those" was a Muslim.

"Dearborn," he said.

"Please?"

"I'm from Dearborn. It's near Detroit. And it's Jah-leel," he pronounced it slowly for my learning. "Who are you?"

I pointed to the cut-out. "I'm Danny Foe."

"All right, Danny Foe," He pronounced my name as if it were one word: "Dannyfoe." "This is my half of the room over here by the window. You got the half by the door. First come first served and all that, right?"

"No problem," I said, although by a simple turning of the twin beds, we could have split the room in the other direction and both had window space.

A look of utter dismay suddenly washed over his face as he looked over my shoulder. "Not already," he said. "I just got here."

I turned to see a navy blue-uniformed police officer filling up the doorway with his six-and-a-half-foot frame. He stared icily at Jalil, but he ignored his complaint before turning his attention to me. "Danny Foe. I'll be damned. Mrs. Barnes said you were up here."

"Officer Sarter?" I asked.

"You're here for the white boy?" Jalil said and laughed. "Man, this must be some kind of *Fantasy* Island."

"*Chief* Sarter," he ignored Jalil and corrected me.

When I left Kelleys, the Chief, who also came from an island family, had only recently returned from serving a tour as a military policeman in the Middle East. He was on Kelleys then working as a part-time officer, riding bike patrol between the downtown bars and marinas on the weekends. Until dark, which was my curfew, he'd let me ride next to him on my bicycle in my policeman Halloween costume. I proudly wore my plastic hat, holster, and badge while we patrolled. Square-jawed, steely-eyed, and broad shouldered, the Chief looked the part of a sheriff in a Hollywood movie.

The Chief called me into the hallway, where he explained that Mrs. Barnes had asked him to stop by and "check up on" Jalil.

"Are you busy?" he asked.

"Just moving in. Why?"

"I need to give a self-defense lesson to a bunch of Girl Scouts over at the 4-H camp."

"Okay," I said with a confused inflection.

"The part-time officers aren't on island yet," the Chief explained, "I need someone to play the Stranger Danger guy." Island lifers always said, "on island," never on *the* island.

"And that would be me?"

"Correct."

"Will I get hurt?"

"Nah. It's just screaming, scratching, and kicking little girls."

"Sounds great," I said facetiously. "But I have one request

first."

"You want to swing past your folks' place."

My throat clenched, and I was unable to answer. I nodded, "Yes."

"No problem," the Chief said.

I popped my head back inside the room. "Nice meeting you, Jalil."

"Yeah. Whatever." He cranked up the volume once more and resumed his unpacking.

"Interesting choice of a roommate," the Chief said on the way out.

"Didn't choose him. We were assigned. But he's cool."

The Chief shot me a dubious glance.

"What do you think, Chief?" Mrs. Barnes called as we passed through the small lobby. "Should I be worried?"

"Don't you worry, Mrs. Barnes. I've got my eyes on the situation."

"You don't suppose I need a metal detector installed do you?"

"No. Like I said, I'll keep my eyes open."

"Okay, Chief. Thanks for checking up."

"No problem, Mrs. Barnes."

Chapter Three

The Chief performed a U-turn on Division Street and directed his cruiser north. "So, what are you doing on island, Danny?"

I gave the short answer, "Working."

"Working? Working where?"

"Island Adventures."

"Island Adventures? Are the Steinbauers opening that dump again this year?"

"Yep."

The name "Island Adventures" was a bit misleading. The holes on the miniature golf course had smelly indoor carpet for greens rather than the typical artificial turf. The wooden boards that encased each hole were warped. The windmill didn't turn and the clown's mouth didn't close. Most of the clubs were bent, and when there was a crowd, golfers sometimes had to share their balls. The golf carts they rented by the hour emitted noxious gas fumes, and the bicycles were single-geared and rode like tanks.

"When do you start?"

"I'm supposed to report to work for orientation tomorrow morning."

"Ahh, Training Days," he said knowingly.

The weekend before Memorial Day weekend had been known as "Training Days" on island for as long as I could remember. Anyone with proof of residence had the run of most businesses at half-off prices. It was the one weekend of the summer season that island lifers – well known for their tightfistedness and curmudgeonly natures – didn't avoid downtown stores, restaurants, shops, amusements, and the park. Service was usually terrible, but it allowed for a soft opening and the training of employees before the official start of the season the following weekend.

We turned off of Division onto Bookerman Road toward what once was my island home next door to my paternal grandfather's. No one had lived in my grandfather's house in the nine years since he'd died. The years of neglect showed. The windows were all broken, and most of the paint had chipped away. What once was a gravel driveway leading to an unattached single car garage was now overgrown with weeds. The garage itself lay in a crumpled heap of wood and glass.

Having caught me sneaking a glance at the charred concrete blocks that once formed the foundation of my parents' home next door, the Chief asked, "Are you all right?"

"The fire wasn't an accident. Was it?" I barely more than mumbled.

"Your folks were having some tough times."

"They sent me into town on purpose that day. Didn't they?"

"Which shows how much they loved you."

"So they lit it themselves?"

"There were suspicions, but it was never officially ruled an arson. Nobody knows for sure what happened. At least no one who's talking. If I remember right, they were having some financial problems. Your dad was in pretty deep to Stan McKillips."

Stan McKillips was a lifer. At that time, at least ostensibly, he was running some sort of handyman and general hauling business, but every islander knew that if anything shady was happening on island or if there was an opportunity to make an easy buck, it was a pretty safe bet that Stan McKillips was somehow involved. He'd occasionally run unlicensed fishing charters; he'd undercut the ferries and transport visitors to and from the mainland; he operated a black market prescription drug service through Canadian suppliers; and he was Kelleys' rogue loan shark. When the lake froze, the ferries dry docked, and islanders were cut off for the winter, there was good money to be made by anyone with ready cash to lend but no soul to prevent him from charging exorbitant interest. Stan McKillips was that soulless opportunist.

"He was there that day," I told the Chief. "I saw him and my dad smoking cigarettes out behind my grandfather's garage."

"The day of the fire at your folks' place?"

"Yeah."

"That wasn't in any of the reports."

"I never told anybody."

"Why not?"

"I was eight years old. I was scared, and nobody asked."

The Chief grew pensive as, I assume, he replayed in his memory the events surrounding the fire, my parents' deaths, and Stan McKillip's potential involvement.

Uncomfortable in the silence, I changed the subject. "My brother blames me. He was already married and living on the mainland. Somehow, because I was here and I lived, it was my fault, I guess."

"No offense, but your brother could be a bit of a piss ant. Besides, people say and do a lot things they don't mean in stressful times. You can't hold folks to every word they say."

"Even piss ants?"

"Even piss ants. Fact is, Danny, there are some things in life we just have to carry."

"Let's just go. I needed to see the place and now I have."

The 4-H camp was a vertical strip of twenty-two acres touching the north central shore of Kelley's Island off of the east-and-west running Ward Road. Its woods, fields, and beach facilitated an abundance of nature programs and outdoor activities for its campers. The second we pulled onto the property, a middle-aged woman with tightly-braided blond hair and wearing a neon green t-shirt, khaki-colored cargo shorts, hiking boots over grey wool socks pulled up to her knees, and black fanny pack emerged from out of the director's cabin to welcome us and to escort us to where a group of junior Girl Scouts, wearing badge-covered vests over their own neon green shirts, were already seated in a semi-circle, on wooden benches, around a dormant campfire pit, near the front of the property.

First, the Chief lectured the kids on the importance of "causing a ruckus" and fighting back should a stranger make an "unwelcome advance." Each child then had the opportunity to put into practice what she had learned – on me. After a half-hour of eardrum-piercing shrieks, kicks to my shins and groin, and a bite or two, I felt sufficiently sleazy and vowed never again to come within a hundred yards of another Girl Scout or to eat a Thin Mint.

As the Chief drove us back into town, I licked my wounds and thought of my interrupted conversation with Daphne on the ferry. "Why are you on island?" I texted her.

Daphne:just visiting

Me:bullshit!!!!!

Daphne:Whatever.

Me:BTW what would you do?

Daphne:?

Me:like in that book. If your next healthy breath were to be your last

Daphne:IDK. What would you do?

Me:spend it with you

Daphne:Dork!!!!!

Me:can i see you later

Daphne:No.

"Don't you kids ever just talk to one another?" The Chief asked.

"Not if we don't have to," I said.

Chapter Four

The Chief offered to buy cones at the Dairy Dock, but first, we stopped at the jail so that he could check to see if either of the part-time officers had arrived on island.

The century-old police station/jail hadn't changed much in the ten years I'd been away. For that matter, it hadn't changed much in the hundred-plus years of its existence. It consisted of a one room office containing a desk with two wooden chairs facing it, a couple of metal filing cabinets against the right wall, and a single holding cell with a cot, a sink, and a toilet against the back wall opposite the desk. It looked exactly like a jail in the old Westerns my grandpa liked to watch.

The Chief was Kelleys' only full-time officer and always on-call. In the summer, he hired one full-time, seasonal officer and an additional patrolman for weekend crowd control. Serious lawbreakers, of which there were few, were transported via ferry to the Erie County Jail in Sandusky. On the occasion that a prisoner was required to be held on island overnight, the Chief was forced either to spend the night at his desk or to take his inmate home with him.

Officer Burns's time card had been pulled and punched, and one of the patrol bikes had been unchained and removed from its stand. A second card remained un-punched and a second bike un-ridden.

A sudden uproar rose on the street. People ran screaming past the large front window of the jail with their arms folded over the tops of their heads searching for shelter. A pattering of thuds assaulted the jailhouse roof. "Hail?" I asked the Chief.

"I don't think so," he said. "The sun's shining."

Something smashed against the window and left the glass splintered in a spider web design.

"Chief, look," I pointed to the center of the spider web, where a blackbird's head barely peeped through with its body hanging bloody and limp from an exposed and jagged edge of glass.

"For Chrissakes! What is this?"

I followed the Chief outside, where hundreds of birds were dropping kamikaze-like out of the afternoon sky. Their bodies crashed against vehicles, the sides and roofs of buildings, onto the street and sidewalk, and into a number of pedestrians. We backed quickly under the cover of the doorway and watched what appeared to be a mass suicide of birds.

Like a passing summer thunderstorm, the rain of birds soon ceased. People slunk from out of their hiding places with looks of wide-eyed terror. Many were spotted with bird shit.

"That's odd," the Chief said.

"What's that?"

"Other than the gulls, what's the most common type of bird around here?" the Chief asked.

"I don't know; I guess ducks."

"Right. Do you see any of either?"

I looked and saw a variety of skull-crushed, broken-necked, black-eyed, and blood-splattered birds among the thousands lying dead in the streets like so many mayflies. Cormorants, sparrows, warblers, and other species mixed in the carnage, but no gulls or ducks. "No," I finally answered. "What about it?"

"Nothing. It just seems odd. That's all." Studying the birds, we stood silent and still until the Chief muttered, "I'll be damned."

The words had hardly passed the Chief's lips when John Patmos, a sort of religious hermit, who lived out on Long Point, a peninsula in the island's northeast quadrant, appeared from seemingly out of nowhere to pronounce, "*So the LORD said, 'I will wipe from the face of the earth the human race I have created—and with them the animals, the **birds** and the creatures that move along the ground—for I regret that I have made them.'*"

As mysteriously and quickly as he had appeared, Patmos continued to walk out of town toward the island's interior.

"You'd just love that wouldn't you, John?" The Chief called after him. "Armageddon. The Second Coming. The Rapture and all that. Go thump your Bible somewhere else!"

"Chief?" I interrupted him.

"I'm sorry. I don't know about God wiping the human race from the face of the Earth or nothing," he turned his gaze first to the north and the 4-H Camp then to the south down Division towards the water then up to the sky, as if trying to make sense of what had just happened, "but it sure looks like Hell has broken loose on this island."

Just then, a forest green school bus, covered in bird droppings and with its wiper blades smearing the excrement across its windshield, came tearing down Division Street blowing its horn. Fishtailing on top of a slippery layer of dead birds and mayflies, the bus arrived in front of the jail with its brakes screeching. It was the bus from the 4-H Camp. The Camp Director sat behind the wheel.

"For Chrissakes, now what?" The Chief said.

"Chief," the Camp Director said through her window, "Come! Quick!"

Back in the cruiser, we followed her back to the camp, where we exited our vehicles and hurried on foot past the director's cabin, a maintenance building, a stone tool shed, and the separated boys' and girls' cabins to the rear of the dining hall, where a red cross marked the entrance to an attached first aid station. The Camp Nurse, dressed identically to the director except for the stethoscope draped around her neck, her sky blue rubber gloves, and the surgical mask over her mouth and nose, met us at the door of the station. Inside, at least a dozen tween-aged girls lay miserable and moaning on green army cots lined against the perimeter of the space.

"What's wrong with them?" The Chief asked. "We left no more than an hour ago. They seemed fine."

"Don't know," the Nurse said. "They just started dropping like flies. I've never seen anything like it. They're burning up, their throats are raw from coughing and vomiting, and they're severely congested but too weak to cough hard enough to break it up or expectorate."

"Expectorate?" I asked.

"Spit," she clarified.

"Is it the flu?"

"Could be. Probably is. But I've never seen the flu come on so fast and hit so many so hard all at once."

"What about Lyme Disease?" The Chief asked. "What have they done recently? These woods are full of deer ticks. They wouldn't be the first."

The Camp Director butted into the conversation. "Officer Dooley from the ODNR (Ohio Department of Natural Resources) led the girls on a wildlife identification hike through the East Quarry yesterday. They were at the beach collecting beach glass first thing this morning, then they used what they'd collected for an arts-and-crafts project. They ate lunch and you did your presentation this afternoon. That's it."

"I thought of Lyme Disease," the Nurse said, "and flu-like symptoms are an indicator, but they don't typically manifest this quickly, nor is it communicable. Besides, what are the odds that they all were bitten? I checked each of the girls for bites anyway but didn't find one."

"What do you want me to do?" The Chief asked. "There's no hospital on island. There's not even a doctor, just a couple of on-call EMTs at the urgent care center. I could call Life-Flight out of Toledo, but that would require at least six trips and their parents may not appreciate the bill if it turns out to be no more than a twenty-four hour bug."

"No," the Camp Director insisted. "There's no need to panic. Let's keep an eye on them, and if they don't get better soon, I'll contact their parents. They can then meet them at the ferry in Marblehead."

She didn't say anything, but I could tell the Nurse wasn't totally on board with the "Wait- and-See" strategy. However, she swallowed her disapproval and returned to tending to the sick girls.

The Chief said, "I'm going to find Officer Dooley to see if he can shed any light on this. For now, I think it would be for the best if you keep the kids here at camp. If there are any changes, call me."

"We will, Chief," the Camp Director answered for both.

An Ohio Department of Natural Resources (ODNR) office was attached to the marina store at the ferry dock. Inside, we found Officer Dooley slumped over the top of his metal desk and burning white-hot. His smallish office reeked of fever.

Chief Sarter nudged the officer. "Dooley? Wake up! Dooley?"

Dooley didn't answer so much as groan then spurt forth a string of unintelligible syllables.

"Help me move him," the Chief ordered. We lifted Dooley under his arms, lay him face down on a wooden bench against the wall, and covered him with a jacket from off a coat tree in the corner.

On top of the desk, the Chief reviewed Dooley's daily activity log. "Says here he was on West Sister Island yesterday morning, the 4-H camp after that, and then did some routine license and boat inspections this morning. That's it," he said and pulled his cell phone from his pocket.

"Who you calling?" I asked.

The Chief, his mind preoccupied turned away and walked to the door, where he looked out across the lake towards the west. "No answer," he said and for a few moments seemed to contemplate his choices. "Let's go."

"Go where?"

"West Sister."

"But no one lives there," I protested.

"Just Smitty, the lighthouse and island caretaker. That's who I was calling."

The Chief unhitched a ring of keys from Dooley's belt and made for the door.

"Are we going to leave him here like this?" I asked.

"What else do you suggest? Where we going to take him? He's too sick to move himself or to be moved by us. Whatever he has must be related to the Girl Scouts getting sick. We need to figure out who passed it to whom and how far back it goes."

The Chief turned the sign on the door to "Closed" and locked the door behind us.

Chapter Five

Approximately twenty miles northwest of Kelleys sits West Sister Island, a twenty-two acre boulder in the Western Basin of Lake Erie. It's federally-owned, managed, and protected as a refuge and breeding ground for the millions of migratory birds that visit it each year on their way south and back. Due to the amount of puke and shit those birds leave behind, local fishermen and boaters have nicknamed it Vomit Island. Nearly three-fourths of the mostly cliff-lined island is covered with towering hackberry trees, and the island floor is infested with poison ivy. A place less habitable for land-based living is hard to imagine. It is a place literally "for the birds." In the 70s, there were many who suspected West Sister to be the burial place for the notorious teamster boss Jimmy Hoffa, who disappeared from outside a Detroit restaurant never to be seen again. An operating lighthouse with a small home and compound for the caretaker is the only human footprint on the otherwise man and godforsaken island. Although the lighthouse has long been fully automated, the State of Ohio appointed position of lighthouse keeper and island caretaker had been promised by the then governor to be maintained until Walter Smith, the fourth generation in his family to serve in that anachronistic position, moved off island. That was fifty years earlier, when no one believed the then twenty-five-year old Smitty would ever choose to stay.

The run to West Sister took just over an hour in a borrowed ODNR open-hulled, eighteen-foot, Boston Whaler. When we pulled up to the floating dock, thousands of birds were bobbing in the water near the shore like apples in a barrel. They thudded menacingly against the hull as we idled in. A low buzzing emanated from the multitude of flies drawn to the birds that lay dead on the beach outside the lighthouse and the caretaker's weather-beaten cracker box home. The stench was god-awful and the lack of birdsong alarming, for it was the middle of migration season.

The Chief brought the Whaler parallel to the dock. A sixteen-foot, aluminum outboard was tied up to the other side. "At least there's that," he said.

"There's what?" I asked.

"If Smitty's boat's here, he has to be here too. Have you ever met Smitty?" He asked.

"No."

"He's a little . . . different."

"How's that?"

"He talks to the birds. Calls them his children and lets them in the house. I've seen him hold his arms out like a scarecrow and have at least ten different varieties of birds land on him as natural as can be."

"Really?" I asked, not knowing how else to respond to the image. I climbed on the dock and tied off the lines while the Chief finished stowing away the Whaler.

"He's a strange bird himself, Smitty, but he's perfect for the job. He's lived alone on West Sister for over fifty years, and I've never heard him complain. Someone from ODNR checks up on him once a month and he has a state-supplied cell phone.

Other than that, he's on his own." As we approached his house, the Chief called out "Smitty!" We had little choice but to step on top of the carcasses of the myriad kinds of birds that littered the grounds like a Civil War battlefield.

Every window in the house was wide open. Yellowed lace curtains blew in westerly-facing windows and out of the easterly ones. No one answered the Chief's call or knock, but the doorknob turned. Even after we'd let ourselves in, the Chief's call went unanswered. From the kitchen, a countertop radio set to an oldies station reminded us that things "Turn, Turn, Turn."

"He's here somewhere," the Chief said.

"Do you smell that?" I asked. The odor was identical to that in Dooley's office if not quite as concentrated.

"Upstairs," he said and directed me with a nod.

We searched all of the second floor rooms but found no one, just some clothes on the floor of Smitty's bedroom and towels in the bathroom soiled with vomit and blood. I covered my mouth and nose with my hand in an attempt to diminish the stench.

"Where the hell could he be?" The Chief asked, apparently unbothered by the smell.

We went to search the pole barn in the side yard. It was the only other structure on the island. The rest of it was so overgrown with thicket, it was impossible to penetrate much less to build on.

The Chief opened the door but couldn't find a light switch. He called into the darkness of the windowless barn but received no response.

"There's no way in hell we're going in there without a light," the Chief said.

He stepped away from the doorway and sent me to the boat to look for a flashlight. I had almost reached the dock when I heard the Chief commanding Smitty to stop. But Smitty, wearing nothing but his soiled underwear like a baby's filled diaper, continued to stumble on his bony legs towards the Chief zombie-like. The Chief, backing away, reached for his gun. Smitty wheezed badly. His skin was nearly blue, his lips cracked and dry, and blood caked his mouth and nose. Smitty was trying to speak but failing. As he drew near to the Chief, he fell to the ground, coughed or spit or vomited all over the Chief's black boots, and died.

"Smitty!" The Chief yelled in an attempt to return him to consciousness and communicability, but he was careful not to touch him or to get too close.

It was too late.

The caretaker was dead.

The Chief hurriedly waded into the bird-filled wavelets lapping onto the beach and allowed them to wash the toxic mess from off of his boots.

"Sorry you had to see that," he said when he returned to where I stood, "but it's about to get worse."

"What do you mean?"

"You're going to have to help me load him into the boat. Whatever caused Officer Dooley, the Girl Scouts, Smitty, and all of these birds to get sick started right here. We're going to take as little of whatever it is as possible off of this island, but protocol is to get Smitty's body to someone who can figure out exactly what made him sick."

When we'd finished wrapping the body in an old canvass boat cover we'd found in the barn and placing Smitty in the boat, the Chief, still wearing a pair of latex rubber gloves he'd removed from the boat's first aid kit, began filling a two-gallon bucket with as many different species of dead birds as he could locate.

"What you doing, Chief?"

"Someone's going to want to look at these too," he explained.

"Any gulls or ducks?" I asked.

The Chief took a look inside his bucket. "No."

Five minutes later, we were speeding east across slightly-undulating waters with Smitty stiffening beneath a bird shit-covered piece of canvas in the back of the boat.

After repeated roaming failures, the Chief's cell phone found service. He pressed one of his emergency contact numbers, switched over to speakerphone, and handed the cell to me to hold up to his ear, as his captaining of the boat required both hands.

"Who you calling, Chief?" I asked as the phone rang.

"Dr. Jennifer Bentham. She's the Director of the Erie County Health Department in Sandusky and my liaison with the Regional Center for Disease Control in Columbus. We go back."

The cell picked up. Over the roar of the twin outboard motors, the thumping of the hull against the troughs of the waves, and the constant splashing, I had to concentrate in order to hear the conversation:

Dr. Bentham:Hello?

Chief Sarter:Jenny, we've got a situation.

Dr. Bentham:So much for small talk, Chief Sarter. You do realize that it's seven o'clock on a Friday night?

Chief Sarter:I know that it's Friday. This can't wait.

Dr. Bentham:What do you have? (Her tone turned immediately grave.)

Chief Sarter:A dead adult male.

Dr. Bentham:Have you called the coroner?

Chief Sarter: Not yet. I think this one falls under your jurisdiction.

Dr. Bentham:Where did you find the body?

Chief Sarter:West Sister Island.

Dr. Bentham:You're kidding me? Who?

Chief Sarter:No, I'm not. Smitty, the caretaker.

Dr. Bentham:Natural or unnatural.

Chief Sarter:No foul play that I can see.

Dr. Bentham:Symptoms?

Chief Sarter:He died before I could question him, but his lips were blue; he had a fever; and he vomited what looked like blood.

Dr. Bentham:Who else knows about this?

Chief Sarter:No one but myself [He twisted halfway round to look at me.] and a deputy [meaning me], but Officer Mark Dooley of the Department of Natural Resources was on West Sister yesterday, and he's sick as well.

Dr. Bentham:Damn it.

Chief Sarter:And, Jenny, there's another thing.

Dr. Bentham: What's that?

Chief Sarter:The birds are dead.

Dr. Bentham:How many?

Chief Sarter:As far as I could tell, all of them.

Dr. Bentham:That can't be possible. Did you collect samples?

Chief Sarter:I did. I'm bringing them with me.

Dr. Bentham:Good. Where's this deputy?

Chief Sarter:(He looked at me again.) He's with me.

Dr. Bentham:And Dooley?

Chief Sarter:Officer Dooley's still on Kelleys. He's incapacitated inside his office. But, Jenny, it gets even worse.

Dr. Bentham:How is that possible?

Chief Sarter:I have a troop of sick Girl Scouts at the 4-H Camp all come down with what I'm pretty sure is the same thing that killed Smitty and made Dooley sick.

Dr. Bentham:What? No sick puppies? [I believe that was sarcasm.]You're going to have to keep them and isolate them all.

Chief Sarter:Keep them? All we have is an urgent care center staffed by volunteer EMTs. It's no more than a triage station.

You know that.

Dr. Bentham:We have no other choice.

Chief Sarter:Okay, but it's your call.

Dr. Bentham:I'm fine with that. You're going to have to keep Smitty too.

Chief Sarter:But there's no morgue or even a funeral home on island."

Dr. Bentham:Chief, I have to examine that body, and I need blood and organ samples from those birds.

Chief Sarter:Okay. Okay. I'll figure something out.

Dr. Bentham:I'll be there as soon as I can.

Chief Sarter:Call me when you're on island.

I pressed the button to disconnect. "For Chrissakes," he mumbled.

No sooner had the words left his mouth than his phone lit up and buzzed. I read the screen. "It's Officer Burns."

"Well, answer it."

Once more, I held up the phone for the Chief.

Chief Sarter:Yeah, Burnsie.

Officer Burns:Davis called and said he can't make it over. His wife's water broke and she's going into labor.

Chief Sarter:Did he get a replacement?

Officer Burns:No. He didn't have time. I could hear his wife screaming at him in the background.

Chief Sarter:Damn it! Not tonight. All right. It looks like it's going to be just the two of us.

Officer Burns:Where are you, Chief?

Chief Sarter:On my way now. Had to make a run to West Sister. Shouldn't be more than thirty minutes out.

Officer Burns:Oh! One more thing. The 4-H Camp Director stopped me and wanted me to tell you they'd decided to take the girls to the ferry and their parents. She said you would know what that meant.

Chief Sarter:No can do! She was supposed to call me first.

You've got to get down there and stop them.

Officer Burns:It's too late.

Chief Sarter:Too late? What do you mean 'too late'? (He reflexively looked at his watch.)

Officer Burns:They just left on the ferry.

Chief Sarter:For Chrissakes! I'll have to try and intercept them. You call the sheriff and get deputies to the dock in Marblehead, then try to raise Captain Russo on the marine radio at the marina. Those kids cannot exit that ferry.

The Chief nodded and I ended the call while he pushed the engines to nearly full throttle.

I had to hold on to the console to avoid being tossed out of the boat or, even worse, onto Smitty. At that moment, I was pretty sure that if I went overboard, the Chief wouldn't come back for me.

In the distance, we soon made out the bow and stern lights of the Janus as we approached from her starboard side. On the Marblehead dock, swirling blue and red lights lit the ferry landing. The Chief got on the boat's radio: "Kelleys Island Chief of Police Sarter calling the captain of the ferry Janus. Repeat. Chief Sarter calling the captain of the ferry Janus. Over."

We waited as the radio static crackled.

"Captain Russo of the Janus to Chief Sarter. Over."

"Captain Russo. Be advised. Do not proceed to dock at Marblehead. Repeat. Do not proceed to dock at Marblehead. Over."

"Um, roger that, Chief. Over."

The engines on the Janus were immediately cut, but her momentum carried her within thirty yards of her dock. The ferry's momentum pushed a surging swell of water up the concrete ramp and onto the landing. The Chief slipped the Whaler in between her and the dock.

As we bobbed in the near shore chop, to our port side, the 4-

H Camp bus sat parked and first in line on the ferry deck with the Camp Director white-knuckling the wheel of what was more-or-less a virus incubator on wheels. Loaded with sick children, it perched with its grill only feet from the raised ramp like a skittish racehorse ready to bolt from its chute. To our right, two sheriff's deputy's cars were parked nose to nose barricading the ferry's dock ramp. Four officers were struggling to keep at bay the mob of parents, confused and desperate, who'd come to claim their sick children.

The radio sprang to life. "Captain Russo to Chief Sarter. Over."

"Go ahead, Captain. Over." The Chief responded.

"Please advise as to a course of action. Over."

"Return to Kelleys. Repeat. Return to Kelleys. Over."

"Roger that, Chief. You are aware there are sick children on board? Over."

"I am. I repeat. Return to Kelleys. Over."

"Roger. Over."

The ferry engines growled as if in sympathetic complaint on behalf of the children, but they reluctantly acquiesced and the Janus reversed her direction. A flood of confused ferry passengers rushed to the rails in an attempt to figure out what was happening and why, but they were at the mercy of *Janus*, stuck between coming and going.

On the landing, the parents breached the blockade. Several ran waist-deep into the water in vain pursuit of the ferry. Their banshee wails pierced the air. Each one seemed to penetrate the Chief's thin emotional armor. Finally, he turned the bow of the Whaler northward and we followed in the wake of the Janus and its precious cargo towards our collective destiny.

Chapter Six

Per the Chief's orders, Officer Burns met the ferry in one of the island's two squad cars. After the Chief snuggled the Whaler up against the ODNR dock, which was only separated from the ferry's slip by a small spit of boulders, he ordered Captain Russo from the wheelhouse and Officer Burns to escort the 4-H bus back to the camp. The ferry ramp was raised, and a heavy chain was strung across the dock. The entire marina was placed on lockdown. Marina dockhands turned away all incoming vessels, and the short line of vehicles and a small group of would be walk-on passengers, who had hoped to board the eight-thirty return crossing, were sent away.

With the Whaler tied off, the Chief radioed the urgent care center for an ambulance to pick up Smitty. It arrived within ten minutes. Chief Sarter waved his arms to direct the EMTs down to the boat. Derek, Daphne's ex, was with them. It must have been his text that prompted Daphne's hurried exit from the ferry that afternoon. One of the others introduced Derek as a summer intern on island. Turned out he was training to be a firefighter.

I felt as if I'd been punched in the heart.

Derek gave me a curt backwards nod of recognition but no

more. He and I certainly weren't friends, but we weren't exactly rivals either. We'd been giving it to and taking it from each other for as long as I could remember. I'd always felt that he didn't trust my friendship with Daphne, but I'm sure he could never quite bring himself to believe she'd ever prefer mine to his.

"Hey, Foe," Derek called me aside. "Did you know Daphne's working over here at Gulliver's? We're going to hook up for a ferry home after our shifts."

"That's great, Derek. If you see her, tell her I said hi, but," I glanced towards the ferry sitting idle at its dock, "I don't think you're going anywhere – at least for awhile."

It had been a lame attempt by Derek to claim Daphne's preference and an even lamer attempt by me to act as if I couldn't care less.

The Chief didn't introduce me to the EMTs, nor did they offer their own introduction. In general, islanders ask few questions and provide even fewer answers. However, one of them looked familiar. I couldn't place the name, but I remembered him from grammar school on island as a bit of a bully. He was a couple of years older than me, but with fewer than ten students, kindergarten through twelfth grade, there was only one teacher in the entire school. Grade levels were combined like in the one-room schoolhouses of the olden days. He couldn't help but recognize me too, but if he did, he wasn't telling.

"You guys are going to have to babysit the body for me for a while," the Chief informed them.

"You've got to be jokin', man," said the tall, skinny one in a soft, Irish lilt. I'd watched him expertly flick the stubby remains of a cigarette onto the rocks before the Chief could take notice and, most likely, reprimand him for smoking on the job. I couldn't tell if his spiked, dirty blond hair, which was peaked in a sort of faux-hawk, was gelled or just greasy and messy.

Because there was such a marginal presence of law on the islands and plenty of opportunities for short and part-time employment – often paid under the table – it was not unusual for "rogues, rovers, and roustabouts," as my island grandfather used to call them, from literally all over the world to wash up on one of the string of islands in western Lake Erie. Although landlocked in the body of the North American continent, the islands had a lawless, last-stop-at-the-end-of-the-world feeling to them, like Tortuga for Caribbean pirates or that cantina in *Star Wars*.

"I wish I were, Andy, but until I can find a freezer large enough to hold him, he's yours."

"That's bullocks, Chief. We're volunteers. I came from tendin' bar at Saturday's. If I'm not back to work in fifteen minutes, I'll lose me only payin' job."

"I'll be as fast as I can. I promise. But I need your help on this. It's coming from authorities much higher than me. Whatever happens, don't let anyone near that body. And keep the kid away from this one," he said in reference to Derek. "And I suggest you glove and mask up," the Chief said before hurrying up towards the marina store.

They didn't.

Still wounded by Derek's presence on Kelleys, I pouted while I watched them unwrap the canvas, stuff Smitty inside a black body bag, and wheel him up the narrow cement walkway that ran to the dock.

After the ambulance had left, the Chief returned with two sets of blue rubber gloves hanging from his pockets and two bottles of Clorox bleach in each hand. He handed me a pair. "You do the bow. I'll get the stern," he said.

I stood motionless holding the bottles, not sure of what he wanted me to do exactly until I watched him glove up then begin to pour and spread the bleach liberally and indiscriminately around the deck. Taking his cue, I did the same in the bow of the boat.

The Chief climbed onto the dock, spread out the canvas in which Smitty's body had been wrapped, and splashed the remains of his second bottle of bleach onto it. "I'm taking this up to the marina and burning it inside a dumpster. Finish up here and meet me at Officer Dooley's office."

When I caught up with the Chief a half hour later, he was visibly upset and pacing furiously outside of the ODNR office as he talked on the radio:

Chief:Burnsie?

Burnsie:Yeah, Chief.

Chief:This is really important. I want you to think. Have you seen Officer Dooley from ODNR tonight?

Burnsie:No. I've been downtown most of the time. He hasn't been down here. I would have seen him if he were. Why?

Chief:I'll fill you in later. I'm on my way. If you see Dooley, hold him until I get there. But Burnsie [The Chief had an afterthought.]. Don't get too close.

Burnsie:How am I to hold him without getting close?

Chief Sarter moved the radio a good two feet from his mouth and contemplated Burnsie's more-than-reasonable question, then he returned it to its holder on his belt and left the question unanswered.

We had just exited the marina under a slow-rising moon when something, bipedal and remotely human in appearance, stumbled across the expansive lawn of one of the million dollar properties along Lakeshore Drive (For clarification's sake: the *properties* were worth millions, not the residences – most of which were old, small, and owned by stubborn islanders who refused to sell to wealthy mainland buyers only interested in turning Kelleys into a cheap Midwestern imitation of The Hamptons.).

The Chief slammed on the brakes and asked, "Did you see that?"

"Yeah."

He positioned the cruiser so that its headlights shined into a front yard, mottled with oaks and elms, a half-a-football-field long. The Chief stepped out and, shielding himself behind his opened car door, he surveyed the lawn. "There!" Once more, the zombie-like figure momentarily flashed into view from among the trees. The Chief threw open his door and took off on a run.

Still seated, I watched as he ran. In my informally-deputized state, I found myself conflicted as to my appropriate course of action, but eventually, I unstrapped my seatbelt and made my way into the black.

"Chief? Chief?"

I tripped over something soft and large on the ground the Chief had somehow run past without noticing and found myself lying flat on my belly in the dampening grass. Scrambling onto my hands and knees, I turned and stared into the bloodshot eyes of the living-dead creature upon whom the Chief had settled the beam of his flashlight.

I rolled repeatedly away until I lay against the Chief's thick-soled, black boots. He chastised me, "Danny! For Chrissakes! Buck up! It's just Dooley."

"Is he alive?"

"Not by much, but at least he didn't get far."

Five minutes later, the Chief and I were downtown, where we dragged Dooley from the back seat of the cruiser into the jail and the cell. The Chief handcuffed one of Dooley's arms to the metal frame then locked the cell door.

"That ought to keep him from walking away again."

"You don't think you're being a little harsh?"

"It's either the handcuffs or I shoot him." There was no sarcasm in the Chief's voice.

"What now?" I asked.

"We wait for Dr. Bentham."

One last look back at Dooley's misery caused me to think he might have preferred the "shoot him" option.

Chapter Seven

After shutting off the lights and locking the jail door in order to dissuade visitors, we walked down Division to the kitchen entrance of Gulliver's, the largest and most popular bar/restaurant on island and where Derek had revealed Daphne to be working. It was hard to wrap my brain around the notion of Daphne holding a job and doubly difficult to imagine her working in a meat market dance club.

Gulliver's sat across Lakeshore Drive with its back to the mainland. Its front faced downtown. In back was a massive party deck; a sixty slip marina for private boaters; a dock it rented to the high speed ferry line that ran constantly between the islands and the mainland from Memorial to Labor Day; and a dock for the "Booze Cruise," a double-deck passenger ship which sailed out of nearby Sandusky. Every Friday night it dropped off a literal boatload of fast and easy-spending partiers for an evening of heavy drinking, dirty dancing, and short-time hook-ups.

Because I was only eight-years-old when I left the island, I'd never been inside Gulliver's, but the Masur twins and I used to motor in on their Kodiak raft and watch an occasional wet t-shirt contest on Saturday afternoons through shared binoculars.

The Chief and I entered the kitchen through a side door. The "thump-thump-thump" of the D.J. warming up his system reverberated off the walls. In front of the bar, a mustered line of waitresses stood at attention in tight, red tank tops over Lilliputian-sized, black skirts and knee-highs. They were gathered on the dance floor and receiving a sort of pep talk from Charles King II, the owner of Gulliver's and one of the wealthiest of the island Lifers. In addition to the bar, he owned a large piece of property and a home on the east end of the island next to the airport. Islanders called it the Playboy Mansion for all of the legendary, late night pool parties the King hosted there full of young ladies gleaned from his staff or siphoned from amongst his patrons.

Eventually, my eyes climbed to the faces of the Gulliver's Girls, one of whom seemed to be simultaneously sneaking looks in my direction while doing her best to disappear behind some of the taller and more well-endowed waitresses. In her skimpy outfit and out of our usual shared context, it took me a few moments to recognize her, but eventually I caught and held her attention long enough to mouth her name, "Daphne?"

An avalanche of total defeat and dejection seemed to overwhelm Daphne, a staunch feminist, upon my outing of her, but before I could reestablish eye contact, the waitresses were dismissed, and she disappeared through the wide opening which led to the party deck and the docks.

Even as an eight-year-old, I knew Charles King II. Like his father before him, he was the perpetually-elected mayor of Kelleys Island Village and known by all islanders as King Charles. He sponsored the Kelleys' entries in the intra-island little league and men's softball league and provided equipment and uniforms for every member of the teams. His father, Charles King Jr., had opened Gulliver's in the sixties. It was the occasion that had begun the transformation of Kelleys from an idyllic, family-oriented getaway and Christian retreat into a favorite destination for few-holds-barred adult debauchery – at least downtown on weekend evenings. Old-timers, like Cleats, and the religious sorts resented the Kings and how they had betrayed their island, but even those Puritanical few couldn't sneeze at the influx of revenue Gulliver's and its imitators, like Saturday's and the more-chill, Jamaican-themed Montego Bay, had generated for the village's coffers. Even worse, they had come to depend on the tax income generated by the bars to fund nearly all of the island's municipal services and to provide enough ancillary income for many of the remaining islanders to hibernate comfortably through each winter on summer's earnings and bogus unemployment checks. Further complicating the matter, the Kings had always made sure to make regular and generous contributions to all of the charities, churches, and civic groups on island.

Finished with the inspection of his wait staff, the King ambled through the kitchen to where we stood just inside the door.

Chief Sarter whispered to me, "Be on your best behavior for King Charles. I need this favor."

The King clearly didn't recognize me, so the Chief introduced me as "one of the Foe boys who used to live on Bookerman."

Unimpressed, the King asked, "What can I do you for, Chief?"

"I need a huge favor, Charles. It's going to sound strange, but it's not for me. It's for the state."

"The state?"

"Well, the Erie County Health Department."

"Them bastards? Are you kidding me? They give me more shit than a summer full of drunks."

"I don't know anything about that, Charles, but this has nothing to do with the cleanliness of your kitchen . . . or restrooms."

"What is it then, Chief? I have a bar to run. It's Training Days weekend you know."

"I need to store a body."

King Charles looked at the Chief for a few seconds as if questioning his sanity. "Why, sure Chief. Just bring it right into the stand-up cooler and lay it down next to the boxes of hamburgers and chicken wings." He paused to allow his sarcasm to marinate. "I'm sure the Health Department will have a field day with that one. C'mon. What is this, Chief? Some kind of set-up? Who's the stiff?"

"It's Smitty, the caretaker and lighthouse keeper over on West Sister, and no, Charles, no one's coming to inspect you. But a Dr. Bentham is on her way to examine the body. I was ordered to preserve him as much as possible. To do that, I need a freezer. So, can you help me or not?"

"What happened to Smitty?"

"Not sure. That's why I need to freeze the body."

King Charles considered the Chief's proposal then said, "I'll tell you what; I'll do it for Smitty. He stopped in here a few times. He was a little weird but a good guy. But in exchange, I want you to get your part-timers to play nicer with my customers. Give a few more warnings instead of the public intoxication and disorderly conduct charges that chase them away to the other bars and islands, then I think we can work something out. Will you do that for me?"

"I can't ignore the law, Charles, but I can call off the dogs a bit."

"Where's the body?"

"He's at the urgent care station. I just need to radio Andy."

"I'll tell you what. I've got an old walk-in cooler in the basement. I only use it for extra beer storage. You should be able to sneak him in there. Will that do?"

"That'll be perfect."

King Charles showed us a separate side entrance to the basement. It was narrow and steep. The basement itself was a regular catacomb, perfect for the Chief's macabre purpose.

After a radio call, the ambulance arrived with Smitty, but it was my former Kelleys Island Elementary schoolmate who backed it down the rear entranceway. Derek rode shotgun.

"Where's Andy?" Chief Sarter asked.

"He said he couldn't stay. Couldn't afford to lose his job. Said we could manage on our own."

"That's just great, and where are your masks?"

"He ain't breathing, Chief, and we ain't kissing him."

"Still, put your masks on."

After we'd finished storing Smitty's body inside the freezer, one of the cooks delivered four brown paper bags oozing grease from the burgers and fries inside of them. "Compliments of the King," he said.

Collectively soured by our undertaking, we sat on the rear bumper of the ambulance and ate in silence until, "Kenny," I said as if disappointedly biting into unsweetened chocolate. "You're Kenny McKillips. Stan's your dad. You were two grades ahead of me at school. You lived on Huntington Lane by the dump with your old man. We shook hands but Kenny's was limp and unwelcoming and mine less-than-enthusiastic.

He stuffed his half-eaten burger back into the bag and turned to the Chief. "Is it okay if we go? We've got to clean up the wagon."

"Sure," the Chief said. "Wipe her down good. You're on call though, right?"

Kenny nodded the affirmative.

Robbed of our bench and with little appetite, the Chief and I threw what was left of our meals into the dumpster.

"Danny, I'm going to find Officer Burns and bring him up to speed. Why don't you walk on up to the dorm and finish getting settled in. I'll meet you at the cruiser in front of the jail in about an hour. I hope to have heard from somebody by then. Sound good?"

I agreed. But after climbing Gulliver's sloping driveway to Lakeshore Drive, instead of heading directly up Division to the dorm, I circled to the rear of the building, where I found Daphne on the raised deck lowering the umbrella tops of picnic tables.

With my elbows resting chest-high on the deck, I said, "Hey."

It took her a few seconds to locate the source, but eventually she spotted me standing beneath her and immediately hustled away.

I followed her along the wide base of the wood-slatted boat dock that butted up against the raised deck. "Daphne, wait."

She doubled back and returned to the corner table at which I first called to her. It was the farthest one from the main bar and out of the sight line of any of her bosses who might have been watching from inside. She leaned over, exposing cleavage I'd never known she had, and pretended to be rearranging the condiments, "What do you want, Danny? Don't you dare make fun of me," she paused in her work and pointed her finger in my face.

I didn't answer. Instead, I asked, "Why didn't you tell me about Derek?"

"Not now. I'm working."

"But why? You've never worked before."

"Well 'before,' my parents were together and the real estate market didn't suck. My mom sells a lot of property on the island. I guess she's known Mr. King for a long time. She got me this job. This uniform is humiliating, but Mr. King said that his best waitresses can clear over ten grand in the summer, mostly because of the uniform."

"Wow, ten grand? I'll be lucky to make a fifth of that renting golf carts."

"Would you like me to ask Mr. King to give you a job? You'd look cute in one of these skirts."

"Ha-ha. What about Derek?"

"He'd be cute too."

"That's not what I meant."

"We planned it a long time ago – before we broke up. My mom helped get him his stupid internship with the volunteer fire department. At the time, I thought it would be fun for us to both be on the island, and if he wasn't going to go to college, I thought, 'At least I'd be dating a fireman. That's kind of hot.'"

"You do know that your entire life is a CW teen drama?"

"Very funny. Until he texted me on the ferry, I didn't even know he'd already started the internship."

"He told me you're taking the ferry home together."

"It's a boat ride, Danny, not a date."

"Well, the ferry's been dry docked. You're not going back tonight. Text me after work. Maybe I can get you a room for the night in the dorm. The foreign workers are stuck on the other side. I'd let you stay with me, but I don't think my roommate would approve."

"You're shitting me. The ferry's still down?" Daphne said, ignoring everything else I said.

"Tell me this," I said, long accustomed to her brushing me aside. "Where is it?"

"Where's what?" Her smirk and half-turn away told me that I was right.

"The novel? Let's go. Give it up."

In ten years, I'd never seen Daphne without a novel somewhere in her possession. When she was three years old, she could recognize words at the college level. She once showed me a video of herself still in a diaper and reading out loud from *Moby Dick* to a gathering of relatives. Outside of the video, Daphne had no memory of the occasion or of the novel. Her mother had her I.Q. tested but was disappointed to learn that despite Daphne's precociousness as a reader, her intelligence was only slightly above average. A psychologist diagnosed her as having Type 1 hyperlexia, which basically meant that Daphne was some kind of savant in terms of decoding written language. As is the case for most hyperlexics, Daphne's peers eventually caught up to her. The only residual benefit was that she developed an early love for stories and the ability to read close to one thousand words per minute. She still rifled through most books, especially novels, at an alarming pace. I'm not sure how much depth of meaning she pulled from that which she read, but, I think, she preferred to read as she preferred to live: near the surface.

She looked slyly over one, then the other shoulder, then she slowly slipped the top half of a book titled, *The Decameron* over the lip of the pocket in the change apron tied around her waist.

"What happened to Shelley?"

"Finished it."

"What's this one about?"

"Now?"

"Yeah. You're not busy and no one's looking."

Daphne set her tray and rag on the table and lowered herself to the deck in as ladylike a manner as possible inside her tiny uniform. She pressed her mini-skirt against herself and sat with her shins on the wooden deck and the backs of her thighs pressed against her calves. She grabbed hold of two of the vertical bars in the railing and pressed her face between them as if she were speaking to me from inside a jail cell.

"It's another on the reading list and another plague story. I just started it, but it takes place in the Middle Ages. There's a plague in a kingdom, so three young noblemen and seven ladies of the court move into a castle in the countryside to avoid the contagion."

"I like those odds," I said.

"Don't be stupid. While there, they decide that each of them will tell a story a day to help pass the time until they can return to the castle."

Just then a manager type appeared on deck. Daphne stood up and said, "I've got to go."

"The dorm," I said. "Think about it. I'll be back later."

Daphne smiled but said nothing.

I hustled uptown, leaned against the cruiser as if I'd been waiting a while, and met the Chief just as he exited the jail.

"You all settled in?" He asked.

"Yes, sir," I lied. "How's Dooley?"

"Not so good, like death warmed over. There's nothing we can do for him until the doctor gets here, so let's go."

"Where?"

"To meet Dr. Bentham."

"Is the ferry running?"

"Nope."

As I grasped the front passenger side door handle of the Chief's cruiser, a thunderous whoosh passed over our heads. The helicopter felt so close, I actually put an arm over my head and ducked.

"That would be her right now," the Chief said.

Chapter Eight

We headed south on the gently-sloping-seaward Division Street past the police station, hardware store, laundromat, and the village park on our left and, the general store, the boutiques, and Saturday's on the right. Straight ahead, across Shoreline Drive, sat *Gulliver's* with a corpse in its basement. From behind Gulliver's, a constant thumping of dance music blared from two decks of dance floors rigged with multicolored Christmas lights as the Booze Cruise pulled into port. Passengers disembarked with drinks already in hand. The mostly mid-twentysomethings poured down the fore and aft gangplanks. Most were still dancing. All were still drinking.

"Shit!" The Chief said, stomped on the gas pedal, and tore across Lakeshore Drive down to the dock. He blew his horn and parted the incoming revelers until he pulled up next to the vessel. "Hey," he called up to the wheelhouse and beeped the horn again.

A tall, balding man in a white captain's shirt and blue shorts appeared through a sliding window. "What can I do you for, Chief?"

"Whitey, what the hell are you doing here. Opening weekend is next week."

"Private party, Chief. A whole group of third years from Case Medical College who just got their residency placements. They rented the boat for the evening."

"Awww! For Chrissakes! Why wasn't I informed? I'm already short a man. How long you on island?"

"Three hours."

"Three hours," the Chief repeated under his breath. "I hope that's enough time."

"For what?" I asked.

The Chief turned towards me. "For Dr. Bentham to figure out what's going on."

The Chief looked back up at the Captain and said, "Don't ship out without talking to me first, Whitey. Do you hear? I mean it," he added for emphasis.

"I hear you, Chief, but why?"

"Just do as I ask, Whitey."

"Okay. I'm sure those kids won't mind."

We drove east down Lakeshore toward the marina, where there was a large parcel of open, flat land conducive for a helicopter landing. By the time we arrived, the chopper was already speeding away. The Chief flipped on the swirling red and blue flashers to signal our arrival and was occasionally forced to blow his horn to disperse scattered groupings of mallard ducks that blocked the way. We drove through the parking lot and down a cart path that wound in serpentine fashion around a section of permanent dockage and led to several widely-spaced picnic shelters inside a large field. Finally, the high-beams spotlighted a tallish woman, wearing a waffle-brown pencil skirt, a frilly white blouse, high heels, and a surgical mask, standing next to a large case and an overnight bag.

"You're bit overdressed, don't you think?" The Chief said after pulling up next to her and popping the trunk.

"When you called, I was in the middle of my first date in six months. Thanks a lot. I barely had time to grab my equipment and a bag."

"Dr. Bentham, this is Danny Foe. He's the deputy I told you about."

I could almost hear the air quotes around the word "deputy."

She looked at the Chief as if he were joking but realized he wasn't. "Nice to meet you, Danny."

Dr. Bentham loaded her equipment into the trunk herself then climbed into the backseat. The Chief turned the car around in the grass, and we pulled out of the marina just as darkness finished circling, plopped down, stretched out fully, and made itself comfortable for the night. Dr. Bentham stuck a couple of white surgical masks inside the caging that separated the front from the back seat and ordered us to put them on.

"Now, Doc, how do you suppose the people downtown are going to react when they see the chief of police in one of these?" He plucked one of the masks from out of the caging and held it between his fingers before dropping it onto the seat beside him. "My job is to prevent riots, not start them."

"At least the boy should wear his," Dr. Bentham compromised, stinging my pride by dismissing me as a boy.

"Put it on, Danny," The Chief said.

As we pulled out of the marina, a fleet of helicopters, each much larger than the one that dropped off Dr. Bentham, swept onto the island. They came from behind us over the open waters to the east. I assumed so as to avoid the crowds downtown and not to startle them with what we all were hoping would turn out to be an overreaction.

"For Chrissakes, Jenny!" The Chief said. "Who'd you call in? The 101st Airborne?"

"Not yet," Dr. Bentham said without a shred of irony.

"You don't think this . . ." The Chief couldn't finish the

unspeakable question, but I knew exactly where his question had been heading: the Cloudmaker.

Whether as a child attending Kelleys Island Elementary or when I transferred to Port Clinton Public on the mainland, at least once a year, we practiced evacuation procedures in the case of a radiation leak or a meltdown from the Cloud Maker. When I was a junior, we'd even gone live when a team from the Nuclear Regulatory Commission found a football-sized crack in the reactor head while conducting a routine inspection. Although the amount of radiation leaked was insignificant and far below an amount that could harm humans or the environment, a worker at the plant panicked, abandoned her post, and rushed to remove her child from school. Before long, cell phones were buzzing in classrooms with rumors of a meltdown. Despite no word coming through the established channels, one district after another initiated evacuation procedures. Many of my classmates ignored what they'd learned in the drills and escaped in their own cars. Similarly disregardful of established policy, many parents freaked out and intercepted their children as they filed toward the busses lined up to transport them out of the evacuation zone. In less than an hour, an unsubstantiated whisper of a rumor butterfly effected thousands of lives.

"West Sister is approximately ten miles from Toledo Energy's reactor," Dr. Bentham said. "Kelleys fewer than twenty east of there. If these bodies and birds have been dead for as long as you've indicated and they died from exposure to high doses of radiation, chances are that an outbreak of radiation sickness is imminent on all of the Erie Islands and possibly a swath of the shoreline. By now, prevailing westerly winds will have blown the escaped radiation directly across the islands. It's too late to evacuate. The only good news is that beyond the islands to the east, there is nothing but open water until New York State. The majority of shoreline communities should remain unaffected."

The Chief looked perplexed. "If there were a leak, wouldn't Toledo Energy have reported it? I haven't been made aware, and it hasn't been on the news."

Dr. Bentham flashed the Chief a look like the one that Mrs. Barnes gave me when I couldn't solve simple math problems as a child. "I did a quick Geiger Counter reading when we landed," she ignored his naivety. "Thus far, there are no signs of unusually high levels of radiation."

"That's good, right?" The Chief asked.

"For now, yes. But if it is a radiation leak, God only knows how it has already affected the Lake between here and there and the thousands of fish caught and eaten over the last couple of days, not to mention the ones fishermen have taken home in their coolers."

The Chief abruptly scooped his surgical mask from off of the seat and slipped it over his mouth, from which I heard a muted, "For Chrissakes."

Chapter Nine

With the constant thumping of techno music and the stomping of dancers overhead, we gathered in the basement of *Gulliver's* in a large, open section of the damp and dark cellar. I could sense occasional movement in the shadows near the walls, which, from living near the water my entire life, I knew to be rats. We all changed hurriedly into orange, full-body biohazard suits and headgear removed from Dr. Bentham's case. We looked like a bunch of half-assed astronauts. Beneath a single 60-watt light bulb hanging from the ceiling, we cleared an old, wooden fish-cleaning table, stained forever with fish guts and blood, and threw a plastic tarp over the surface. It would have to serve as the examination table. As Dr. Bentham organized her sparse equipment – just enough for a quick, surface examination of the body – the Chief and I removed Smitty from the freezer and delivered him to the table.

I fought swells of nausea as Dr. Bentham used a scissors to cut off Smitty's clothes and examined his naked, Smurf-colored corpse from head to toe. No crease, crevice, or orifice was left unexplored. Speaking into the recording app on her phone, Dr. Bentham said things like, "patient zero," "no signs of trauma," "clear evidence of both vomiting and diarrhea," "lungs full of fluid," "heliotrope cyanosis," and "redness at the back of the throat."

"Was the patient feverish when you encountered him?" She asked the Chief.

"Yeah, he was burning up."

"That would be consistent with radiation sickness as well."

Finally, as if she'd been avoiding the obvious yet unthinkable diagnosis, Dr. Bentham removed a Geiger counter from her bag and made several passes over Smitty's body. I couldn't see the meter nor hear any unusual clicking, but my hearing was somewhat obstructed by the headgear.

"Nothing," she said.

"Nothing!" The Chief echoed enthusiastically. "That's great! This is good news, right?" He looked at me through the plastic visor of his headgear to share his joy and relief at the catastrophe avoided, but I noticed that Dr. Bentham was paying no attention to the Chief's celebration, and her expression only seemed to grow more concerned.

The Chief, disappointed that he was dancing with himself, turned back to Dr. Bentham. "Jenny? What's the matter? "

"Let's go outside," she said.

After the body was returned to the freezer, the three of us stripped out of our protective suits and climbed the stairs to the back drive of Gulliver's. Dr. Bentham removed from her case a yellow sheet of plastic with four black, inter-linked circles on front somewhat resembling a black rose. It was the international warning symbol for a "Biological Hazard." I only knew because those same words were printed in large black letters beneath the circles.

"Subtle," the Chief said from where he and I stood near the dumpsters.

"This basement is officially a hot zone until we're otherwise convinced. That means nobody goes in or out without clearance from me and inside a biohazard suit."

"That's just great. I can't wait to tell the King," the Chief said. Luckily, the sign was not visible from the street, and the King didn't use the basement.

"I need to examine Officer Dooley. Right away," Dr. Bentham said.

"Dooley? What for? If there was no radiation on Smitty, why would there be any on Dooley? It must just be a 24-hour flu bug or something."

"Chief," she began, "this isn't a radiation event."

"Not a radiation event? What do you mean? What else could it be?" the Chief asked.

"Those helicopters that landed at the marina were carrying virologists from the National Biosurveillance Initiative, veterinary pathologists from USAMRIID (U.S. Army Medical Research Institute of Infectious Diseases), and a special ops unit. They're part of an emergency response team organized by the Department of Homeland Security to rapidly detect, assess, and respond to outbreaks of disease in humans and animals and to deliver their findings to local, state, national, and international public health officials: from my little office in Sandusky to Columbus to the CDC (Center for Disease Control) in Atlanta to the WHO (World Health Organization). If the lighthouse keeper's death wasn't caused by radiation but by something in nature, believe it or not, the situation may be worse. The symptoms found in that cadaver . . ."

"Smitty," the Chief interrupted as if offended.

"As found in Smitty," Dr. Bentham acquiesced, "are, as you suggested, consistent with the flu but not the garden variety you're thinking of but the Avian Flu."

"The what 'flu?" I asked.

"Avian. The bird flu. Typically, it doesn't infect humans. Even when people have been infected, it's been mostly through chickens or turkeys that had been crammed into overcrowded and deplorable conditions in factory farms or markets. It has rarely been able to spread from person to person. Where it has, it has proven to be limited, inefficient, and unsustainable – mostly amongst poultry handlers."

"Then, why all the doom and gloom?"

"Viruses mutate, redesign, and adapt themselves to new hosts. Sometimes, they even jump species. It's called zoonosis."

"Like rabies?" the Chief asked.

"That's one type, but a rabid animal is relatively easy to avoid, so very few people are ever infected."

"*To Kill a Mockingbird*," I said.

They both looked at me as if I had two heads.

"It's like in *To Kill a Mockingbird*. When Atticus shoots the rabid dog."

"How about that mosquito one?" the Chief asked, ignoring my allusion. "West Nile?"

"Absolutely," Dr. Bentham answered. "And much scarier because of the number of potential carriers of the virus. Nearly three hundred people died from it during an outbreak in New York in 2012. Mostly the elderly. So far, however, its virulence has proven relatively weak."

"Or Zika," I said.

"Even worse," Dr. Bentham said, this time recognizing my contribution.

"Shit this place swarms with mosquitoes in the late summer," he paused to think. "But not so much in May. What about the mayflies?"

Dr. Bentham shook her head. "No. Mayflies don't bite or sting and are not eaten, so there is no means of transmission. But go back to your rabies example and think of how many dogs live with people. Think about the potential for contracting and spreading a zoonotic illness from dogs if no bite from or ingestion of the animal is necessary for contracting the virus. Imagine if it could spread in the air we share with our dogs."

"That could be devastating," the Chief said.

"It actually happened not long ago in Colorado. It barely made the news because it was quickly identified and controlled, but a pneumonic plague was spread from a pit bull to its owner through its cough. It was the first recorded case of such a dog-to-human contamination in the United States, but it was limited to the dog's owner and three veterinary employees, and it was never passed from person to person. Now think of the number of birds in the world, and think about the devastation they could inflict on the human population should a bird-borne virus jump into that population and subsequently become passable from human to human. Think of the difficulty in containing or eradicating such a virus."

"It could be even worse than dogs," the Chief said.

"Much," said Dr, Bentham. "Because the virus that causes the bird flu has not commonly infected humans, we have virtually no immunity to it or vaccines to prevent it, and the antiviral medications we have are designed to treat a much lower pathogenic form."

"That sounds bad," the Chief stated the obvious.

"If a virus killed the lighthouse keeper and has acquired the capacity to spread through the air from person to person, a deadly influenza pandemic is not only possible but probable. It will make that Ebola panic a few years back look like pink eye."

"Okay. I get it. This disease is bad, but worse than a nuclear meltdown?"

"It's not only a matter of what is worse. If word spreads that there has been a radiation leak, the response will be localized and the panic manageable. Most people will say 'too bad for those people living near the reactor' – just like Chernobyl or Fukushima – but if we announce the potential for a lethal flu pandemic . . ." She momentarily left her speculation open to interpretation. "The human collective unconscious has deep-seated memories of the plague. The Spanish Flu virus of 1918-19 originated in birds and is estimated to have killed 80 to 100 million people worldwide. It won't take much to jostle those memories awake and to cause a panic unlike one this country, even the world, has ever witnessed. Trust me, in terms of avoiding mass panic and the chaos that would ensue, an isolated outbreak of radiation sickness would have been the lesser of two evils."

"Dooley," the Chief said as the full weight of the situation dawned on him.

"That's right, Chief, and we need to get him and those Girl Scouts diagnosed and, if necessary, quarantined as soon as possible. Smitty, surrounded by thousands of wild birds, may very well have contracted the disease from direct contact with bird excretions. He probably did. In which case, there is no real threat to anyone else, but if Officer Dooley, who only had contact with the still-living lighthouse keeper, not the birds, contracted it from the lighthouse keeper through inhalation and then passed it on to those girls . . . ." Dr. Bentham paused as the nightmare flash forwarded in her mind, "we may have evidence of a spillover of the virus from bird to human to airborne human to human transmission. Even worse, if this virus somehow gets off this island and onto the mainland, there is potential for a catastrophic outbreak. So, where is Dooley? I assume you have him detained somewhere."

"He's locked up in the cell in my office."

"Good. By now, the advance team will have contacted the Coast Guard and Border Patrol and they will be forming a cordon around the island. The ferry will remain shut down and the airport closed. No one will be permitted on or off this island until we know exactly what we are dealing with," she said.

I thought of Daphne and asked Dr. Bentham for a spare surgical mask.

"What about the Booze Cruise?" the Chief asked. "It departs for the mainland at 1:00 a.m. That's close to fifty drunk and unruly people who are going to want to know why they're being detained."

"Get me to Dooley. If he has a case of the common flu, we could be out of here before they ever know what nearly hit them, and you two need to round up anyone else who may have come into contact with Smitty. He's Patient Zero."

We placed the bucket of dead birds inside the trunk of the Chief's cruiser and drove to the jail, where Dr. Bentham examined Dooley. The Chief and I stood across the room behind his desk and, although we wore masks, all but held our breaths. Dr. Bentham, in full spacesuit, didn't seem particularly concerned for Dooley's well-being. She paid him neither curative nor compassionate attention, strictly clinical. She made no attempt to alleviate poor Dooley's misery or to respond to his crazed ramblings.

After drawing several vials of his blood and storing them inside her case, Dr. Bentham finally turned toward us. "I need you to get me, these samples, and those birds from West Sister back to the marina. The pathologists will have established a field lab by now where everything can be tested and compared with Smitty's blood and tissue samples. How about the EMTs who transferred the body? I assume you have them under quarantine as well."

The Chief's crestfallen expression was a more-than-adequate, if less-than-desired response.

"You're kidding," Dr. Bentham said.

"Jenny, I didn't think. I'm a cop, not a doctor. It's not like I deal with this kind of shit every day."

"You weren't supposed to think," she said, angrily. "You have a manual with established protocol."

"I have binder after binder with 'established protocols.' I'm also the only full-time officer on an island whose population more than quadruples during the summer."

Dr. Bentham softened, but said, "You should have known.

It's your job to know. You need to track down those EMTs and get them to the marina as soon as possible." She paused. "Now!"

Dr. Bentham agreed not to place a biohazard sign on the jailhouse door, but the Chief made sure the lights were off and the jail was good and locked when we left.

"Why us?" I asked the Chief after dropping off Dr. Bentham, her samples from Smitty and Dooley, and the dead birds at the marina, where a string of large, white medical tents had been erected and a perimeter formed by armed soldiers. "Why can't some of those special ops guys in the choppers track them down?"

"I suppose," the Chief said, "we're less likely to cause suspicion, and we can perform the search and removal more surgically than a bunch of soldiers in gas masks unfamiliar with the place."

Chapter Ten

By the time we arrived back downtown, the music was blasting out of the open doors of the bars, and the mayflies had begun to flit beneath the light poles.

"What about our masks, Chief?"

"I suppose we'd better wear them. If nothing else they'll block the smell of those damn bugs."

"Won't people ask questions?"

"On this island, near eleven o'clock on a Friday night? It's going to take a hell of a lot more than a surgical mask to raise suspicion. Hell, we'll probably start a trend. Next week, all of the animals will be wearing them."

That was the first time I'd heard the Chief use the island Lifers' favorite pejorative for Kelleys' weekend bar patrons: animals.

He took off his uniform shirt so that he wore a tight-fitting, v-neck, white t-shirt over his navy blue pants. Except for the slight graying around the temples of his military-cut, sandy brown hair and the absence of a single tattoo, the well-muscled Chief didn't look much different from a lot of the guys, half his age, peacocking in and out of the bars.

"Let's go," he said, crossed the street, and entered *Saturday's* through the side door on Division Street. Andy had said he had to get back to work. That made him the easiest of the two EMTs to locate. It also put him in the most direct contact with the unwary and unprotected public.

I followed in the wake cut by the Chief's wide frame. He carved an impressive swath through the sea of partiers standing shoulder to shoulder or dancing nose to nose and crotch to crotch. At nearly six-and-a-half-feet, he was able to see over the tops of most heads in our search for Andy. "Stay here and keep your eyes open." He literally had to scream down at me. "I'm going to ask at the bar if he reported to work. Maybe we got lucky, and Andy never showed up."

I smiled my assent but I was scared shitless. The volume of the music and the heat generated by the pressing and writhing of bodies added to my discomfort and primed the nausea in my guts. One dude was apparently offended by my mask and asked if I thought "he stunk or something." A cute girl asked me if I wanted to play doctor. I did, but she wasn't serious, just drunk.

I watched the Chief approach the bar. He leaned way over to talk to a bartender who wasn't Andy. When he returned, he yelled, "The bartender said Andy left a while ago. He also said that Andy was coughing a lot and complaining about not feeling well."

"That doesn't sound good," I yelled back.

Our attention was drawn to a ruckus in the back of the bar. Driven by instinct, the Chief pushed me through the crowd to the front of a line snaking out of the men's room. His size was enough to temper anyone's sense of unfairness. The one stall was closed, but a stench rose from it that was borderline demonic and causing nearly everyone nearby, including me, to gag.

"It's Andy," the Chief muttered even before he gave the stall door one quick pop with his shoulder and knocked the sliding bar lock right out of its screws and onto the piss-stained, linoleum floor. Inside, Andy had either shit or puked all over himself or both. His dirty-blond goatee was stained red with coughed-up blood and sputum. "We've got to get him out of here," the Chief said.

"We can't walk him through that crowd like this," I said.

"You're right."

The Chief pulled his badge from his pants pocket, stepped out from the stall, brandished the badge, pulled grown men by their shirt collars from their spots in front of the urinals, and escorted them out of the door with their peckers still hanging out until he, Andy, and I were the only ones remaining inside the men's room.

He then called Officer Burns from the two-way clipped to his belt.

Chief:I need you to disperse the crowd watching the fire outside of *Saturday's*.

Burnsie:I'm there now, Chief. There's no crowd or fire.

Chief:Just open the doors and move the people. I'm about to start one.

Burnsie:What?!

The Chief ignored Burnsie's question and furiously unwound one of the rolls of brown paper hand towels from its wall dispenser as if he were reeling in a fish.

"Get the other one," he commanded me.

The Chief piled his armful in one sink and I placed mine in the other. He took off his thick black rubber-soled boots, placed one on each pile, pulled a lighter from his pocket, and lit the towels.

Thick, black smoke from the burning soles soon reached towards the high ceiling and its exposed pipes.

"What exactly are we doing here, Chief?" I asked while waving the acrid fumes from my face.

"We're clearing the place so we can get Andy out without infecting half the bar."

The Chief yanked open the door and starting fanning the tar black smoke and pungent smell of burning rubber into the bar space.

Some dude called out, "Fire!"

A girl screamed.

"There'll be a stampede," I was forced to yell over the dance music that flooded into the restroom.

"Let's hope," he yelled back.

One after another, a series of the glass domes over the sprinkler heads burst. Water sprayed down upon us and in the immediate area of the restroom. I watched as revelers pushed and shoved and made their way out of Saturday's. A pair of girls, doused by the sprinklers and knocked to the floor, sat huddled, and soaking wet as if dejected losers in a wet t-shirt contest. They hugged and cried hysterically even after the crowd had passed by and over them. I crossed the flip flop and sandal-strewn space and helped them to their feet and to the door, which had been ripped from its hinges and where I heard the island's lone fire truck's siren finally piercing the night in harmony with an ambulance. When I returned to the restroom, the Chief was finishing dousing the fires in the sinks, while Andy moaned on the floor.

"What now?" I asked.

"We wait."

"For what?"

"The firemen to arrive and for Burnsie to clear the area."

Though not insignificant, the structural damage was limited to the restroom. Compared to the lives potentially saved, it was well worth it.

The first volunteer firemen through the door were Tom and Terry Sanderson, identical twins and island Lifers.

"The fire's under control fellas," the Chief said, "but we're going to need a stretcher."

Tom and Terry both saw Andy's legs sticking out from the

stall and started in his direction, but the Chief quickly blocked their way. "Send in Kenny," the Chief ordered. "And tell him to put on a mask."

A few minutes later, Kenny entered the bar alone.

"It's Andy," the Chief told him then said, "You're going to have to come with us."

"Why? What for? What's this about?"

"Just listen. Here's what we're going to do," the Chief said. "We're going to wheel Andy across the street to the jail and put him in the cell until we can safely transport him elsewhere."

"Is it the same thing . . ." Kenny began.

"That killed Smitty?" The Chief finished Kenny's question. "Yeah, it looks like it."

I could almost hear Kenny doing the math in his head: Smitty's dead and Officer Dooley and Andy are sick. There was little question who was next in the pattern. He panicked, broke for the Division Street door, and ploughed into and fell on top of Officer Burns, who was entering. Kenny quickly performed a push up off of the officer, whose hat had gone flying, and was out the door and into the night before the Chief could reach him.

"What was that all about," Burns asked as he righted himself, rubbed his jaw, and put his hat back on.

The Chief didn't answer him. "We're going to have to find Kenny, but right now, we need to get Andy out of here. How's it look outside?"

"Clear as it's going to be," Burns said. "Most of the crowd's already moved on to Gulliver's and *Montego Bay*."

I pulled as the Chief pushed the stretcher. Officer Burns provided interference through the diminished gathering of the curious. Catching a whiff of the effluvium rising from our cargo, the throng happily parted before us. I'm sure it wasn't the first near-comatose individual, reeking of shit and vomit, they'd seen transported from an island bar. When we crossed the street, I stopped, lifted my mask, and puked into a nearby trash bin. I blamed it entirely on the stench, and the Chief seemed to buy it, but in the hollows of my insides, I feared it was more than that.

Inside the police station, the Chief deposited poor Andy inside the cell, on the floor, with Dooley. He handcuffed him to a vertical bar of the cage and locked the door. Officer Burns was sent in search of Kenny.

"Quick, take your clothes off," the Chief ordered me.

I stared at him, stupefied by his request.

"Let's go. We're taking no chances. There's no shower in here, just that sink and toilet in the cell." He grabbed a bottle of hand sanitizer from off his desk. I'll pour some on you, and you rub it all around. I'll get your back where you can't reach, then you'll have to do the same for me."

The full enormity of the situation seemed to be washing over the Chief. I think he sensed his always-tenuous control over island events slipping through his fingers.

"But."

"No 'buts' Danny. This is some bad shit we've fallen into."

I stripped, stood naked, and did as I was told. As I rubbed myself down, the Chief, hairy-assed naked himself, stuffed everything but our shoes inside three layers of black, plastic garbage bags, then he opened an antique, iron floor safe, which sat behind his desk and was used to store prisoners' valuables. He locked the bundle inside. After the Chief finished stashing the clothes, he "did my back," then he performed the self-scrubbing routine, and I applied the sanitizer between his shoulder blades. He pulled two fresh uniforms out of a locker: his own spare and one for me left behind by a fired part-timer. It wasn't a perfect fit, but it was close enough and it was clean.

After delivering Andy to the marina field lab, we left Officer Dooley handcuffed to the cage between the seats in the cruiser and waited outside the tent for some answers and directions from Dr. Bentham.

"It appears that it is zoonotic, and it looks like it jumped," she said when she finally emerged from the tent. Her tone was as dispassionate as if she were giving the time and temperature. "We haven't processed the results of Andy's blood work yet, but Dooley clearly contracted it from Smitty who caught it from the birds. There's little doubt that Dooley passed it on to the girl scouts. Who they've transmitted it to, time will tell and so on."

When I heard Dr. Bentham's prognosis, my knees wobbled, flesh crawled, and insides turned queasy. I had little idea of the apocalyptic slide on top of which we were perched, and when I say 'we,' I mean the entire damn species, but it was obvious that she did.

"I have to make a bunch of phone calls. You need to get Officer Dooley to that campground. That's going to be our quarantine zone. If we're lucky, no one else has been infected. The facts that we're on an island and are aware of the virus's existence are the two things we have in our favor. If we get ahead of it, we may be able to choke off what's already here and prevent its spread. What about the other EMTs?"

"We're still looking for them."

"Find them," she ordered the Chief. "It's not a very big island."

"What about the people on the mainland?" The Chief ignored her implied insult.

"With the ease and amount of contraction we're seeing here, should the virus make it to the mainland, it could spark an outbreak of unprecedented proportions. It's a little known fact that all three pandemics of the twentieth century had first mutated in birds before shifting into the human population."

The Chief's expression didn't change any more than if someone had told him that one of the tourists had dumped a golf cart into the lake – not an uncommon occurrence on the island.

"And," Dr. Bentham began again, "if either of you start to feel even the slightest bit ill, get your asses to the 4-H camp immediately and quarantine yourself. Also, you both have had close contact with every one of the infected, so wear those masks. If you have been infected, you've also become carriers, and you're most contagious now, before the symptoms appear. If I could afford to, I'd bench both of you right now. I'll meet you two back at the jail within the hour," Dr. Bentham said and disappeared inside the only non-white tent. I assumed it to be a field command post.

The Chief volunteered to transport Dooley himself. He said there wasn't a need for both of us to risk infection any more than was necessary. After slipping a mask over Dooley's mouth – a bit like putting on a condom after the sex – the Chief carried the sick ODNR officer to the cruiser and lay him in the back. With the windows wide open and the flashers swirling, the Chief drove away towards the camp.

Before hiking back to town, I convinced myself to come clean with Dr. Bentham and confess that my head had been pounding for the past half hour, my throat was sore, and my body felt like it had been run over by a truck. I stepped inside the command post and found her in the middle of a very serious conversation on what looked like an old-school handheld walkie-talkie. When she saw me, Dr. Bentham responded with a look as if I'd walked in on her stepping out of the shower. Between the seeming urgency of her phone call and the look she'd given me, it was clear that I wasn't welcome, so I immediately backed out of the tent, took off in a jog toward town, and blamed my discomfort on fatigue and the stress of the long day, and I kept my mouth shut.

Chapter Eleven

It was past midnight, when I hurried down to Gulliver's to warn Daphne.

I found her busing tables inside. "Do you have a minute to talk?" I asked.

"Yeah, but just a minute. I don't want to get in trouble on my first night. By the way, what's up with the mask, Michael Jackson?"

"It's no joke, Daph. The mask is what I need to talk to you about. I brought you one. At least wear it while you're talking with me."

"I suppose I can take a quick break," she said and followed me outside around back to the docks, where we sat with our feet dangling over the side no more than two feet above the black water.

"Do you see that twenty-seven foot Catalina sail boat just inside the break wall? It belongs to the King. Stay there – at least for tonight. He never takes it out. I don't think it has ever moved. It'll be safer than staying in the dorm."

"Danny, slow down. What are you talking about? Does this have something to do with Derek?"

"No. I told you the ferries have been shut down."

"I thought you meant temporarily? For how long?"
"I don't know."

"Why?" She asked.

"Look, I don't know everything, but it looks like there's a nasty virus loose on the island. Some infected people have already died."

"A virus? You mean like in *The Andromeda Strain*?" she asked almost excitedly.

"I don't know. I've never read it. Don't you ever just watch television?"

"No," she said curtly. "How do you know all of this? And if the virus is here, shouldn't we be getting *off* the island?"

"Of course," I said. "You're right. But they have some kind of protocol. It's all I've heard all day: protocol this and fucking protocol that." I was growing increasingly tired, frustrated, and scared, so I was venting to Daphne. "I've been with the Chief of Police all night and some doctor from Sandusky. I helped the Chief recover a dead body. It's in a freezer in the basement."

"Yuk! Here?"

"The doctor said it's some kind of bird flu."

"Is that why there are so many dead birds all over the place?"

"Yes. It's bad, Daphne. Really bad."

"I'm sure you're blowing it out of proportion. I'll call my mom. She'll know what to do."

"Okay. Look, Daphne. I have to meet up with the Chief. But you can't tell your mom what I've told you. Make something else up. The Chief doesn't want a panic. For now at least, people are safe here, but their first instinct will be to return home, where, according to the doctor, the risk of their spreading the infection is great and will only increase over the next couple of days. So keep it to yourself for now and just stay on the boat, okay?"

"I don't like it," she said, "but I will." She added, "For now."

I wasn't convinced. She may have been simply telling me what I wanted to hear, but I had to get back to the jail to meet the Chief and Dr. Bentham.

When I returned, Dr. Bentham was outside the jail smoking a cigarette. She didn't question my whereabouts.

"You caught me," she said, dropped the cigarette to the sidewalk, and snuffed it out beneath the sole of her high heel. "It's a bad habit from med school of all places. It helped me stay awake when studying. Now, it just calms my nerves when I'm really stressed."

My eyes rolled over.

"I know. Those are excuses and I need to stop. I mean, what kind of example am I setting? Blah, blah, blah. Danny? Are you alright?"

My knees buckled. My throat felt gripped by the strong hands of Panic, and I began to hyperventilate.

Dr. Bentham swung one of my arms around her shoulders and guided me inside to the Chief's desk chair. "Cup your hands to your mouth and breathe into them," she instructed me.

Gradually, I got my breathing under control, but my heart still pounded, my mind still raced, and my words poured out at a mile-a-minute, "Am I going to die? I mean, I was right there with those Girl Scouts. One of them bit me. And Officer Dooley and Smitty and Andy. How can I not be infected?"

"Is this what you wanted to talk to me about back at the marina?"

I nodded in the affirmative.

Dr. Bentham hiked her knee-length skirt just enough so that she could squat in front of me. Her nylons groaned as they stretched. "I don't know if you've been infected or how it will end. I wish I could tell you differently, but I just don't know. I guess time will tell. What I do know is that there is no undoing what has already been done. All we can do from here is protect ourselves the best we can. These things aren't automatic. Everyone's different. Some people are more susceptible to infection than others, and some people's systems are better at fighting it off. We'll just have to see. I do know that panicking will only make it worse."

I took a couple of deep breaths and nodded my head.

"You're going to be all right," Dr. Bentham said in a tone lacking conviction, just before I passed out.

BOOK TWO

"Don't worry (don't worry) 'bout a thing,
'Cause every little thing gonna be all right!"

From "Three Little Birds"
By Bob Marley

Chapter One

*Day 2 – Saturday, May 25, 201_*

Delirium.
Snippets and shadows.
"If I could only get up, I would show them."
Thirsty. Always thirsty.
Hot. Cold. Hot. Cold.
Drowning!
My mother pushes me on the tire swing attached by a rope to a limb in a tree in our backyard.
"I want to walk!"
Everything hurts. So heavy.
"Officer Sarter, I have to go home. The streetlights are on."
Fire trucks.
Breathe!
Girl Scout zombies!
Swallowing swords of fire.
The whoosh of helicopters.
"I really need to go for a walk."
A lady in a mask runs a wet washcloth over my skin.
"Where are my pants?"

"Daphne Moyer is so hot?"

"Let me up! I have to get out of here!"

A murder of crows on the rooftop. An unkindness of ravens on the wire.

"Danny. Danny, it's me."

"Daphne? How did you find me?"

"You said you were helping the chief of police."

"Is he here?" I asked.

"No. No one's here. I let myself in. They've got you strapped down like a mental patient."

"I'm sick, Daphne. I'm so sick I'm not even sure if you're really here or if I'm having a fever dream."

"I see that. Don't worry about me. I'm wearing my mask."

"That wasn't really my point, but I'm glad. I wouldn't want you to get sick."

Daphne had transformed the plain white mask I had given her into a tie dyed field of crayon colors. Hot magenta, electric lime, orange-red, and razzle-dazzle rose all burst forth in fireworks patterns on her mask. She wore a pair of black-with-white-piping, satiny men's soccer shorts, whose waistband had been rolled several times to keep the shorts from sliding off of her slender hips. On top, she wore a tie dyed wife-beater under a zippered black hoodie with a smiling Bob Marley on the left front half and the chorus to "Three Little Birds" emblazoned in words of alternating red, yellow, and green – "Don't worry about a thing. Cause every little thing's gonna be all right" – on the right half.

"What's with the outfit?" I asked.

"I've been living on that sailboat behind Gulliver's. I found the clothes and a tie dye kit. I thought if I have to wear this mask to talk to you, it may as well be cheerful. I did a bunch of men's undershirts and boxers too."

"Please, don't go all hippie and stop shaving your legs and

armpits."

"You're gross," she said. "Danny! Don't go back to sleep yet. I need to talk to you. I can't stand that boat. It's making me seasick. I talked to my mom. The ferries still aren't running, and she thinks I should move. She gave me an address for a client's house that she's been showing on the island and told me where the hide-a-key is."

My skin tingled as the ice cold tip of a red Sharpie scrawled the street name and house numbers across the palm of my hand.

I asked, "What about your dad?"

"He didn't answer his cell last night, and now I can't get any service on my phone."

I changed the subject. "What happened after I left you at Gulliver's last night?"

Daphne sat down on the edge of my cot. "Some cop with a bullhorn announced that all of the ferries were being grounded indefinitely, all islanders should return to their homes, and visitors would be put up in the dorm or the hotel. Should I have gone to one of those?"

"No. You did the right thing. You're better off where you are – away from people – but you shouldn't have come to see me."

"I had to."

Afraid that she would leave and afraid to be left alone if I didn't say something to make her stay, I asked, "Whatcha reading now?"

"The last of the books I brought with me. It's called *After London*."

"How is it?"

"Real science-y."

"How's that?"

"In the story, extreme climate change has returned the world to a state of nature. Kind of like that *Discovery Channel* series that Mrs. Kubitz showed in biology class. Remember? All of the buildings and roads are gone, even in like New York City and London, and the whole world is covered in vegetation again. It's a botanist's dream."

"Sounds interesting," I lied.

"It's not," she said. At least not yet, but I've only finished part one, and the jacket promises that part two is 'a riveting adventure.' We'll see."

Daphne suddenly stood up.

"What's wrong?" I asked.

"Someone's coming."

The last thing I remember of that Saturday is Daphne leaning over, kissing my torpid forehead through her tie dyed mask, and disappearing as if in a dream – a very bad dream.

Chapter Two

*Day 3 – Sunday, May 26, 201_*

For most of the day, I continued to drift in and out of consciousness with my throat raw and my lungs full of fluid. When I was awake, I alternated between spells of teeth-chattering chills and white hot fevers punctuated by violent fits of coughing and vomiting. Blurred images and concerned voices of vaguely familiar people came and went. At one point, I swear, my dead grandfather and parents were in the room, but they stood back as if embarrassed.

Chapter Three

Day 4 – Monday, May 27, 201_

Early in the evening, the fever relented. I could once again draw deep breaths, and I knew that I, if not the world around me, was returning to normal.

A man's voice slowly seeped into my awareness. "Danny, Danny, Danny," it prodded.

For a moment, I thought it to be my brother's. I figured that I was back in Port Clinton, had overslept, and was late for school.

"Danny, it's Chief Sarter."

"Chief Sarter?" I questioned as if it were the first time I had heard the name. "Where am I? What happened?"

"You're in jail."

"Is that why I'm in handcuffs?" I took a quick spatial inventory: the cot on which I lay, a toilet, sink, and a Visqueen curtain, which had been draped against the cell bars. "What did I do?"

"You didn't do anything, son," the Chief said as he removed the handcuffs. "You've been sick. The handcuffs were to keep

88

you from hurting yourself or infecting anyone else. For a while there, you were thrashing around and trying to get out of bed."

"Am I going to die?"

"No. Your fever broke. You're going to be fine now. Scared the hell out of us though. You ran a temperature over 104F for quite some time."

"Where's Daphne?"

"Who?"

"Nothing. Why am I alive?"

The Chief bent over me and undid the cuffs. "Are you talking under the immediate circumstances or do you mean in an existential sense? In either case you're asking a question that is only answerable by someone at a much higher pay grade than I'm pulling, but if you want my opinion, it's completely random."

"Chief, where did you learn to talk like that?"

"I'm a big *Rush* fan, and I did parts of two years of community college before I enlisted. Philosophy 101."

I sat up too fast. The blood rushed to my head and nearly caused me to faint. Only the Chief's steadying hand prevented me from rolling off the cot and onto the concrete floor.

"I need to get to work," I said. "Saturday is orientation and Training Day."

"First off, it's Monday night, and second, I don't think Island Adventures is going to open this season."

"Not open? Why not? It's tourist season."

"I'm afraid there won't be a tourist season this year. A lot has happened since you took ill. For one, the Steinbauers are no longer with us."

"They got off the island?"

"You could say that. They're dead. I found them this morning. Did it themselves. The plague has struck the island. Hard"

"Plague?" I began to stitch recent memories back into

coherent form.

"Plague. The avian flu. The bird flu. H5N1. Some are calling it 'The Blues,' but it doesn't matter what you call it. It kills the same."

"Have you found Kenny?" I asked.

"Not yet. He must have gone into hiding, and we just don't have the resources to look for him right now. Besides, if he has gotten sick, as long as he's hiding, he's probably not infecting anybody else. He's as good as in our custody and in isolation."

"What about that doctor-lady and her team at the marina?"

"I'm here; they're gone," Dr. Bentham answered as she entered the cell through a slit cut down the middle of the Visqueen curtain.

Wearing only a pair of boxers that weren't my own and which left me to ponder who exactly had undressed then dressed me, I crossed my arms across my chest to cover as much of my nakedness as possible.

"Don't sweat it, honey," Dr. Bentham said. "It's been a while, but I have seen it all before – mostly dead guys," she added.

She'd changed out of her "date clothes" from Friday night and into a form-fitting, sky blue, long sleeved, button down, cotton shirt and a pair of navy blue, stretch twill pants with a bottom that flared over open-toed sandals. The new ensemble still left her way overdressed for the island and the occasion.

"Here," the Chief said and tossed me a pair of white socks, the stiffest pair of jeans I'd ever felt, and a green t-shirt with "Kelley's Island, OH, an Island for All Seasons" screen-printed around a map of the island on the front. "I got them at the general store along with those undershorts. [That answered that question. Yuck.] Get dressed. Then, if you're up to it, step outside. You could use some fresh air, and we need to talk."

"Should I wear my mask?"

"I'm not going to tell you not to," the Chief said. "But, we don't have near enough to supply everyone on island. In my line of work, I've known of people who have been killed for a whole lot less."

After they'd left, I tried to check my phone for missed calls and messages, but there was no service. I reached up to rub the sleep from my eyes and saw red flash before them. On my hand was the address I thought I had only dreamed Daphne had inscribed. Before washing off the marker, I committed the address to memory.

When I emerged from behind the Visqueen, the office was empty but the television sitting on a corner filing cabinet was on. The Chief's and Dr. Bentham's voices filtered in from outside. I paused to listen to a reporter interviewing a man identified by the graphics beneath him as the Assistant Director of the Division of Community Health Services for Erie County. The Director was insisting that, although tragic, the radiation leak from Toledo Energy's nuclear power plant had been contained and limited to the Erie islands and that state and federal officials were doing everything possible to treat those unfortunate enough to have been on the islands when the leak occurred. The islands, he said, would remain under quarantine for the foreseeable future, and the waters of the Lake's Western Basin would be similarly off-limits to boaters and fishermen. As soon as the interview was finished, the screen went black as if it were deliberately cut. I used the remote from off of the Chief's desk to flip through some channels, but each one displayed the same message of "No Signal" floating through its space and bouncing off its walls like a Pong ball in perpetual play.

"What is happening here?" I asked the ghosts of lawmen and prisoners past.

Outside, the Chief and Dr. Bentham, neither wearing surgical masks, stood against the yet-to-be-replaced window of the jail. From the sleeping bag rolled up and stashed behind the desk and the scattered women's personal items and beauty products, I deduced that Dr. Bentham had been living out of the jail while I was sick.

Although the downtown looked the same, the second that I stepped outside the jail, I knew that something wasn't right. For one, above our heads, some kind of four-legged drone was making slow, circular sweeps of the downtown. In addition, usually by Sunday night, the tourists have fled the island and the Kelleys' workers and Lifers have wiped off their put on smiles and have reemerged from behind their counters and bars, from inside the restaurant kitchens, from off the charter boats, and from their private properties – which many kept private with "No Trespassing" signs in their yards and loaded shotguns stashed near their front doors – but they were nowhere to be found. Oddly, a steady beat of music, accompanied by sporadic hoots and hollers, wafted down Division Street.

"There's Lazarus," Chief Sarter greeted me. "We thought you were a goner for sure."

I ignored his biblical allusion and failed prediction and directly addressed Dr. Bentham.

"I thought you said there was no radiation poisoning."

"That's correct," she said. "I did."

"But I just heard the man on the news say there was and that all of the islands have been quarantined," my voice quivered as I spoke. "And where's that music coming from?" I asked the Chief.

"Slow down, son," Chief Sarter said. "There's a lot we need to catch you up on. We *are* under quarantine. There's a flotilla of naval, Coast Guard, and Border Patrol vessels surrounding the entire island, and as I'm sure you've noticed," he stopped and pointed to the sky, where no more than a couple hundred feet in the air the whizzing of tiny helicopter blades attached to a Space Invader-looking drone could be heard passing overhead.

"We're being watched," he said.

"Unmanned Aviation Vehicles," Dr. Bentham said, "UAVs or drones, equipped with cameras, being operated from one of those vessels the Chief just mentioned."

"They're all over the island," the Chief interjected. "And you thought the mayflies were bad."

"Anyway," Dr. Bentham continued, "if they don't like or are confused by what they see coming from the cameras on those drones, they send in the big boys."

"Big boys?" I repeated as a question.

"Fully-crewed, locked and loaded Black Hawk helicopters," the Chief explained. "As for the music, it's coming from the Village Dorm. It's some of the visitors who got stuck on island when the quarantine went into effect, mostly the Booze Cruisers and a few folks who were camping at the state park. The birders chose to nest at the Kelleys Island Hotel on the west end."

A quick look down to the foot of Division proved the Booze Cruise to still be on island.

"And the radiation?" I turned to Dr. Bentham. "I thought you said it was some kind of flu."

"That part is a little trickier," she said.

"What do you mean?"

"There never was a radiation leak. That's just the story they're selling to the public."

"They?" I asked.

"The government. Remember what I said about the lesser of two evils? That would be the radiation leak. What you had and what they don't want anyone to know about is a newly-emerged strain of the bird flu."

"Then, why am I not dead like the others?"

"Who knows? For some reason you beat it. You're the lucky one. Even the Black Death didn't infect everyone, and everyone it infected didn't die . . ."

"Just most of them," I interjected.

"Not quite but there are always a few exceptions like yourself. Nature is like that. You're a fluke," Dr. Bentham said. "The flu didn't kill you, but you still carry the virus. It's highly unlikely, but it's possible that you could still pass it on."

"I don't understand any of this," I said, dizzy with confusion.

"Few people do, but as the Chief said, the entire island has been quarantined, and residents have been asked to confine themselves to their homes as much as is possible."

"But, why? Why not transport them to the mainland and get treatment for the sick?"

"There is no treatment," Dr. Bentham said. "Like I said, it's an entirely new strain of virus. For now, we're applying the same strategy on the island as the army and CDC are applying to the island as a whole."

"The CDC?"

"The Center for Disease Control has ordered a quarantine of the island. Their goal is to isolate the infected and prevent as much human interaction as possible until the virus burns itself out. If we're lucky and we're vigilant in our response, we may be able to stop it from spreading. They call it 'Operation Chokehold.'"

"Where is your team?"

"Evacuated."

"Then . . . ?" I began.

"Why am I still here?" She correctly inferred my question.

"Yes."

"I knew the protocol. Hell, I helped write it. But when the chopper landed to evacuate the team, I couldn't board. I couldn't abandon all of these people or leave Chief Sarter with one deputy and a sick eighteen-year-old kid."

"But what about . . ."

"My family?"

Damn, she was good at that game.

"A mother in a nursing home, but she doesn't even remember my name."

"So they just abandoned us, and no one is coming to help?"

"The strain is too virulent to risk sending in more medical personnel. The plan is to choke the flu off at its source, minimize losses, and prevent its spread at all costs."

"Even at the cost of our lives and everyone else on the island?"

"Yes," she said matter-of-factly.

"But what about the infected birds? They can't quarantine all of the birds. Won't they just fly to the mainland and spread their flu?"

"To other birds? Maybe. But remember: Smitty lived on a protected Wildlife Refuge on West Sister, a major springtime stop for wild migratory waterfowl crossing the lake. He was surrounded by bird feces, saliva, and vomit. He was particularly vulnerable. There's little danger of people being infected on the mainland in a similar way. Waterfowl avoid humans as much as they can. The real danger is the mixing of the waterfowl with the poultry that ends up in the food supply, but we've dealt with that before. Even worse is what we're seeing here: the direct spread of the virus from one human to another, but as far as we know, no one currently on the mainland has been infected, and the only possible human carriers are and must remain on this island."

"You mean Officer Dooley and Andy."

Dr. Bentham exchanged a look with Chief Sarter that chilled me. "I mean all of us."

"They're dead. Aren't they?"

"Officer Dooley's deceased," the Chief answered.

"This virus is faster-acting than anything the world has ever seen," Dr. Bentham said. "Dooley's contact with Smitty was relatively prolonged."

"What about Andy?"

"It doesn't look good for him either," the Chief said. "He's at the campground with the other infected."

"Others? You mean the girl scouts?"

"Them too," the Chief said, "turns out that Dooley contact with quite a lot people before getting sick, and Andy mixed and poured drinks and served plates of food for a couple of hours before we got to him, and we have yet to find Kenny or that intern. I just haven't had the time. The reality is that, right now, we just don't know how many people it has spread to."

"There are a number of others isolated in cabins and tents at the 4-H camp with manifestations of early symptoms," Dr. Bentham said. "For now, we've been letting people believe the radiation story. It tends to keep them indoors and isolated. I've been doing what I can to comfort the infected and to ease their suffering, but there's nothing I can do to prevent the virus from running its course, which, except for you, has always resulted in death. There are no other medical personnel at the campground, only me and some guards."

"Guards?"

"With orders to shoot to kill," the Chief added.

"Lucky for us," Dr. Bentham jumped in to soften the image forming in my mind, "that has not been a problem. The disease is so virulent that most of its victims quickly fall incapacitated."

"That's 'lucky'?" I asked.

"Compared to the Walkers it is," the Chief added.

"The what?" I asked, as the complications cascaded and I grew increasingly mortified.

"For some reason," Dr. Bentham said, "some of the infected, at the infection's worst point, show a dangerous proclivity for walking, which, if unchecked, adds to the danger of its spread."

I remembered a point during my sickness when a lucid consciousness of my life-in-death condition washed over me like an unanticipated, ice cold wave come over the bow. I remembered a surge of adrenaline and struggling against the handcuffs that kept me chained to the cot and wanting, needing – more than anything – to get up and move, as if to prove to Death that he had the wrong guy.

The Chief tagged back in. "The real problems will arrive later if and when the non-infected decide to hide their diseased family members and friends, or they attempt to break them out of quarantine. That's why the guards, and that's where you're going to be particularly helpful."

"Me? Why me?"

"Now that you've had the virus and survived, you're most likely immune," Dr. Bentham explained. "You probably can't catch it again."

"That means," the Chief said, "you're going to help me search homes for the infected and for guns."

"Wait. You said 'most likely' and 'probably.'"

"We can't be a hundred percent certain without tests and time, and we have neither," Dr. Bentham said.

"That's just great," I complained. "I still can't believe they've just left us?"

"In the late nineties," Dr. Bentham began, "a strain of the bird flu broke out in the poultry markets of Hong Kong, and just this past winter in Tennessee, the only means they had to combat it in either case was to slaughter millions of birds. It sounds drastic, but it proved effective. The world hardly even noticed."

It was the Chief who responded to that news. "Wait. You're not suggesting they'll . . ."

"I'm just telling you what worked. With today's speed and ease of travel, this virus will spread around the world in fewer than forty-eight hours if it gets off this island. If word leaks of what's happening here, there will be chaos beyond anything this country's ever experienced. Whether we like it or not, in comparison, the four to five hundred some odd people who may die by letting the virus run its course here until there are no more hosts is an acceptable loss by any measure."

"Including us?" The Chief asked.

"Including us," Dr. Bentham confirmed, "and it wouldn't be the first time."

"Aw, c'mon. I've never heard . . ."

"Of it happening before?" Dr. Bentham finished his claim of disbelief. "Of course you haven't. But our governments aren't always exactly truthful. The news that gets reported isn't always what actually occurred, and history is easier to invent than you'd like to think, especially today."

"So in our case, by being told and believing the cause for the blockade is radiation poisoning, the world remains blissfully ignorant," I said.

"Right."

"What can we do?" the Chief asked.

"Contain the flu ourselves. Isolate it. Show signs of life. Survive as long as possible."

"I know there's a blockade, but what's to prevent us or anyone from making a run for it?" I asked.

"Listen," the Chief said.

As if on cue and with irony to spare, the sound of a Coast Guard *rescue* helicopter approached south from the mainland.

"As if the drones aren't enough, the army and Coastie choppers make regular fly-overs, scanning the island and enforcing a no-fly zone," Dr. Bentham said. Above them are fighter jets."

"Fighter jets!"

"Do you remember, Tom Phillips? He ran Island Airlines?" The Chief asked

I shook my head in the negative.

"It doesn't matter. Saturday night, he took off in his Cessna 172 under the cover of darkness and tried to escape east towards the open water. He didn't make it a mile offshore before being blown to bits."

"There's got to be some way off of the island," I said.

"Actually, Danny," Dr. Bentham said. "*We* can't let that happen. Our only chance is to survive *here*. There are only two proven methods for successfully controlling a recently-shifted virus: isolation or eradication. If potentially-infected people start attempting to run the blockade, the switch to the latter strategy will be immediate."

"What do you mean?" I asked.

"Remember those chickens in Hong Kong and Tennessee?"

"You can't be serious. This is America. They wouldn't do that," I said, still clinging to an unreasonable reasonableness.

"In terms of the greatest good for the greatest number of people, it's the right policy," Dr. Bentham said. "As I've said, history is full of manufactured fictions to cover up hard truths that the public would've found unpalatable."

"I have to call my brother," I said. "Let him know I'm all right."

"No can do," the Chief said. "We've been cut off. There's no phone service, the internet is down, and all satellite and radio signals are being jammed. There aren't even any pigeons or ravens to tie notes to. As far as we're concerned, there is no mainland."

"It's all part of the plan," Dr. Bentham added. "Although, I never really thought I'd live to see it implemented, much less be on the business end of it."

"But I'm not the only one with family or friends on the mainland who must be demanding answers. I can't believe they'll just sit back and wait for their loved ones to catch this thing and die no matter what they believe caused it."

"Sure, there's probably an uproar going on right now, but in the end, what can they do?" Dr. Bentham asked. "They're being told that we're dying of radiation sickness. The local and national news programs are probably ratcheting up the fear factor by showing all sorts of footage of victims from previous atomic and nuclear catastrophes. Networks are lined up along the Marblehead shore with their cameras aimed our way. You can see their satellite trucks from here. The public, including friends and families, will reluctantly accept the necessity of the harsh measures being taken here. They may not like it, but they will accept it. What other choice is there? And again, we're talking fewer than five hundred families. It'll run in the news cycle for a couple of days – like a passenger jet crash, a cruise ship sinking, or an earthquake – but the media focus will soon move on to other stories, and everyone else will move on with their lives."

"What about food and other supplies?" I asked.

"Nothing's coming," Chief Sarter said. "What we already have is it, and sadly, alcohol is what we have the most, and there're no farms and little livestock on island. I've asked King Charles to convince the other restaurant and bar owners to temporarily cease in the sale of alcohol, to pool their food, and to establish a community pantry out of Gulliver's. We don't want masses of people gathering anywhere. They've divided up the island and are going to run a sort of Meals-on-Wheels program and deliver one supper a day to each home as long as supplies – and people – last. The General Store is damn near emptied out already. When people's cupboards and refrigerators start running out, we're going to have a major problem on our hands if we're not organized and unable to convince them to pool all resources and efforts. All of which is why, tomorrow, you and me are going to start searching homes for the infected and to confiscate weapons."

"People aren't going to like us taking their guns, Chief."

"The risk of their being armed when supplies start running low is worse than pissing them off now before the entirety of the situation sinks in, and this bird flu shit really hits the fan. Tomorrow," the Chief said, "before we begin our search, we're holding a community wide meeting to organize and to inform folks of the gun collection." The Chief turned to Dr. Bentham. "It's been a long day. Now that wonder boy is okay, I'll run you back to the camp." He then shifted his attention to me. "There are a few things left in the mini-fridge. Help yourself. You must be starving. I'll be back in the morning."

Chapter Four

*Day 5 – Tuesday, May 28, 201_*

I woke with a sore back from a restless night spent on the cot in the cell. My lips and throat burned from inhaling vapors of the Clorox bleach that had been used to sterilize the space after Officer Dooley's and Andy's removal. Once I'd reoriented myself to the living nightmare in which I was trapped, a full realization of the direness of our condition returned. But bird flu or not, my bladder was full and screaming to be emptied. However, the toilet inside the cell was backed up and the water in the bowl was lapping over the rim.

Outside, I slipped on my mask and entered into the shadows cast by the buildings on the east side of Division. A surveillance drone briefly hovered over me then whizzed over the downtown toward the marina. After it had passed, I headed south to Memorial Park, where I knew there was a port-o-potty. All of the shops and restaurants were closed, and the streets were empty and quiet except for that incessant thumping of party music still coming from the Village Dorm. A ghost town feeling had replaced the usual sense of anticipation such mornings once inspired, when the downtown merchants waited for the ferries to begin dumping off the tourists to be separated from their dollars.

A village pick-up truck with a snowplow attached passed me as it pushed dead birds, mingled with mayflies, into piles at the foot of Division Street. I didn't exactly recognize the driver, but he had a face I thought I knew, should know, or would know. From beneath his black ball cap, the swarthy complexioned driver smiled my way and exposed a red, gummy mouth full of yellowing teeth.

I waited for the shivers to exit through my scalp and toes, gathered myself, and turned into the park. The grass was spotted with rotting blackbirds, robins, and sparrows. I carefully crossed the park without stepping on any of the open-beaked carcasses, whose wide-eyed stares left me with the uneasy feeling of being watched from a perverted, bird's-eye-view.

Full from the weekend, the port-o-potty was disgusting. When I exited still squeezing my nostrils, I nearly walked straight into Daphne, who stood expectantly outside the door of the port-o-potty dressed in her tie-dyed mask, flip flops, and a maroon-and-gold Lebron James Cleveland Cavaliers basketball jersey, which she wore like a mini-dress. She held a brown cardboard box of supplies to her chest, but she dropped it and hugged me harder than I'd ever been hugged in my life.

"Oh, Christ!" I said. "You scared the shit out of me!"

"Smells like it."

Mortified by her suggestion, I pointed at the port-o-potty and said, "*That* wasn't me."

"Just kidding, stupid."

"It's all yours," I said.

"Are you crazy? I'm not going in there."

"Then what are you standing here for?"

"I was waiting for you. I saw you cross the park. I was going to knock, but I was afraid you'd piss down your leg."

"Ha-ha," I said.

"You're cured then?"

"Yeah. I guess I should be dead, but instead now I'm most likely immune like some mutant X-man or something. All I need now is a superhero's name and a costume."

"How about the Fluke?"

"That's the second time I've been called that."

"What's your superpower?" she asked.

"I don't know. Not dying I guess."

"That's not very sexy," she said.

It had only been two days since I'd seen Daphne, yet there was already something different about her. She was looser, more playful – the opposite of what I expected given the tragedy of the situation. I wasn't sure how to respond to or even if I liked the carefree Daphne. Looking back, I think she'd already adopted a strategy of denial and was overcompensating for the direness of the circumstances. Either that or she'd looked Death's inevitability squarely in the eyes and decided the best thing she could do was to enjoy the day she had. Just to be sure, I leaned a little closer and subtly sniffed for a whiff of alcohol or pot. Smelling neither, I changed the subject. "What are you doing downtown?"

"I was getting some supplies from off of the King's boat. My scooter's right over there." Daphne pointed to a red Vespa parked on Lakeshore Drive across from *Gulliver's*. There's a whole fleet of them at the house. It's huge by the way. There's a pool, a home theater with a game system and hundreds of DVD's, a game room, and best of all, the owner had already stocked the pantry and freezer for the summer."

"Sounds great, Daph. Hey, by the way, have you seen Derek by any chance?"

"No. I told you we broke up," she said defensively.

"The Chief is worried that Derek may have been exposed ·to the virus I told you about and, if so, that he could spread it to others."

"I haven't seen him," she reiterated her denial.

"This whole thing," I mused. "It's unreal. Just a few days ago, we were graduating from high school."

"I know. It's crazy – like some novel. The way I see it," Daphne said, "the old rules don't apply anymore. It's like another dimension in the multiverse. As long as we're here, we should make the most of it and do all of the things our parents and teachers and ministers told us not to do. Don't you see? This is like a get-out-of-reality-free card. In a few days or weeks, it will be over. We'll be back home, and things will be normal again, and in three months, we'll start college."

"I'm not so sure."

"About what?"

"About any of it."

"Whatever," she said dismissively.

"There's going to be a meeting at . . ."

"Nine. I know. In the ball field at the park. That other cop stopped me at the intersection and told me."

"So, why don't you stay for the meeting?"

"I don't think so, but, hey," she said brightening once more. "You used to live here, right?"

I nodded, "Yes."

"Then tell me: Is there a library on this island? I need the rest of the books on my reading list."

"What's up next? Something apocalyptic-light, I hope."

"You won't believe me."

"Try me."

"Camus' *The Plague*."

"That figures. There's a library, but . . ."

"Why bother? Right?"

"Well, yeah."

"I just told you. This all will pass, and college starts in three months."

Finding no use in bursting her bubble of optimism, I turned

and pointed north. "It's a mile or so up Division Street. Connected to the school."

"Great. That's all I needed to know."

"Wait," I said. How will you get in?"

"There's always a way in. It's the getting out that's hard."

"I have no idea what that means, but listen. The librarian job, when it's filled, is part-time. So the library is almost never open, but every islander knows how to get in anyway. The front doors are going to feel locked if you pull on them normally. They're supposed to seal magnetically, but the right-side door has never shut correctly. If you pull hard enough and lift as you pull, the seal will break and the door will open."

Daphne nuzzled up close so that her breasts rubbed against me. "You're absolutely sure you can't blow off this Chief guy, skip the meeting, and come see the house? It'll be fun. It has its own beach and a fully-stocked bar."

"You don't drink."

"I didn't drink – past tense. I'm doing a lot of things I never used to do. Like in the *Decameron*, the prince and the courtiers and ladies wait out the plague with music and dancing. They feast and they drink and tell stories of life and love. As long as I'm stuck here, I want to live like that."

I took a minute to reconsider her offer (and her breasts), but I said, "The Chief's really counting on me." It sounded lame in my own ears.

"Suit yourself." Daphne rose onto her tiptoes, kissed me on the cheek through her mask, and ran in her girly way to her scooter, where she strapped down her box of supplies with bungee cords before hiking up her jersey-dress, straddling the seat, and buzzing away.

Just as Daphne disappeared up Division, I saw Chief Sarter approaching from East Lakeshore Drive. He spotted me still standing near the port-o-potty, beeped his horn, and waved me to the cruiser.

"Everything come out all right?" He asked.

"Very funny," I said.

"Get in. We have to pick up Dr. Bentham at the camp and head over to the park for the meeting."

"I'll meet you there, Chief. I need to eat something first. I think my appetite's coming back."

"Check Montego Bay. I've ordered all bars and restaurants closed, but if you tell them I sent you, Tomas might rustle something up. He makes the best cup of coffee on island, but don't be late to the meeting."

Other than its bar and a small kitchen, Montego Bay was completely out of doors and open to the sky. It was the newest bar/restaurant on Kelleys and was located on Lakeshore Drive right next to the oldest and the locals favorite dive bar: The Village Pump. The sign out front of Montego Bay claimed it served "Jamaican Blue Coffee So Good It Will Change Your Latitude." The owner, Tomas Brown, was the "1" indicated on the most recent U.S. census, representing Kelleys Island's full-time African-American residents. A naturalized Yank, Tomas flew the Stars and Stripes next to a red, yellow, and green striped Rastafarian flag at the entrance to his slice of Jamaican paradise. The patio "floor" consisted of six-inch deep, imported white sand. A strict SHOES = NO SERVICE policy was enforced on the patio. To that end, a bank of cubbies to house patrons' footwear while on Jamaican soil (or sand) had been built-in the three-foot high concrete block wall that separated Montego Bay from Ohio. At that hour of the morning, the sand was cool against the soles of my feet, and the mellow steel-drum tunes emanating from hidden speakers were soothing against my soul.

Hoping an employee or Tomas himself would take notice, I took a seat in one of the four swings dangling around a high-top table near the street. The swings, which functioned in lieu of stools, hung from chains hooked into mostly-hidden crossbeams beneath a canopy of phony palm fronds. The trunk of a fake palm tree shot up through the center of the table like Jack's beanstalk. Alongside a variety of other Montego Bay souvenir apparel, I noticed a "Three Little Birds" hoodie, like the one Daphne had worn when she visited me in the jail, hanging for sale behind the outside bar.

An aromatic trail of Arabic coffee rode the back of the light offshore breezes that swept through the patio, teasing my nostrils and making my tongue hard.

"We're closed by order of de big Chief," a Jamaican-sweetened accent called from a pick-up window.

"Please, just a cup of coffee and a donut or something," I begged. "I'm working with the Chief. He said maybe you'd serve me."

A caramel-skinned, barefoot, hemp ankle bracelet-wearing waitress – inside a pair of cut-off denim shorts, unbuttoned and failing to cover the string side ties of a lemon yellow bikini bottom that matched her top – emerged onto the patio. She smiled and handed me a laminated and limited breakfast menu. With my blood still flowing warm from Daphne's flirtatiousness, I was immediately smitten by the waitress who introduced herself as Paula. "If you are with de big Chief, I guess I can get you someting."

"Are you Tomas's wife?" I asked in an uncharacteristically forward manner.

She burst out in laughter. "No, mon," she managed to say through a giggle. "I'm his niece, Paula. Here for de summah."

Embarrassed over whatever faux pas I had committed, I ordered a cup of regular flat bean roast coffee and some kind of cinnamon fritter. The entire experience was dizzyingly surreal in its ordinariness, considering the nightmare unfolding on the north side of the island at the 4-H camp and that, from where I sat, I could look past Lakeshore Drive, beyond the vessels of the blockade, and to the mainland coast to where life went on as normal beyond the evacuation zone.

Paula's slow trudge away through the deep sand, which made her bare heels turn outward with each step and her shapely calves and backside all the more alluring, left me mesmerized. Alone again and swaying in my swing, a line from a John Donne poem, which we'd read in senior English, popped into my mind: "No man is an island entirely unto himself." I thought: "Bullshit. Even the islands have islands."

"Get it to go," the Chief's voice called from the street, where he had temporarily stopped his cruiser. Dr. Bentham sat in the passenger seat.

After the Chief had pulled away, Paula returned with a fritter wrapped in a white paper napkin and my coffee inside a Styrofoam cup. "I heard de big Chief," she explained.

I reached for my wallet but she stopped me.

"It's on de house," she said.

"Do you think," I said, mustering courage I rarely had mustered before, "when all of this is over, you and I could . . . could . . . you know . . . go get a cup of coffee or something?"

Paula smiled and wiped the table that didn't need wiping. "Or someting," she said.

"Awesome," I said then climbed out of the swing, put my shoes back on, and headed for the meeting.

Chapter Five

When I arrived at the ball field, Officer Burns was directing foot traffic through a wide opening in a dilapidated, redwood-colored snow fence that circled the field. Stan McKillips, wearing a sun-faded, red ball cap, had backed his truck up against the fence and sat in a nylon-strap lawn chair in the truck bed drinking a beer as if attending a tailgate party. The gathering had also attracted the attention of one of the surveillance choppers rather than a drone. It hovered and circled, hovered and circled.

Folks were arriving as if they walked on the surface of an alien planet. They approached nervously and stood far from the people around them. Some held handkerchiefs to their mouths and noses. Some wore bandanas like Wild West bank robbers. Others wrapped winter scarves over their faces. Still others wore dust masks as if they'd just come from power-sanding a floor. Dr. Bentham moved through the crowd distributing an insufficient supply of surgical masks she'd found at the urgent care clinic to the unprotected, but there weren't nearly enough for everyone. Most people moved in isolation and kept their distance from all others. One gentleman, clearly inspired by the island's blockade by government vessels and the overhead surveillance, arrived dressed as a Revolutionary War Minuteman. He carried a yellow "Don't Tread on Me" flag in one hand and a homemade sign listing outbreaks of what he considered episodes of governmental tyranny:

Ruby Ridge.

Waco.

Bundy Ranch.

Kelleys Island?

Clusters of wispy cirrus clouds canopied a blue and birdless sky. The grass was overgrown and spotted with puddles from recent rains. In one, a mallard mother duck, dressed in her drab brown plumage and oblivious to the proceedings, sat with her splashing ducklings while a lordly drake, with grey wings and belly and its iridescent-green head and neck, stood watch nearby. White puffballs of cottonwood rode a light westerly breeze: a springtime snowstorm.

I sneezed.

No one said, "God, bless you."

Knowing that the virus had transformed a sneeze into a weapon for potential mass destruction, Dr. Bentham shot me a scolding glance, prompting me to remove my surgical mask from my back pocket and cover my mouth and nose. "Sorry," I apologized sheepishly.

The Chief's cruiser was parked in the soggy centerfield grass beyond the baseball diamond. Through its p.a. system, he encouraged those gathering to enter within hearing range but to keep a proper distance from one another, but before he could formally call the meeting to order, a barrage of questions rained down upon him. Each followed by seconding voices.

"When will the ferries start running again, Chief?"

"Has the radiation leak been fixed?"

"Was it a terrorist attack?"

"Are people sick on the mainland?"

"Obama?"

"Why won't our phones, internet, televisions, or radios work?"

"Whoa, people! Please! We will answer all of your questions as best as we can, but we can't answer them all at once. Dr. Jennifer Bentham is here from the Erie County Health Department and the Center for Disease Control out of Columbus. She knows more about what's happening than anyone, but I can tell you myself that the ferries will not be going anywhere anytime soon. No one currently off the island will be allowed on, and no one can leave."

A roar of disapproval rose from the crowd.

The Chief raised his arms in an attempt to quell the uproar. "Please," he said, "let Dr. Bentham explain."

Dr. Bentham took the square, handheld microphone, stretched the cord, and began. "Thank you, Chief Sarter. I'd like to begin by reiterating what the Chief said: for our own protection, no one can be allowed on or off of the island. We are under a federally-enforced quarantine, which means, at least for the immediate future, they're not going to allow any of us to leave Kelleys."

An indecipherable cacophony followed her announcement.

"They can't," Dr. Bentham said loudly over their complaints.

"Why should we trust you? You're one of them," the Minuteman's voice bellowed and many concurred.

King Charles raised his hands to quiet the rising tide of anger. "Let's have order, people. Let the doctor speak."

"What's happening is not the result of a radiation leak," Dr. Bentham said.

"That's not what the news was saying before my TV stopped working," a woman's voice squawked from behind one of the many veils.

"I'm aware of that."

"If it's not radiation, what is it?" the unidentifiable woman asked.

"It's the Avian – or bird – flu," Dr. Bentham continued. "It's serious – very serious. It has the potential to decimate the majority of the species."

"Of birds?" The woman asked.

Dr. Bentham paused to consider her response. "No, of humans."

"Then that's what's been killing the birds," Cleats stated the obvious. Dr. Bentham's doomsday warning had apparently affected him like water off a duck's back, in other words, not at all.

"Yes," Dr. Bentham answered with no air of condescension nor with a desire to reiterate her ominous warning.

"If it's not a radiation leak, then why has the reactor been shut down?" The King, like Cleats, was unable to absorb the near decimation of the human species scenario Dr. Bentham had suggested. Their thoughts were still centered on a radiation event.

"It's all part of the plan," Dr. Bentham answered almost apologetically.

"What plan? Whose plan?" The King continued to prod. "I'm the mayor here, and I never heard of such a plan."

Dr. Bentham remained evasive. "They want the world to *believe* it has been a radiation event. It's a better story for them. Most likely, all of us have already been reported as dead or beyond saving, and they're not letting anybody close enough to the island to discover and report differently, especially the media."

"That's ridiculous," the King said, but Dr. Bentham ignored him and continued.

"Trust me, they're knocking on wood, kissing their crosses, and doing their happy dances considering how lucky they are that this outbreak is occurring here on Island No. 6."

"Island No. 6?" The Chief asked.

"I'm sorry. That was Kelleys Island's original governmental designation when it was first officially claimed by the U.S. They use that name as a means of de-personalizing what must be done here. To them, the island is only a number. We're all merely numbers."

"You said, 'they're 'lucky.'" The King said. "How so?"

Realizing it wasn't necessary to her being arrested, Dr. Bentham handed the microphone back to the Chief. "Think about it. If there had to be an outbreak of the bird flu virus in the human population – and it has always been a matter of when it would occur again and where, not if – what better place than here, on an island? Based on the migratory routes of wild birds, they've suspected for a long time that when the day came that the virus jumped from birds to humans, it would be along one of these routes. All of which pass over several population dense areas. Should it have jumped in one of those, it would have been virtually uncontainable. Many people would have died before it could have been identified and choked off – if at all. But here – as long as nobody comes or goes – it can, theoretically at least, be isolated and stopped."

"How will they do that?" The King asked.

"They already have," she said. "On the mainland, the National Guard will have already established a mandatory evacuation zone within a fifteen mile radius of the actual nuclear plant – with Fukushima fresh enough in people's minds, I doubt that they will have received much resistance. And all of the five inhabited islands, as you can see for yourself, have been encircled by U.S. and Canadian naval vessels, their coast guards, border patrols, and law enforcement. The blockade also helps them sell the radiation leak story."

"She's right," one of the nameless seasonal residents chimed in. "You can see the ships from my porch. They've been there since Friday night. Just sitting."

Several others also reported having seen the ships from various points on the island.

"Our only choice is to cooperate with the quarantine," the Chief said, coming to Dr. Bentham's aid by investing whatever good faith he'd earned with islanders over the years into the discussion. "Enforce it ourselves. Prove to them that we are on their team and no threat to the mainland."

"But my children and grand babies live on the mainland," an elderly woman complained.

"You wouldn't want to risk passing it on to them would you, Mrs. Grey?" The Chief said.

"But I'm not sick," Mrs. Grey said.

"And the quarantine should allow us to keep it that way. All of this is temporary. Everyone needs to be patient. It will pass and we will all go on with our lives," the Chief spoke with affected optimism.

"Just wait a minute," the King said after having partially digested Dr. Bentham's explanation. "Let me get this straight. You're saying they're selling the crisis to the public as a deadly but containable radiation leak and the blockade as necessary to keep people out when it's actually designed to keep *us* and this bird flu virus in?"

"That's exactly right," she answered.

"For how long? I mean, I see how the radiation story buys them time and calm in the short term, but they can't enforce a blockade and a no-fly zone forever. The cost would be astronomical," King Charles said.

"Compared to allowing this virus to spread, the cost is negligible. Not even considering the human toll, imagine the economic impact of a widespread epidemic on not just this island but the country and even the world should it be forced to battle this flu. There could be no mass transit, no manufacturing, no commerce, no schools in session, no public sporting events, no tourism or travel, basically, nothing that would require large numbers of people to occupy shared space. But, here's the good news for them: the virulence and death rate of this strain is proving to be such that they won't need to enforce the blockade 'forever.' We're only talking days or weeks at the most if we don't take the drastic but necessary steps to isolate and contain the virus ourselves."

"So they're just going to sit out there until . . ." The enormity of the conclusion to his own speculation landed on him hard, and the King couldn't continue.

"Until what," Mrs. Grey asked, still not having wrapped her head around it.

"For all of us to die of this bird flu, to starve to death, or to kill each other off. That's it. Isn't it, Doctor?" The King asked.

Dr. Bentham's silence confirmed his conjecture.

"There's got to be a way of reasoning with them," the ever-politic King said.

"Charles," the Chief jumped in once more, "there's not even a way to talk to them. I've tried."

"What's with that Muslim (He pronounced it Moose-lum.) fella who was on the ferry?" Cleats asked apropos to nothing.

"He has nothing to do with any of this," the Chief said.

"You mean to tell me it's a coincidence that this Muslim shows up on island and people start getting sick? Sounds fishy to me," Cleats said.

"I don't 'mean to tell' you anything. Trust me," the Chief said. "The kid is no terrorist."

"Seems to me," the King said, bringing the discussion back on point, "our choice is either to stay here and die or to try and run the blockade. There are hundreds of boats on this island. They can't stop us all."

"Not only can they stop you, Charles, they will," Chief Sarter said. "Remember, they blew Tom Phillips right out of the sky. They didn't have a choice. None of this is personal, people. It's survival. Potentially, by now, every single one of us has been exposed to the virus, and, if we have, we would most likely spread it into the mainland population should we get off the island. Hell, Charles, even if you did manage to get past the blockade, where would you go? You don't think they'd be waiting for you the minute you tried to dock? By now they have a complete list with every one of our names on it.

"Our only choice," the Chief continued, "is how we play the hand we've been dealt. We should accept the blockade, work together, and live long enough to prove to them that we're capable of burning the virus out by not giving it anyplace to live – kind of like the way they fight forest fires out West. The other option is to panic, grow careless and selfish, and die. It's a long shot, but if we're careful and organized, we can work together and maybe even beat this thing. Which means that we must be willing to stay in our homes, to isolate the infected at the 4-H camp, and to surrender our dead for mass burial. For now, socialization and sentimentality are our enemies. Danny and I will begin making rounds today to remove to the 4-H camp anyone from your homes who is showing symptoms. I have Officer Burns organizing a shore patrol to keep guard at all marinas and boat ramps and to prevent anyone from leaving. He could use some volunteers to help keep watch. Captain Russo has agreed to play undertaker. He asks that you place a black cloth of some kind in a front window or door to signal your need for his services. He will be making regular rounds.

"What will we do for supplies, Chief? Damn near everything on island has to be ferried or flown over," Tom Hobbs, owner of the general store, asked.

"We'll have to make do with what we have. As for the long term – should it be necessary – many of you have vegetable gardens; there is plenty of game on island; and we can always fish."

"The Chief's right," Captain Russo, the owner and operator of the freight and passenger ferry, entered the conversation.

"We must be self-reliant as a community yet entirely communal as individuals."

"What are you talking about, Captain?" Cleats asked. "That makes no sense."

"There are peach trees and apple trees and wild berries and grapes growing on many of our properties. They should be made available to everyone."

"Sounds like commie crap to me," Cleats said.

"Sounds like survival," Russo shot back.

"We have a right to our own property," the King said.

"That's correct, Charles, under normal circumstances. But these are anything but. If we would all temporarily give up the right to hoard what is ours," Captain Russo said, "we could all benefit from the *entire* island, not just our tiny parcels. We would all surrender some rights temporarily but remain at least as free as we were before, if not more so, because we may also benefit from each others' surplus, and the general good is served. It's a win/win but only if we are all willing to cooperate. One island of one mind. Everyone subject to everyone else for their survival and happiness."

"I don't like it," Cleats said.

"No offense, Captain, but you and the Chief are both talking nonsense," the always practical Tom Hobbs, the owner of the general store, said. "Give me a break. Twenty-four more hours of this and we'll be at each others' throats. And you talk as if they'll sit back and let us build our own paradise here, but that would take time that we don't have and they can't give us."

"I'm not sure I know what you're talking about, Tom," the Chief said.

"It has nothing to do with cost, but the King here was half right when he said that they can't keep us here forever. Even if some of us do somehow manage to survive the virus, the reality is that they can't keep us alive at all – here or anywhere else. They can't have us blabbing about this bird flu if, as Dr.

Bentham says, they have sold this to the world as a radiation leak. How would they explain it when, months from now, we show up alive and with no signs of radiation poisoning?

"They're counting on us dying off like the damn birds. They're just watching and waiting to verify that the annihilation is complete," Hobbs pointed to the helicopter. "Then they'll swoop in, clean up, and move on. That's it. All signs of life and organization like your little Meals-on-Wheels program, the hospital or whatever you want to call those death tents at the 4-H camp, and especially this little meeting we're having right now is a threat to that plan. What it all boils down to is regardless of what we do to govern ourselves, each day that we survive, the risk of the truth slipping out increases, and the pressure grows for them to speed up the process of our dying."

"What exactly are you saying?" Cleats asked for clarification as if it weren't crystal.

"What I'm saying is what everyone here already knows, but only those Booze Cruisers at the Dorm have had the courage to admit." He paused and looked around at his audience. "None of us are getting off this island alive. When Officer Dooley died, we all died with him."

I noticed that the Chief appeared to be temporarily stunned by Mr. Hobbs' stark take on the situation.

"What should we do?" Mrs. Grey asked.

"Accept that, if we choose to do nothing or to extend our stay as the Chief suggests, we are already dead. I'm with the King on this one. Those who are willing should organize a simultaneous mass escape, but the Chief's right about one thing as well. Most of us won't make it, but there is the small chance that a few will."

A pensive mood and prolonged silence infected the crowd as they weathered Tom Hobbs's brainstorm.

"Tomorrow night there will be a new moon. At midnight, I say, with the Captain's permission of course, we set the automatic pilot on the ferry for its course to the dock at Marblehead. That should provide a small and temporary diversion; it won't take them long to see that the ferry is unmanned and without passengers. If we're lucky, it will, for at least a few minutes, force them to divert their resources and focus their attention on the ferry. At which time, any of us who are interested should haul ass off this island. Run without lights in as many different directions as we can. Every man for himself. Look for a seam in the blockade. If by chance you make it through, run aground or drop anchor and swim ashore, somewhere away from lights, docks, and marinas."

"No!" Dr. Bentham emphatically interjected. "How can you be so selfish? The symptoms of the disease don't manifest themselves for at least twenty-four hours after infection. Right now, any one of us could be a walking viral time bomb. During the incubation period, even though he doesn't know he's sick, the patient is highly contagious. If any of you make it to shore who are infected, you will pass it on to an unprepared population. It will spread like wildfire. It would be mass murder, and it would be your fault."

"What if you're wrong, miss? What if we're not sick, and they get tired of waiting for us to die? By whose authority are you asking us to stay?" Hobbs asked. "The government's that has shown itself willing to shoot us out of the sky and that you and the Chief have made clear are just itching to massacre us?" He answered his own question. "I say we have as much a right to live as anyone else. The Captain, he's half-right too. Our guiding principle should be good, old-fashioned, American self-reliance. As long as we're here, I take care of myself and mine. You take care of yours. But, you set one foot or hand on what belongs to me, you're going to lose that foot or hand. The strong survive. That's Nature's law. Not mine. Survival of the fittest is the *only* law that matters anymore."

"Well, Tom," the Chief said, apparently recovered from his temporary disillusionment in Dr. Bentham's plan, "I believe you're really going to hate what I have to say next. I have no choice but to forbid you or anyone else to leave, and I'm going to collect your guns until this is over."

"I told you so! I told you so!" The Minuteman said over the roar of disapproval that rose primarily from the Lifers who made up the majority of the crowd.

"You've got to be kidding, Chief," Mr. Hobbs said while failing in his attempt to stifle a sarcastic smile. "And just how do you plan to make us stay, and how do you propose to take our guns? That badge you're wearing is nothing but a hunk of metal until this thing passes. Like I said, it's only Nature's laws that matter now, not mans'."

"I don't want to make you stay, Tom, and I don't want to *take* your guns. Not if I don't have to. But I would like to *trade* for them."

"Trade them for what?" Hobbs asked. I was as clueless as he was.

The Chief walked around to the rear of his cruiser. Dr. Bentham shot me a knowing glance as the Chief popped the trunk.

"For these," the Chief said, as he removed a box.

"Whatchu got, Chief," the King asked.

"Flu shots," the Chief said as if announcing a royal flush. He reached inside the box and pulled out a syringe sealed inside a plastic wrapper with an accompanying vial.

I swear every person in the park took one covetous step toward the Chief.

"I have enough of these for everyone on island. I've been around long enough. Shoot, I've hunted with most of you myself. I know what guns you own. When we finish here, Danny and I will start coming around to every home on island. Give me your guns; I'll give you enough flu shots for you and yours. No guns; no shots. It's as simple as that. You can either choose to take your chances with the rest of us or choose to take your chances with the virus. But I guarantee you ain't getting past that blockade, and you can't kill this virus with a bullet."

I noticed Dr. Bentham doing her best to hide a smile. I think she was genuinely proud of the Chief's manipulation of events.

"So," the Chief addressed the crowd, "I probably can't stop you from taking part in Mr. Hobbs's plan, but know this: if y'all go through with it, not only are you putting at risk the health of the mainland population, you're condemning those of us who remain to an immediate execution. They can't let it go down that way. I'll say it again: our only hope – as slim as it may be – is to endure as long as we can, playing by their rules, and hope to force them to play another card. If you stay and turn in your weapons, I'll provide you with a flu shot. If you choose anything else, you're on your own. You all have a choice to make."

John Patmos, barefoot and – despite the heat – dressed in a brown monk's robe, arrived from the east, parting the crowd as he came forward. "The plague is God's will. *For the world is passing away, and also its lusts; but the one who does the will of God lives forever.* Only God can save you. *For it is He who delivers you from the snare of the trapper and from the deadly pestilence.* No guns or medicines can alter what God has ordained."

"Oh, for Chrissakes," the Chief complained. "Save it, John."

Despite the Chief's harsh words, there were those who said, "Amen," some who crossed themselves, and others who fell to their knees in prayer.

Patmos didn't stay to argue socio-political philosophy with Russo and Hobbs or gun control with the Chief. He simply continued his trek across the field towards downtown. As he progressed, some rushed forward to kiss his robe and to ask for his blessing. A few new converts followed in his sandaled footsteps.

The meeting was thus destroyed as two separate factions of the likeminded formed and caucused around Russo and Hobbs. Russo's people were primarily his neighbors on the northwest corner of the island – all highly-educated, liberal-minded, relative newcomers, and part-time residents who ran successful businesses on the island and had created a sort of suburb complete with subdivisions, block watches, and neighborhood associations in their new corner of the world.

Hobbs's disciples were the longtime island Lifers, most of whom lived on the southwest quadrant and scattered in the island's interior. They lived mostly in dilapidated trailers; fishing shacks; or older, modest homes, having watched the majority of prime lakefront real estate bought up by outsiders. Their exclusivity was primarily based on a shared xenophobic dislike for, well, anyone really but especially for mainlanders and the tourists who strayed from downtown and interloped onto their properties either accidentally or while sightseeing for local color.

A small segment of those gathered – mostly from the sunrise side of the island, which in recent years had become a sort of enclave for seasonal residents – remained unaligned and milling about.

A second helicopter approached from the west and joined the original. Together they flew in low and hovered noisily over the Chief's cruiser, where he, Dr. Bentham, and I had gathered. The roar of their engines and blades made any further public discussion impossible. The choppers dipped their noses and began to move like cowboys riding herd and dispersed the people, who ran covering their heads with their arms, away from the park and to their respective corners of the island.

"Well," Dr. Bentham said, "that went swimmingly."

"You can't save people from themselves, Jenny," Chief Sarter said. "If we're lucky, Hobbs won't be able to convince enough of the others to go along. He needs big numbers, or his plan doesn't stand a chance."

"Where'd you get the flu shots?" I asked, filled with hope.

"They're leftovers," the Chief said. "I took them from the urgent care clinic this morning. Last fall, the health department screwed up and sent us enough for ten times the number of year-round residents we have. They must have used summer census numbers by mistake. Plus, many of the Lifers don't trust vaccines and never took their shots."

"Do they actually work?" I asked.

"No," Dr. Bentham answered. "They're worthless. The flu virus is so volatile; the vaccine for it has to be reconfigured each season based on the best predictions we can make as to what will be its most likely formulation. And the genome sequence of this particular virus has never been seen before."

"But they don't know that," the Chief said, "and with no internet, they won't be able to Google it."

"It won't take them long to figure it out when people start dying anyway," I said.

"I know that, but the shots should buy us enough time to barter for some of the guns and to keep enough people from choosing Hobbs's Hail Mary attempt."

"You do realize how wrong this is?" Dr. Bentham said.

"The way I see it," the Chief said, "at least until this thing plays out, the slate's been wiped clean of wrongs and rights. There's just survival. For now, I figure we all have a better chance if we don't help this bird flu along by killing each other first. So, we're going to collect as many guns as we can now, and we can apologize for our white lies later."

"Sounds like you're going all *Lord of the Flies*," I said.

"I've never read the book, but if it has anything to do with keeping order and saving a few lives, then call me Beelzebub.

Here, put this on," the Chief said and tossed me an official badge of the Kelleys Island Police Department.

"Are you serious?"

"Absolutely. It gives you authority."

"If you say so, Chief," I said and pinned the badge to my t-shirt, which was too thin and loose-fitting to support the weight of the badge.

Chapter Six

After we had returned Dr. Bentham to the camp, where she was overseeing the confinement and treatment of the sick, the first stop in our search for the infected and for guns was the Village Dorm. If nothing else, I was happy to have the opportunities to put an end to the infernal music that was serving as the soundtrack to the horror film that had become our lives and to stop by my room, take a shower, and change back into my own clothes.

The Chief removed a can of red spray paint and another of black from a box in the backseat and told me to keep a sharp eye for anyone who looked like they might be infected.

"What's with the paint?" I asked.

"Just hope we don't have to use it."

The Chief knocked on and shook the locked, glass double doors, but no one came to answer. Apparently, Mrs. Barnes had abandoned her post.

"Chief," I said.

"Not now, Danny."

"Chief," I said again.

"Not now, Danny. I'm going to have to go find a key. I have a bunch in…"

"Chief," I interrupted and tapped him on the shoulder.

He turned. "Danny, I said . . ."

That's when he saw me holding my dorm key out and in front of my face.

Clothes were strewn all over the lobby. Over the weekend while I was sick, the Chief had dropped off boxes of unclaimed clothes from last summer's lost and found for the Booze Cruisers and others who'd crashed in the dorm. He had also used the Police Department's credit card to darn near empty out the souvenir stores, beach shops, and boutiques of much of their adult-sized clothing. Unclaimed T-shirts, board shorts, and bikini tops, bottoms, and cover-ups littered the lobby.

The music rose from the basement, making it the logical place to begin. It was an open communal area with lounge furniture, big screen televisions, a karaoke/disc jockey station, a tile dance floor, pool and foosball tables, and vending machines, which had already been ransacked. Twenty to thirty bathing-suited bodies were sprawled all over the room.

The Chief stepped over body after contorted body. He made his way to the sound system, pulled its several plugs, and put an official end to the rave. The basement looked like Jonestown meets Spring Break.

"Hey! Who shut off the music," the voice came from the top of the basement stairs.

"It's the Chief of Police."

A young man slowly materialized from toes to head: a pair of flip-flops; red and white floral board shorts; a shirtless, lean, angular torso with perfectly-manicured chest hair; a face with two day's stubble and Mediterranean features; and dark curly hair spilling from a backwards Cleveland Indians ball cap. Although there weren't even any windows in the basement to allow in sunlight, he wore a pair of mirrored Aviator sunglasses.

"Sorry, bro," he said. "Didn't know it was you."

"What happened here?" With a nod of his head, the Chief indicated his concern for the lifeless bodies littering the basement.

"Oh, they aren't dead, Chief. They're just sleeping or drunk or both. A bunch of us decided to throw an end of the world party – at least until the alcohol runs out. We've got a fully-stocked cafeteria and a few dudes made a beer run."

"And who exactly are you?"

"I'm Giovanni Dioneo; my friends call me Geo."

"Where you from, Geo?" The Chief asked.

"Cleveland. East side. Murray Hill neighborhood in Little Italy. You know it?"

"No. I'm afraid not."

"Came over on the Booze Cruise with a bunch of college friends."

"Are you in charge?"

"Me? In charge? Nah. Nobody's in charge here."

"Look, Geo. We're here to collect any weapons and to locate anyone who is sick and in need of our help."

"That's cool."

I don't suppose you've noticed if any of these," the Chief scanned the passed out bodies, "friends of yours were carrying any weapons, did you?"

"Nah. No way. We had to pass through a metal detector on the dock back in Sandusky even to get on the boat or ship or whatever. There aren't any weapons here."

"Good. I'm going to take your word for it. Could you do us a favor and rouse these folks while my partner and I do a sweep of the rest of the dorm? Make sure they're all just hung over and not sick?"

"No problem."

"Is there anything I can do or get for you guys?" the Chief asked.

"We're good, Chief. Like I said, plenty of food and drink, at least enough to last for . . . well, you know."

"Don't be so morbid, Geo. We had a town hall meeting of sorts at the ball field this morning. I think that, if we work together, we can beat it."

"Maybe. Maybe not. We talked about it, and we think otherwise. These kids may not look like it, but most of them are really smart." He nodded to the scattered bodies.

Neither the Chief nor I were convinced.

"Pardon my language, but our consensus is that we're fucked. Tommy there, in the plaid shorts, he was a biochemistry major. Karen, over there in the Cleveland Cavaliers shirt: neuropathology. I studied biomedical engineering. Based on that cooling tower to the west, Tommy's sticking with the radiation event, but I'm not buying that bullshit. Karen's going with SARS, which would be bad enough. But I'm thinking something avian. What? H5N1 or even H7N1?"

"You're the winner, Geo, but let's keep it between us."

"Then they all owe me a beer, and now I'm even more convinced that we're fucked."

"You really think this is your best option then? Locking yourselves away and partying?"

"What's the other choice? Sit scared in some room like those bird lovers at the hotel waiting to die?"

"Or maybe, to live," the Chief said.

"That's not an option, Chief. That's a fairy tale. There's a reason they have us caged up on this island. This bug is a nasty one, and they can't afford to let it loose on the mainland. We both know that. We're being amputated like a frostbitten finger."

"You're a smart guy, Geo, but I think you're being too pessimistic. I'd like you and your friends to join the community and put some of that brainpower to work, but suit yourselves."

"I'll run it past them when they 'wake up,' but I wouldn't expect much. We're a pretty disillusioned bunch. For eight fucking years, we watched our liberal arts and business school buddies party and live it up while we studied our asses off because we were going into medicine to make the big money and laugh the last laugh, then this shit happens," Geo paused in his reflection. "Oh well, what are you going to do? We've got a lot of making up to do and short time to do it in."

"You're sure there isn't anything you need?"

"No. Like I said, we're good. You know, *Carpe Diem* and all that. We'll just keep the doors locked and eat, drink, and be merry – if that's all right with you. Who knows? Maybe you're right, and we'll all get lucky and ride it out."

"Okay, Geo."

"Come to think of it, Chief, there is one thing you could get for us."

"What's that?"

"Condoms. I mean, between you and me, what's the difference? But smart as they are, not all of these chicks do their math so good."

"I'll see what I can do," the Chief said.

"Thanks, Chief."

The Chief and I each took a floor. Most of the doors were wide open and the rooms empty. We knocked on every door and looked for the symptoms. I took the second floor with the added intention of visiting my room and, as I've said, taking a shower, changing clothes, and getting my stuff.

My key smoothly retracted the dead bolt to my room; however, the door would hardly budge. Through the sliver I was able to open it, I saw that much of the room's furniture had been stacked against the door.

"Jalil!" I called but received no response until I pounded on the door with my fist.

"Stay out!" Jalil warned from behind the barricade. "I'll fuck you up, man!"

"Jalil. It's me. Danny."

"Danny? Danny who? I don't know no Danny."

"Your roommate."

"Let me see your face."

I put my face up to the crack I'd opened.

"Are you with them?"

"With who?"

"The crazies in this dorm, dog."

"No. I just came to get my stuff. What's going on? Let me in."

"I don't know. How do I know that you're not with them? That this isn't some kind of trick?"

"I guess you'll just have to trust me."

"I'm hungry. Do you have food? I haven't eaten in two days."

"Not with me, but I can get you some."

"Back away down the hall, so I can check you out."

I did as I was told. When Jalil's head appeared, his face was haggard and eyes sunken. I pulled down my mask so that he could see my face.

"Jalil. Are you sick?"

"No, I'm not sick. I told you. I'm hungry, dog. I haven't slept and I've been pissing onto a towel in the trash can. Some of these drunk fools wanted to kill me. First night here, they spotted me for a Muslim and started talking crazy. They said I released some Anthrax on the country or some shit like that. Kept screaming at me about 9/11 and chanting U – S – A! U – S – A! If it wasn't for that Jersey Shore Guido, they would have killed me. These rooms don't have televisions. My phone gets no reception, and I can't get my laptop to connect to the internet."

"Let's go back inside the room," I said. "Pack your stuff while I take a shower. When I'm done, we'll go. I'm here with the Chief of Police. We can get you fed and explain everything once we get out of here. Sound good?"

"Yeah. What choice do I have, dog? But hurry before they come back."

"I wouldn't worry about them. Most of them are passed out in the basement or hiding in their rooms, but I have to ask one more time. You're sure you're not sick?"

"I told you, dog. I'm tired and I'm starving to death, but I'm not sick or nothing."

When we reached the lobby, the Chief was already there and waiting.

"Chief, you remember Jalil?"

The Chief looked at Jalil then at me with clear concern.

"He's not sick. He's been hiding in his room without food for a couple of days. He's coming with us."

The Chief didn't look too happy about the addition. There was nothing about Jalil's side-turned ball cap, oversized white t-shirt, sagging cargo shorts, and skater shoes that the Chief didn't find absolutely repulsive, but I think he understood the potential danger Jalil faced if left alone on island.

"Did you find . . ." not sure of Jalil's knowledge of the epidemic and perhaps not wanting to alarm him by saying "bodies," the Chief said, ". . . anything?"

"Nothing. How about you?"

The Chief held up two fingers. "Couple of waitresses from Gulliver's. Roommates. I shut and locked their door and marked it with a black cross."

I immediately ran down the hallway until I found the cross. I hesitated, then opened the door. Neither of the waitresses was Daphne. I closed the door and dropped my head against my arm, pressed against the door. Logic told me neither could have been Daphne, but logic had been rendered all but useless and had given way to panic. I'd had to check. I wondered where and when the roommates had caught the virus and if Daphne had been likewise exposed.

The Chief and Jalil caught up to me.

"Shouldn't we . . ." I started.

"Not now," the Chief said. "We'll let Captain Russo know. He'll handle it."

"Whatchu talking about? And what's up with the tag on the door?" Jalil asked.

"Let's go," the Chief said without providing the explanations. "We all need to eat, but, son," he looked directly at Jalil, "you're not going anywhere with me until you pull those pants up and put your damn cap on straight."

"Are you serious, Chief?" I asked.

The Chief didn't even blink.

Begrudgingly and with attitude, Jalil complied.

"Shelves are nearly empty," the Chief apologized and handed us our breakfast through the windows of the cruiser – a couple of energy bars, saltines, and cans of cream soda, which he purchased at the general store. We ate inside the car.

"What's going on, dog?" Jalil asked between chews and swallows. "And what is that smell?"

I turned around in the front passenger seat so as to face Jalil. "What?" I asked, "No mayflies in Dearborn?" I reached out the passenger side window to extract one of the recently-landed insects from off of the windshield.

"May what?"

I held the noxious bug by its gossamer wings against the cage separating the two of us. "Mayflies," I said.

"That's what you call those bugs? I thought they were some kind of mutant mosquito from that nuke plant. Do they sting?"

"No. They don't do much of anything. The fish eat them. Other than that, they're pretty worthless, really." I flipped it out the window, where it was scooped up by the breeze and deposited farther down the sidewalk.

"They smell like," Jalil hesitated, "death."

Fearful that Jalil's presence would only make the already suspicious population less likely to cooperate, the Chief suggested that Jalil stay behind in the jail.

"Is it safe?" I asked, considering that I had spent three days inside of it battling the virus.

"Compared to what?" The Chief answered. "His chances out here?"

"Good point," I said.

"It's been bleached to death. If any germs are alive in there, we don't stand a chance against them anyway," the Chief said.

After the treatment he'd received in the dorm and even after we'd caught him up on the events of the past few days, Jalil was more-than-willing to hole up inside the jail with his headphones, laptop, and surgical mask and take his chances.

Chapter Seven

In the brief interval since the meeting in the park, it was as if the island's inhabitants had counted off by fours and divided into teams. They had splintered themselves according to their different histories with the island and their various theories for survival. Boundary lines were drawn and the island was quartered.

Captain Russo's cooperative settled into the northwest quadrant. By far the least populated section, it consisted largely of transplanted islanders who'd opened businesses and moved to the island. They lacked the stubborn isolationism of the native born, the blind faith of Patmos's followers in the northeast section, and the split citizenship of the seasonal residents in the southeast corner. Those who subscribed to Hobbs's conflict theory, mostly island Lifers, entrenched themselves inside their homes in the southwest quadrant with the fervor of Doomsday Preppers.

The northeast quarter, re-named New Jerusalem by Patmos, filled with those surrendering to faith, seeking a theocratic order, and preparing for a moment of rapturous reunion with the returning Christ. They'd settled into the smattering of whitewashed wooden cabins on the grounds of the Baptist Bible

Camp, which had been operated by the Ohio Baptists Council for over fifty years but had yet to open for the approaching summer and was therefore vacant. Each Patmosian wore a black cross on their surgical masks. The southeast section, which was primarily filled with seasonal islanders, remained shapeless and ill-defined. The residents there had no desire to join or form a confederation of any sort. They just wanted to get back to their real homes on the mainland.

This fracturing into new and autonomous regions greatly negated the Chief's authority but not his resolve. He remained as determined as ever to hold the island together, and he was willing to employ extreme measures to maintain some sense of community on the island, without which, the most dangerous threat was not the Blues but one another.

Division Street became a sort of Berlin Wall and the downtown a demilitarized zone, the heart of the island through which its lifeblood flowed and without which no quarter could survive. Other than the Booze Cruisers in the dorm and a few of the seasonal employees who lived in tiny apartments over the establishments in which they worked, no one stayed downtown. But the number of citizens from the different factions already on the streets and sidewalks as the Chief and I set off on our mission made it clear that the downtown would continue as a place of limited commerce and news gathering for as long as there were products and services to sell and rumors to spread. An uneasy neutrality had been established downtown, and wary citizens of all four provinces came, conducted their business or pleasure, and went with a wary eye on his or her neighbors.

The Chief's plan was first to visit all of the homes along the island's perimeter beginning with Hobbs's people, the Lifers, whom the Chief believed would only grow more uncooperative, cantankerous, and insular as the crisis wore on. From there, we'd continue in a clockwise direction.

We stopped at a few double-wide trailers and cottage-sized homes of longtime islanders. Many of the properties were less than *Homes and Gardens* worthy, yet others were quaint, inviting, and well-maintained. There were very few full-time island families with children left on Kelleys, which I guess was a small mercy. At nearly every home, dead birds had been shoveled into piles and into garbage cans. At the homes of the less industrious, they were merely left where they fell to Earth. Recognizing the Chief as one of their own and starved for information and/or conversation, most of these folks greeted us at least lukewarmly and allowed us to perform quick searches for the infected, and the majority willingly turned over firearms in exchange for the bogus flu shots.

At nearly every third or fourth home, the flu had nested. In some, the infected person's housemates demonstrated love and tender care beyond the limits of reason and self-preservation. In others, we couldn't take their "loved ones" off their hands and out of their breathing air space fast enough. If the home contained a still-living victim of the virus, we spray painted the grass in front with red crosses as a warning for others and delivered the patient to Dr. Bentham at the camp. If it were too late, we painted a black cross and left the deceased for Captain Russo to collect.

Between West Lakeshore Drive and Beach Road sat Sunset Acres, a private community populated entirely by Lifers who were the remains of generations of proximal in-breeding between no more than ten to twelve island-family lines that had all but run out. Hand painted signs on plywood sheets at the entrance to the enclave warned KEEP OUT! When the Chief and I pulled into a dirt driveway beside one of the clapboard shacks, we heard a heated argument spilling through its paper thin walls.

We rushed inside through the aluminum screen door, sans the screen, to find Tuck Sutherland, who I thought was near death's door ten years earlier before I even left the island, crouched and cowering in a corner of the front room holding a cushion from off the couch out in front of himself like a shield. He wore only a wife beater t-shirt, which was struggling to contain his sagging old man boobs, yellowing boxers, and black dress socks pulled up to his knees.

His wife, who looked quite a bit like a "Smurfy" Albert Einstein, was clearly infected. She stood over her husband inside a threadbare, linen nightgown and rained spit down upon him.

"Mrs. Sutherland, stop!" The Chief commanded her, but she continued to dredge up globs of bloody phlegm with which to shower her husband.

"Mrs. Sutherland!" The Chief actually drew his gun. "I'm not kidding."

Smug in my presumed immunity, I couldn't help but smile at the absurdity of the scene. The Chief, however, did not appreciate my dark sense of humor in that particular moment and shot a smile-eradicating glance in my direction. I wised up fast.

I think it was more from exhaustion than fear of the Chief's gun, but the old woman stopped her assault and collapsed onto the cushion-less third of the couch. "He tried to kill me," she managed to accuse her husband between labored breaths.

"You're crazy, old woman!" Mr. Sutherland screamed at his wife.

"He came at me with a pillow," she said. "He was fixing to smother me in my own bed. Didn't want to risk catching the Blues his self. That's the thanks I get for all the years of caring for and putting up with his filth."

"You was flat on your back. Gurgling like you was drowning," Mr. Sutherland rebutted. "I was fixing to prop you up."

"He's lying. I saw his beady eyes. He was going to murder me."

"We're just going to have to sort it all out later," the Chief said. "For now, Mrs. Sutherland, you'll have to come with us. We can't risk you spreading this thing."

"So, the bastard wins after all," she said resignedly.

"There are no winners, Mrs. Sutherland," the Chief said. "Only losers of different degrees." And again I wondered if he were waxing philosophical in general or just in reference to our current nightmare.

She grabbed a ratty housecoat from the back of a chair. When we reached the door, she turned to her husband and promised, "I'll see you in hell, old man."

As the Chief escorted Mrs. Sutherland to the cruiser's back seat, I stood on the porch and listened as Tuck sobbed inside and begged his absent wife and god for forgiveness.

Occasionally, we spotted a looter on foot or a group of them working from out of a vehicle. If he recognized them, the Chief recorded their names in his little black notebook, but we never gave chase. The Chief said he'd deal with the looters later, that the island itself had become a sort of prison anyway, and that our focus needed to remain on identifying the infected and the dead.

In some of the homes we visited, we were forced to play doctors, asked to analyze inhabitants' symptoms – both real and imagined. In others, we were psychologists, shown open psychic wounds and emotional scars incurred over lifetimes of futilely pursuing happiness. Still others made us confessors and required us to hear long-hidden secrets of adultery, thievery, and incest, even one of murder. Tears and lamentations were heard in almost every house. By the end of the day, it would be nearly enough to make me believe that Patmos was right, that the bird flu was an act of the divine cleansing of man and his depravities from god's Earth.

The last driveway on West Lakeshore before one was forced to turn east onto Titus Road was narrow and well-camouflaged. Unless you knew what you were looking for, you'd never notice it from the road. It wound through thick trees and undergrowth until it eventually turned to concrete and led to what could only accurately be described as a compound, invisible from the road and protected by an arched, black wrought iron, sliding security gate.

"Who lives here?" I asked as the Chief pulled up to the gate, next to a speaker box, and into the frame of a camera mounted on the fence and aimed directly into the vehicle.

"Captain Russo and his wife and kids."

"From the ferry and the meeting this morning?"

"That's him. You remember the Newman family. They ran the ferry line when you lived here, but when none of their kids wanted to take over the business, the old man decided to move to Florida and to shut down the ferries, which would have left this island in a world of hurt. Out of nowhere, Russo swoops in. Turns out he'd made a fortune in construction and waste management in Cleveland. He had an off-the-boat great-grandfather from Sicily who worked on the island back in its quarrying days, and although he'd never even been here before, Russo bought the ferry line dirt cheap, sold his other businesses, got his captain's license, and he's been running the ferries at a loss ever since. The Captain lives on island until the lake freezes, but his wife and kids are only here a few weekends in the summer. For the most part, they keep to themselves."

The speaker box squawked. "What do you want, Chief Sarter?" The squeals of children could be heard in the background of Teresa Russo's voice. She was in her early thirties and at least twenty years younger than her husband.

"Morning, Mrs. Russo. We're going door-to-door to keep folks updated on the situation and to check for the sick."

"We are all fine, Chief. Go away, please."

"No can do, Mrs. Russo."

There was a prolonged period of silence that was finally broken by the whining of a large engine then the whipping of helicopter blades. Suddenly, a chopper marked with the orange stripe and insignia of the Coast Guard rose over the treetops of the compound and whisked away towards the East.

"I thought you said, no one comes or goes from the island?" I said.

"I did," the Chief answered.

"Yeah, well, I guess some things are the same everywhere: money flies; poor folk die."

The security gate activated and slid open.

We pulled up to an Italian Tuscany style home. Built on the highest point of the island, it was three stories high and topped with a widow's walk. Though fancy, it was actually much smaller and less gaudy than I had expected. A Range Rover sat inside one of the opened garages, and a tricked-out, eight-seat golf cart and a fleet of ATVs were parked inside the other. In place of a lawn, a heli-pad had been poured in front of the house.

Captain Russo appeared on the elevated porch to greet us.

"Nice trick, Captain," the Chief said. "Using a Coast Guard chopper."

"What can I say, Chief? Mine's in the shop, and it pays to have friends in," he pointed to the sky, "high places. No?"

I wasn't sure if he meant pilots, the military chain of command, God, or all three.

With his wife and kids spirited away, Captain Russo, whose dark tan, salt-and-pepper hair, and weather-beaten but chiseled features gave him the appearance of an aging movie star, invited us in. "Come in, Chief. Do your search."

The interior looked like something from *Architectural Digest*: natural light poured in from massive windows and through skylights in the ridiculously high and gabled ceilings, fireplaces in nearly every room, marble countertops and tabletops everywhere, gorgeous wood cabinets, and real hardwood floors throughout.

Captain Russo walked us out back to where sat a guest house, a large pool, and a cabana with a full outdoor kitchen and swim-up bar all surrounded by an eight-foot high and spiked, black wrought iron fence and thick woods.

"Keeps the deer out of the pool," he explained and nodded towards the fence.

Our host detached a pool skimmer from its clamps on the fence and began to scoop dead birds and mayflies from the surface of the water.

"Why aren't you on that chopper, Captain?" The Chief asked the obvious question.

"I could ask you the same thing, Chief. I know you have a wife and child on the mainland. You could have gotten off this rock before they applied the choke, but here you stand as well." He tossed a net full of birds and insects over the fence and into the woods.

"This is my job."

"You're wrong, Chief. It's not your job; it's your life. When I bought the ferry line, I made this island my life too, but I could not ask the same of my wife and sons."

"Well, you are a far wiser man than me, Captain," the Chief said then changed the hurtful subject. "We've brought you a box of surgical masks and rubber gloves and a two-way radio in order to communicate the locations of any bodies you might need to collect. There are two waiting in the dorm and several back in Sunset Acres. I marked their yards with a black X. Probably the sooner you can get those out of there the better."

"I'll get right on it. Cleats and a couple other of my guys have agreed to help." He paused before adding, "For a price. Even at the end of the world, money talks, Chief."

"That it does, Captain. That it does. There's one more

thing."

"What's that?"

"Your guns. I know you got some, and I can't let you keep them. I'll store and tag them for you. Give them back as soon as this thing passes, but in the meantime, we're all better off unarmed."

We left carrying an antique, double-barreled shotgun that the Captain said belonged to his great grandfather, a handgun, and a sneaking suspicion that there were more where those came from.

Chapter Eight

After a canvass of the rest of what the Chief had begun to call "Russoville" on the northwest corner of the island, we traveled east on Titus Road toward where it connected with the northern end of Division Street. I noticed a wedding band on the Chief's finger and remembered Captain Russo's mentioning of the Chief's wife and child. "I didn't know you were married, Chief," I half-declared, half-asked.

"*Were* is right."

"Then why the ring?"

"I don't know. It just seems to make life easier."

"Divorced?" I asked.

"Yep. She couldn't take it."

"What? You being a cop?"

"No. For the most part, being a police officer here is like being a playground monitor. Not a whole lot of danger. She couldn't handle the island – the people or the place. She was a mainlander. I never should have taken the job after my time in the service. I wasn't the same guy she'd married."

We turned right onto Division Street and headed towards downtown. We passed the state park, where if the flu had struck one week later, hundreds, if not thousands, of Memorial Day Weekend campers would have been staying and, by now, probably dying. The Chief wanted to search the few houses on Division in a north to south course before we'd check in with Dr. Bentham at the 4-H camp then progress toward the homes on the eastern half of the island.

On our left, we passed the island cemetery, the school, and library, where I'd earlier sent Daphne. The strap of my seatbelt bit hard into my collarbone when the Chief unexpectedly pressed heavily on the brake in the middle of Division Street.

"What's up, Chief?" I asked.

He pointed to a three-story, corner-lot, Victorian home on the right side of the street at the north corner of Bookerman Road and Division. A red Ford F-150 pick-up truck was backed up to the side porch and nearly full of boxes and bags of groceries and supplies.

"Something's not right," he said. "That's Mrs. Barnes's house."

"Yeah. So?"

"Mrs. Barnes is a widow. She lives by herself, has no family, and she doesn't drive a truck."

He whipped the cruiser into the side yard and blocked the pick-up just as a man, around the Chief's age, and a kid, maybe thirteen or fourteen, with handkerchiefs over their mouths and dressed in blue jeans and long sleeved flannel shirts, emerged carrying a big screen television, which they gingerly placed inside the truck bed.

I think it was the sheer audaciousness of the looters theft in broad daylight and seemingly without the smallest compunction that caused the Chief to take a stand, or maybe it was the fact that it was because it was Mrs. Barnes who beas being victimized. The Chief had once been a student in her classroom as well. I'm not sure of his motive, but he suddenly seemed determined to draw a hard line against the emerging lawlessness on island.

"Hey, Chief," the older of the two said nonchalantly when he him with his service revolver drawn and steadied across the top of the cruiser in a two-handed firing position.

The Chief lowered his weapon. "Stan! What do you think you're doing?"

Although his hair had grayed a little and his face had been eroded by island wind and sun, Stan McKillips wore the same shit-eating grin he wore the day of the fire. According to the magnetic sign slapped against the side of his truck, Stan's current gig was running a septic tank and boat bilge pump out service. I remembered that my grandfather, following his goodly inclination to grant even the most suspect of characters the benefit of the doubt, had referred to Stan as a "Jack of all trades, yet a master of none." I also remembered that the Chief, back in those days and less graciously, called Stan a "worthless piece-of-shit." Clearly, the Chief's characterization had been more accurate, and his opinion hadn't changed.

Stan ignored the Chief's question, and through the wooden toothpick bobbing in the corner of his mouth, he asked, "Who you got in the squad car there, Chief?"

"That's one of the Foe kids."

"Is it now?" Stan's face lit up with a smile that exposed his tobacco-stained teeth and red gums. "I knew your daddy," he called to me. "You remember me, boy?"

I shook my head but couldn't bring myself to vocalize the lie.

"You need to put all of this stuff back, Stan, the Chief said."

"Aw, c'mon, Chief," Stan complained. "Mrs. Barnes ain't coming back. Everyone knows she's at that death camp of yours and that doctor lady's."

That was news to us, but Mrs. Barnes certainly could have gone on her own. The 4-H camp wasn't far from her house. The Chief walked over to the pick-up bed and began rifling through Stan's scavenged items. He removed a can of shaving cream and a man's grooming kit. "Where'd you get this stuff, Stan? I don't believe Mrs. Barnes shaves."

"Maybe she should," Stan said. "Might've found a husband if she had."

"That's not funny," the Chief said.

"We ain't the only ones out scavenging, Chief. What're you gonna do? Shoot us? Arrest us all? Where you gonna put us if you do? That one-cell jail of yourn? If you were smart, you'd be out like us rather than running around playing cops and robbers."

"We've been looking for your son, Kenny. We think he may have been exposed to the virus."

"Don't know where he's at. He's a grown-ass man. None of my concern anymore what he do."

The Chief seemed to consider Stan's answer and to realize he wasn't getting anywhere. "At least put the television back," he said, clinging to the thinnest thread of authority.

Stan looked at his helper, then back at the Chief. "All right, Chief, we'll put the TV back, but don't stop us again. It's every man for his self from now on. Badge or no badge." He turned his back. "Get your end, boy," he ordered his helper. "We'll do what the Chief says," he paused, "for now."

The boy was none too happy about having to lug that 60-inch big screen back inside, but he said nothing and did as he was told.

The Chief walked back to the cruiser like he was returning to the dugout after striking out in the bottom of the ninth with two outs, the bases loaded, and the tying run on third. He stood defeated at his door with his arms resting on the roof of the cruiser. I mirrored his pose from my side.

By way of explanation and a half-ass apology for McKillips, the Chief said, "Stan did a tour overseas in Desert Storm."

"Was he an MP too?" I asked.

"No. He was with the Red Horse out of Camp Perry over in Ottawa County."

"The what?"

"Red Horse. It's an acronym: Rapid Engineer Deployable Heavy Operational Repair Squadron. He was part of a road building crew. Stan wasn't a very nice guy when he left, but he came back a real asshole."

Chapter Nine

We stopped to check on Dr. Bentham at the 4-H camp, where she was overseeing the treatment of the infected. The Sanderson twins, Lifers, volunteer firemen, and charter boat captains, whom the Chief had deputized and placed as guards, met us at the entrance. Thinking I may be another delivery of the infected, they inspected me closely.

"What's the count?" The Chief asked.

"Lost three overnight," Dale answered, then asked, "Find any more?"

"Not since this morning. Going to swing over to the east end before taking on Patmos. I asked the Captain to organize a burial detail. He should be round soon to collect those bodies."

"What's he going to do with them, Chief?"

"Families aren't going to like it, but I want them buried in the quarry off of Bookerman. The Captain is going to fire up one of those backhoes, dig a deep trench, place the bodies inside, and cover the hole with stones. Dr. Bentham here?"

"In the park office," Dale said.

The Chief pulled the cruiser into a gravel-covered driveway outside what had been the director's cabin. Dr. Bentham met us at the door of the cabin, which she had converted into a sort of command post around which tents for the infected had been erected between her command post and the campers' cabins, which had already been filled with patients. The tents were situated so that through the office windows she had a three hundred and sixty degree view for monitoring the infected. "Let's talk outside in the open air," she said in lieu of a greeting. "Andy's dead," she added without segue.

"Shit!" The Chief said. "I'll get him and the others out of here quick as I can."

Occasional groans sounded from the widely-spaced tents. A wooded area with an outdoors challenge course was situated between what were designated as the boys' cabins and the overflow tents.

"What are you doing for them?" The Chief asked.

"Ibuprofen. Water bottles. Blankets. Not much I can do. Just treating symptoms," Dr. Bentham said. "Don't forget, Chief, I'm a pathologist. I'm not that kind of doctor. My bedside manner is for shit."

"Well, you're the closest thing we've got. Did you secure them with the temporary restraints I gave you?"

"I think they're in enough misery without me handcuffing them to their cots."

"It's for their and our own good," the Chief was short with her, but quickly retraced his steps and adjusted his tone of voice. "If you could, get me a surgical mask and those restraints. Danny and I'll do it."

Past the Chief's shoulder, I sensed movement in the woods. A late middle-aged woman, shoeless and dressed in a long and loose-fitting night gown, had emerged from one of the cabins and was weaving her way in our direction through the outdoor challenge course with her arms upraised like a mummy walking. She mumbled a string of unintelligible requests. Her skin was waxen and blue, her hair greasy and matted.

"Mrs. Barnes! Stop where you are!" The Chief called to our

150

ex-elementary school teacher, but she continued towards us oblivious to his command.

She drew closer. The three of us instinctively backed towards the cabin.

"Mrs. Barnes," The Chief repeated. "You need to stop right there."

As she reached within twenty feet of our position, she suddenly coughed a spray of frothing, crimson blood in our direction. Its residue ran down her chin and stained the front of her cream-colored nightgown.

I watched the Chief unfasten the snap on his holster. "Mrs. Barnes, I can't ask you again. Please. Stop."

From no more than ten feet from where we stood, pressed against the front outside wall of the office, I saw tears flowing from Ms. Barnes's bloodshot but remarkably childlike eyes – just before her head exploded.

At first, I suspected the Chief to have pulled some Wild West quick draw maneuver, but his gun was still holstered, and the stunned expression on his face mirrored my own. The double click of a cartridge being ejected drew my ears to the campground entrance. "Don't none of you move," Tom Sanderson ordered as he examined each of us, one-by-one, through the high-powered scope positioned atop his .30/06 rifle.

"What's he doing?" I asked the Chief under my breath.

"Checking us for any of Mrs. Barnes," he said.

The last to be examined, I felt what I prayed to be a bead of sweat forming over my upper lip, but for all I knew, it was a splash of the infected blood, or worse. I wondered if Tom knew of or even understood the process of infection and resistance that accounted for my probable immunity. He seemed to train the crosshairs of the scope directly on my face for an inordinately long time until I felt rivulets of perspiration running down my cheeks and I was imagining each to be a river of Mrs. Barnes's blood. I wondered if I'd hear the shot or feel the bullet. I wondered if they'd throw my body in the quarry. I wondered why I turned Katie Jenkins down when she begged me to go all the way after prom two weeks earlier. I wondered why I ever applied for the job on that fucking island.

After an agonizing couple of seconds, Tom methodically lowered his weapon. "Shoot to kill were your orders, Chief," he explained emotionlessly.

I fell to my knees and wretched what little I had put into my stomach onto the grass. Dr. Bentham and the Chief reflexively backed away.

"It's okay. Everyone just relax," the Chief said and raised his hands. "He's not sick, at least not with this flu. It's the excitement. He just watched a woman get her head blown off for god's sake." With that, he stepped directly in the line of Tom's fire. When my convulsions stopped, the Chief helped me off of the ground. "Go inside with Dr. Bentham and get yourself some water then come on back. We need to clean up out here. Jenny, could you?"

"But, Chief," I whined.

"For Chrissakes, Danny, I don't want to hear it. This is one of those choices you don't get to make. For whatever reason, you're here right now and in this place and I need you. So, buck up. Put on a mask, gloves, whatever will help you get through this, but we're going to collect what's left of Mrs. Barnes and prepare her for pick up. Then, we're going to restrain the rest of the infected with those temporary cuffs."

Our restraining of the infected was met with no resistance. They were all too sick to put up any kind of fight. Most were too weak to even talk. I swear a few even looked longingly at the Chief's sidearm and were disappointed that all we did was chain them to their sickness rather than grant them release.

When we had finished and returned to the office, both of us

made somber by our chore, Dr. Bentham greeted us from the front steps, where she sat crunching numbers inside a spiral notebook. "How many you figure are on the island, Chief?" She asked.

"Counting Lifers and visitors, I'd guess no more than five hundred. Probably fewer."

"So, including Officer Dooley, Andy, the girl scouts, the Steinbauers, the two waitresses from the dorm, Mrs. Barnes, today's additions, plus the others in the tents, that's about twenty infected on the island in three days, give or take. Correct?"

"Don't forget the Golden Boy," the Chief indicated me with a nod of his head.

"Right."

"That's what we know of. We have nearly half the island yet to search."

"Okay. For shits and giggles, let's conservatively throw in a few more," Dr. Bentham said, surprising but not disappointing me with her potty mouth. "That's twenty-five."

"Which means," the Chief piped in, "at this rate, there will be one hundred dead in . . .?"

"About twelve days," I was good in math. "And all five hundred in about 60 days or . . ."

"Two months," the Chief finished my calculations.

"With maybe twenty, like Danny, who survive or somehow escape contraction," Dr. Bentham said.

"Hobbs is right. That's too long and too many," the Chief conceded.

"But remember," Dr. Bentham said, "those figures only hold if its spread progresses arithmetically. These types of epidemics tend to accelerate exponentially over time."

"Is there any chance of a vaccine or inoculation of some sort being developed in two months?" the Chief asked.

"None," she said. "These numbers are fairly consistent in

known Avian Flu outbreaks among bird species, but this is some kind of super virus. In the previous cases we're aware of, it took nine to ten days to cause death in a human, but we're dying in forty-eight to seventy-two hours from contraction. Typically, from the isolation of the virus strain to the development of a vaccine, it takes up to six months to a year – at least."

"Which means?" The Chief asked.

"We're dead," I said. "One way or another."

"Maybe," the Chief said, "we will all be among the lucky ones."

"With the amount of close contact we've had already and what our jobs are still going to require, that's highly unlikely," Dr. Bentham said.

"There is another option," I said.

Chapter Ten

"It's out back," I said. The Chief shifted the cruiser into park in my grandfather's driveway. "Bring your flashlight."

"Flashlight? It's the middle of the . . ."

I assume he said "afternoon," but I was already out of the cruiser.

My grandfather's property – which my brother had inherited but in which he had zero interest – sat on the crest of a small hill that sloped away from the back of the house and toward the downtown and south shore. It wasn't much of a hill, but on the relatively flat island, it was adequate to provide a small slope for sledding when I was a kid.

As we tiptoed through the overgrown yard, doing our best to avoid stepping on the bird carcasses, it took a conscious and constant effort for me to restrain the flood of images and memories that were pressing against the mental levees I had constructed ten years earlier to constrain my grief and that I continued to buttress ever since.

I stopped in the middle of the backyard and did a slow 360 degree turn.

"What you looking for, Danny?" the Chief asked.

"There," I said, pointed, then made my way towards a pile

of rocks barely visible amidst the high grass. I dropped to my hands and knees and crawled the last few yards before, one-by-one, I removed the rocks to expose a thick square of weathered plywood, which had all but become one with the surrounding soil. After a few moments of digging and prying, I was able to lift the plywood to reveal a hole in the ground no more than three-feet in diameter.

"What's this?" the Chief asked perplexed.

"Shine your flashlight down it," I suggested rather than answering his question.

With no room for Dr. Bentham to join us, the Chief did as I asked.

"For Chrissakes," the Chief said, as, together, we stared in shared wonder at the kaleidoscope effect created by the flashlight's beam ricocheting purple and blue off of quartz crystals that lined a cavity inside the island limestone no more than fifteen to twenty feet from the surface. "What is it?"

"Grandpa said that geologists call it a geode, but when the cavity is this large, I guess you'd call it a cavern."

"How did you find it?"

"The summer of the . . . of the . . . fire. I was helping Grandpa drill for a new well when he said the bit seemed to 'cut through Hell's roof.' When we looked, this is what we found. He made me swear not to tell anybody."

"Don't tell anybody? He could have opened this up to tourists and made a living from it. Did he know how many people pay six bucks a pop to visit one of these on South Bass Island?"

"I'm pretty sure he knew, and I'm pretty sure that's why he didn't want me to tell anybody."

We stood up and backed away in order to allow Dr. Bentham to take a look. When we reconvened, I made my proposition. "If ventilated, I'd bet there's room down there for at least five people and their provisions. It has a constant, comfortable temperature in all seasons and it's dry. I'm not saying it would be luxurious, but we could survive."

Their interest clearly piqued, the Chief and Dr. Bentham exchanged a long look before the Chief said, "Let's think about it. If nothing else, it could be a last resort. Think of it as Plan B. It might even be a good idea to start stockpiling whatever supplies we can get our hands on. For now, let's cover it up before one of those drones makes a pass. We've got to get back to work."

"Where's that leave us, Chief?" I asked after we had dropped off Dr. Bentham at the 4-H Camp and returned to canvassing the island for guns and the infected.

"Pretty much just the eastern half of the island, which is far less populated than the western half."

The northeastern corner, past the airport, was almost entirely forested and unpopulated except for the wilderness bible camp, where Patmos and his growing number of followers had hunkered down. It was obvious that the Chief was in no hurry to get there. "We'll start with the Seasonals on the southeast quarter," the Chief said.

Chapter Eleven

During good economic times, it never fails that some mainland schmuck – typically one who has grown enamored with the island and fooled by its phony hospitality during a weekend visit – will take a flyer on purchasing cheaply some interior island property with the dream of building a housing development, which, they stupidly believe, will attract droves of buyers dreaming of some idyllic island lifestyle and make the developer rich. It also never fails to fail. An inland property on one of the Lake Erie islands may as well be a pasture in the middle of Kansas for all of its real estate value.

After a fancy name for the development is posted on a sign displaying available lots at the entrance to the subdivision, a model home might be constructed with a lake view – if you crane your neck and peer through a small break in the distant trees and past the actual lakeside homes – and maybe one or two suckers will buy lots and build smallish homes only soon to find the claustrophobia of island life and the inhospitality of the Lifers unbearable and their getaway homes being offered on the market at a staggering loss. Paradise Lanes was one such development. It included Melody, Memory, Fernwood, Cedar, and Orchard lanes.

Because so many trees had been cleared for the construction, there were far fewer dead birds littering the area; although, we were forced to wait when a group of mallard ducks, including a couple of drakes, waddled across East Lakeshore Road like they owned the place. We drove at a snail's pace up Melody Lane across Orchard Lane back down Memory Lane with the Chief repeatedly calling on his PA for any residents to please show themselves, but driveway after driveway was empty of cars, and no signs of other life were visible until we turned north onto Fernwood Lane, where three concrete slab driveways in a row were occupied by what were clearly "island cars." Island cars were pieces-of-shit cars, behind the wheel of which most people would never allow themselves to be seen on the mainland.

The Chief's repeated calls from the street went unanswered. "Damn," he said, "we're going to have to get out and search these."

"Do you know who lives here?" I asked.

"Not personally, no, but I know it's a sort of family thing. Beck is their name. It's an older couple and their grown kids with their grandchildren. They bought lots and built these small, pre-fabricated houses a few years back. I believe their intention was to move here full time to live 'off-the-grid,' as one of the sons told me. Apparently, they were fed up with what they called 'the godless and socialist direction of America and came here thinking they might escape it. Look around the houses. What's missing?" The Chief quizzed me.

I took a few seconds to study the exterior of each of what couldn't have been more than two-bedroom homes before I said, "Satellite dishes!" They were ubiquitous on the island and typically the first addition to new island homes, sometimes even before water had been tapped and electricity had been made available to use them.

"That's right," the Chief said. "These folks have kept to themselves and have been pretty scarce around town."

The Chief had clearly been made nervous by the lack of activity. He hesitated a moment and took a deep breath before undoing his seatbelt and exiting the cruiser. I joined him in the mostly dirt front yard.

"Are you ready?" the Chief asked.

"Let's go," I said. I was pretty sure nothing could be worse than what I'd witnessed and took part in back at the 4-H camp.

I was wrong.

As we expected, the front door at the first house was locked, and no one answered our repeated knocks. We crossed a pair of ragged lawns and got the same results at the second and third houses. We were about to come down off the porch when we heard the sound of a baby's muffled crying followed by the panicked voices of a man and a woman in a heated debate.

Instinctively, the Chief unsnapped his holster and positioned his hand over the butt of the revolver. "Come on out folks," he called. "We can hear you in there."

More argument was followed by a man's voice which ordered us to "Go away. Unless you've got a search warrant, you have no right to be on this property."

"I don't have a warrant," the Chief called while signaling with his hand for me to walk around back and to try and get a look inside a window or backdoor. "We just want to make sure y'all are all right and have everything you need. Now which one of you Becks am I talking to?"

"It's Donnie, and don't lie to me, Chief. We know about the concentration camp at the 4-H camp."

I could hear their shouted conversation even as I made my way around the side of the house.

"It's not a 'concentration camp,' Donnie. It's a sort of field hospital. We can't let those who've been infected walk around spreading this thing, and we can't treat anyone who we don't know is sick."

Through a small crease in the curtains over the backdoor

window, I could see through the kitchen and into the front room, where Donnie Beck stood cradling a double-barreled shotgun and talking to the Chief through the door. His wife seemed to be pleading with him to do something. The baby, crying, lay on its back in a portable play pen. I came back around and reported the situation as I'd seen it to the Chief.

"Donnie? What about the rest of your family?" The Chief asked.

"They're all dead. Mom and dad down with the sickness. My sister-in-law, Janet, and the girls too." There was a prolonged pause before Donnie added, "My brother blew his brains out this morning, and now my boy is sick. I don't know what to do, Chief, but if I give him to you, I know I'll never see him again."

We could hear the poor man sobbing between sentences, his wife's pleading, and the baby's wails all mixing in anguished disharmony.

"Donnie. Mrs. Beck. Listen. You folks are gonna have to trust me. I have flu shots in the cruiser. If you just slide out your weapon, I'll get them for all of y'all."

"I don't know, Chief," Donnie said.

"What do you mean you 'don't know'? What options do you have Donnie? Just hand out the shotgun, butt end first, and I'll get them shots."

Mrs. Beck's entreaties grew in intensity along with the volume of the baby's cries until, finally, the deadbolt was slid over, the front door cracked open, and the shotgun was passed through. The Chief indicated for me to take hold of it. After I'd secured the gun, the door opened fully. In the doorframe, against the unlit background stood a tall and haggard-looking Donnie Beck, dressed in work boots, blue jeans, and a wife-beater undershirt. A scraggly growth of a ruddy beard had taken root along the jaw line of his pallid face. His eyes were deeply sunk into their sockets over a face mottled by freckles. The sharp smell of fever seeped from his pores.

The Chief and I exchanged knowing glances. "Donnie, are you healthy enough to drive one of these here cars?" (By then, I'd grown fascinated by the Chief's ability to change his manner of talking based upon the person with whom he was speaking.) "You're sick too. I'm going to need you to come along to the camp with the baby. We can get you your shots there, and you can stay in a tent with your boy." He turned to Donnie's wife and said, "M'am, you can come if you'd like. All three of you can be together until this thing runs its course. It's your choice."

Donnie's wife headed immediately for the original model, wood side-paneled, Chevy Caravan parked in the driveway and being held together by its rust. Donnie followed on his wife's heels, slipped in the driver's side, and fired up the reluctant engine. She marched around to the sliding door and placed the baby inside its car seat, then, without a kiss for baby or husband, a word spoken, or a backward glance, she marched right back into her house, shut, and dead-bolted the door.

Donnie no sooner had his hand on the door handle intending to chase after his wife before the Chief's service revolver was pointed directly between Donnie's eyes. "She made her choice, Donnie," the Chief said.

Donnie froze in his seat but called out through his open window, "Baby? Baby? You can't be serious. C'mon, baby. We're a family. We're gonna stay together. You're all I have left." Ignoring the Chief's revolver, he pulled the latch. The car door groaned on its hinges, and opened a few inches.

"Donnie!" The Chief yelled. "For Chrissakes! I don't want to, but I will shoot you. Is that what you want? Don't you want to live, Donnie? Remember the flu shots. Think about your baby. You can fix all of this later. She's not herself. This flu has changed us all. It will pass and things will be normal again, but not if you make me kill you here. There's no undoing or fixing that."

Donnie turned his attention to the Chief then snuck a glance at the baby in the backseat, and the accumulated wisdom of the Chief's words seemed to overpower Donnie's impulse to chase after his wife. "Okay, Chief."

"Good," the Chief let out a deep breath and slipped into what sounded like an elementary school principal's tone of voice. "Here's what we're going to do. You're going to drive to the 4-H camp. We're going to follow you. If you try anything stupid, when I catch you, there will be no questions asked or second chances. Do you understand?"

Donnie's focus had returned to the little house that contained his wife and that once seemed the key to his and his family's happiness. Tears flowed in streams over his cheekbones into the scruff of his beard. I imagined him recalling what must have been the excitement and promise of those heady, first days on what they all thought to be an Edenic island only to see it all destroyed by a too-tiny-to-be-seen virus. I wondered if he recognized the irony.

Finally, he said, "I understand."

The Chief sent me to the cruiser to retrieve a can of spray paint with which I marked the front doors of all three houses, two with black crosses and one with red. Outside Donnie's door, I heard the anguished cries of his wife, I suppose defending herself to her god. "I want to live. I want to live," she repeated over and over.

After convoying to the camp and leaving Donnie and his son with the useless flu shots under the guard of the Sanderson brothers and care of Dr. Bentham, the Chief radioed Captain Russo to collect the bodies of the Beck family, and we continued on our mission of little mercy.

Chapter Twelve

After picking up our canvassing of the Seasonals' quarter and coming up empty down several gravel-covered and pothole-pocked lanes, we continued north on Monaghan Road toward our eventual run-in with Patmos. Before that, however, there were several far off-road homes to search and the King's Playboy Mansion, which sat adjacent to the airport and its single landing strip. At the moment we passed, it was living up to its nickname. There were at least half-a-dozen girls, all in bikinis, sunning themselves by and lounging in an in-ground pool. A handful of shirtless young men in board shorts mingled among them. Three of them were the frat boys who'd hassled Jalil on the ferry ride over. The rest were all either *Gulliver's* employees or reveler-refugees from last Friday night. The grey-haired King Charles, wrapped around the waist in a terrycloth towel, which exposed his basketball-shaped paunch and spindly legs, stood Hefner-like near the diving board lording over, yet clearly a crasher, at his own party. He lifted a drink inside of a tall glass to toast us as we passed.

"It's good to be the King," the Chief said as he returned a cursory wave.

"Aren't we going to stop?" I asked with more-than-a-little

disappointment in my voice.

"Nah. They all look pretty healthy to me."

"What about weapons?" I asked desperately.

"The King's not a gun owner. He runs a tight ship at the bar, and he can be a real prick as mayor, but he's more lover than fighter."

Dejected, I turned my head and watched the bikinied girls disappear.

Just past the airport, the street sign identified the next private road as Rebecca Lane. When the Chief turned onto the unpaved road, I saw Daphne's mother's face lying in the grass staring heavenward. Someone had clearly uprooted the sign on purpose, most likely to discourage any of the island's other refugees from squatting there themselves. I immediately looked for the ghost of the address Daphne had written on my palm when I was sick in the jail cell: 213 Rebecca Lane.

"The Sennett family lives down here," the Chief said, "and there are a couple of summer homes. I didn't see any of the Sennets at the meeting this morning. Let's hope they've been off island and aren't sick and holed up inside."

He pulled into a stone driveway next to an old barn at the end and on the left side of the lane. Though one arrived at the barn first, it was actually the back of the property. The front of the house faced the open waters to the east.

"This is the Sennetts' place. They live here, but they run a little bed and breakfast near downtown. I'll check it out." The Chief then pointed across the lane, where another path, marked by two address posts labeled 211 and 213 Rebecca Lane, cut into the field and led to two properties also directly on the water. "You check those two. They should be empty."

One was nearby: a still-boarded up cottage with a massive satellite dish and a rusted pick-up truck on blocks in the yard. The other was a large, stone and cedar, two-story home with landscaped grounds, and an expansive lawn. Its many-peaked roof rose like a mirage over a line of pines that separated the disparate properties.

I ignored the obviously-vacant cottage and headed immediately towards the larger home, whose address matched the one given to me by Daphne. As I crossed the front lawn, the automatic sprinkler heads popped out of the ground to perform an aquatic, synchronized salute to my arrival. Forced to run round, duck under, and jump over jetted streams like a cat burglar through a field of infrared laser beams, I arrived at the porch with only a few drops of damage.

No one answered the doorbell at the heavy oak front door, so I made my way around to the rear of the property, where a ground-level, granite stone patio sprawled beneath a first floor wooden deck and a house-wide, lake-facing balcony on the second. A cello-shaped, in-ground pool/hot tub combination lay in front of an outdoor cabana and pool house. Beyond the back yard, I heard his and her giggles rising from a small private beach of brown sand, which had been trucked-in from the mainland.

I sidled up to the northeast corner of the pool house to get a better view. Knee-deep in the water, Daphne and Derek played and splashed one another like children. Derek wore a pair of tie-dyed boxer shorts. Daphne was barely in a white bikini she must have found inside the house. They swam out into deeper waters. After a few moments of treading water, they raced toward the motley-striped beach towels laid out on the beach. When the rising shore forced them to their feet, they sprinted, holding hands, with Daphne trailing the entire way.

I wanted to throw up. Instead, I turned and hurried off of the property back to the Sennetts' family barn across the road, where the Chief was waiting inside the cruiser.

"Anybody?" The Chief asked in abbreviated fashion.

"No," I said. "They're both empty. How about you?"

"Nope. Nobody home. They must've got stuck on the mainland. Lucky bastards. Well," the Chief said, "we can't delay it any longer. It's time to go see Patmos."

The Chief decided he'd need more than my support to face Patmos, so we swung by the 4-H camp once more and picked up Dr. Bentham. As we drove east on Ward then north on Monaghan, the Chief filled us in on John Patmos. On weekends, Patmos witnessed in Memorial Park, where he gave his end-of-days sermons with the fervor of a Pentecostal camp meeting preacher. On good days, he was ignored. On bad, he suffered vicious ridicule. However, neither reaction to his apocalyptic warnings discouraged him from continuing. To his credit, according to the Chief, unlike most "Bible-whoring charlatans," he never took a nickel or tried sell bogus relics. He never pretended to heal anyone, and he never babbled like an idiot in pretend tongues. For years he had lived a hermit's life in a crude shack on the tip of Long Point, a mostly uninhabited peninsula that extended from the northeast corner of Kelleys, but with the arrival of the Blues, Patmos had asserted himself and found his purpose and audience. At the base of the peninsula where Monaghan Road dead ends, lay the Bible camp, which, since the epidemic, Patmos had claimed and converted into a sort of cultic community with himself as its leader all David Koresh-like.

When the epidemic struck and the island-wide quarantine was announced, his ramblings suddenly seemed prophetic. Many of those who had previously spurned him and those hearing him for the first time looked to Patmos for guidance, protection, and hope. The Chief said that as I lay sick in the jail cell during the chaos of that first weekend, Patmos, emboldened by his newfound status as a respected seer and deliverer, stood in the park and announced that the Second Coming was at hand and that he would be founding a religious colony on the

167

grounds of the Bible camp for those who had been or wished to be "born again unto Christ" and who longed to be counted among those selected by God for salvation. Within hours, a number of Lifers, Seasonals, and tourists were making the pilgrimage to the Patmos camp in vehicles crammed with supplies and settling into its many one-room cabins. There they were newly baptized in the Lake's waters.

"Oh, for Chrissakes," the Chief moaned when we entered the camp and saw Patmos and approximately thirty of his converts congregated inside a large, covered picnic shelter. Wearing open-toed sandals; frayed khaki cargo shorts; and a blue, collared, and short sleeve Newman Ferries work shirt with "John" stitched in red inside a white patch on his left breast, he paced frenetically in front of his gathered sheep and preached without prepared notes, sans a microphone, and with only occasional visits to a Bible set on a lectern. The shaggy, dark-haired, and bearded Patmos looked remarkably younger than a man who had to be in his mid-forties. Long, lean, and broad shouldered, he had a swimmer's body and a handsome face that made it hard to dislike him or to reconcile his ascetic lifestyle with the good looks that would have opened numerous doors (and legs) in the secular world.

After the Chief parked the cruiser, we all exited, leaned against it, and listened to Patmos proclaim a mixture of quoted and paraphrased biblical text and his own rantings. I have no doubt that he marked our presence, amplified his vehemence, and directed his message our way.

> "*They continually mocked the messenger of God, despised His words and scoffed at His prophets, until the wrath of the Lord arose against his people, until there was no remedy. Oh Beloved, sing to the Lord a new song . . . all is not*

*yet lost. Sing His praise from the end of the Earth!
You who go down to the sea, and all that is in it.
You islands, and those who dwell on them. I,
John, your brother and fellow partaker in this
tribulation, am on this island because of the word
of God and the testimony of Jesus.*

But may it never be that I would boast, except in the cross of
our lord Jesus Christ. Because, like Sodom and Gomorrah, these
islands have forsaken Him and provoked Him to anger with all
the works of their hands. His wrath will be poured out on this
place, and it shall not be quenched! Do homage to the Son . . .
How blessed are all who take refuge in Him!"

I could almost hear the Chief's eyes rolling in his head.

" . . . *therefore the land mourns and everyone
who lives in it languishes along with the beasts of
the field and the birds of the sky . . . it has become
a dwelling place of demons, a prison for every foul
spirit, and a cage for every unclean and hated
bird ... For all the nations have drunk of the
wine of the wrath of her fornication, the kings of
the earth have committed fornication with her,
and the merchants of the earth have become rich
through the abundance of her luxury.*"

Patmos smiled seductively and his voice became pleading.
"Come out of her, my people, lest you share in her sins, and lest
you receive of her plague."

"There can't be a half-a-bird brain among them," the Chief
said, looking at those gathered.

As if directly addressing the Chief, Patmos said, "For many
walk, of whom I often told you, and now tell you weeping, that
are enemies of the Cross."

"I can't take this nonsense," the Chief said and walked away from the shelter towards the mostly rock-lined north coast of Kelleys, where he began to pick up and throw rocks into the Lake toward the distant Pelee Island in Canadian waters. Beyond the Chief, I noticed that the waters north of Kelleys were being patrolled by Coast Guard cutters flying the red Maple Leaf of Canada. Our containment had become an international priority.

Dr. Bentham and I remained listening.

> " . . . *Now this will be the plague with which the Lord will strike all the peoples who have gone to war against Jerusalem; their flesh will rot while they stand on their feet, and their eyes will rot in their sockets, and their tongue will rot in their mouth.*"

He continued like that for nearly fifteen more minutes, then after an altar call and a laying of hands, Patmos's sheep scattered maskless into the late afternoon. Many cast unwelcoming glances in our direction before they disappeared into various residential cabins, a large game room, or the cafeteria building. Some of the faithful settled beneath the shade of trees and continued to pray, which caused me to notice, for the first time since our arrival, birdsongs emanating from the branches and the occasional darting of a warbler or wren from tree to tree.

I thought I recognized the last worshipper to emerge from out of the picnic shelter. "Kenny!" I called, but on seeing me, he immediately turned towards the stone administration building. I was about to chase after him when Patmos approached and interposed himself in my sight line between Kenny and me. When I craned my neck to reestablish visual contact, Kenny was gone.

"In my vision," Patmos said, "*I saw an angel standing in the sun, and he cried out with a loud voice, saying to all the birds which fly in mid-heaven, Come, assemble for the great supper of God.* Look around, young man. The birds are abundant here and my flock free from the plague. I can offer both of you the guidance of my divine visions. I can offer you life here and in the hereafter through the redeeming cross of Jesus. Other than death, what does the Chief offer?"

"Right now," Dr. Bentham replied, "he provides the best opportunity for survival. What you're doing, meeting in large numbers in close spaces is madness and a sure means of spreading disease."

"Excuse me, Miss . . ." Patmos extended his hand and directed his ice blue eyes into her green.

"Bentham. Doctor Jennifer Bentham," she said, ignoring the handshake.

"Do you really believe, Miss Bentham, that whether you or any of us lives or dies will be the result of our own choices and doings?" He clearly and purposefully used the old-fashioned "Miss" and completely ran around the "doctor."

"I believe there are precautions one may take to reduce the risk of infection, yes," Dr. Bentham answered.

"Then you are a fool, but you are a fortunate fool, for truly, I say you have come to God's holy place of refuge at these end times. See." He opened his arms and half-rotated his torso towards the campground. "None are infected."

As if on cue, a group of mallards took flight from where they'd been resting and feeding in the near shore shallows and continued their journey north.

"That may be so, Mr. Patmos."

"Call me John."

"Okay, John. That may be so, but the reality is that this island is ground zero for what could be a devastating pandemic. Maybe, through some quirk or because of its relative isolation, no one out here has yet to manifest the symptoms of the virus, but, trust me, it's only a matter of time, and when that happens, this sort of living in close proximity and gathering for community prayer and meals is equivalent to mass suicide. You may as well start mixing the Kool-Aid."

He actually smiled at her allusion to Jonestown. "Have you no faith in God, Miss Bentham?" he asked.

"If it's okay with you, I'll put my faith in the lessons of modern medicine and, if I hedge my bet with an occasional prayer, I'll do that in private."

Patmos, unfazed by her logic, smiled even wider at her answer, which revealed teeth as white as angels' robes. He turned towards me and drew me into their conversation, "Are the two of you familiar with Psalm 91?"

We both shook our heads to indicate no.

From memory, Patmos recited:

> "He that dwelleth in the secret place of the most High shall abide under the shadow of the Almighty.
>
> I will say of the LORD, He is my refuge and my fortress: my God; in him will I trust.
>
> Surely he shall deliver thee from the snare of the fowler, and from the noisome pestilence.
>
> He shall cover thee with his feathers, and under his wings shalt thou trust: his truth shall be thy shield and buckler.
>
> Thou shalt not be afraid for the terror by night; nor for the arrow that flieth by day;
>
> Nor for the pestilence that walketh in darkness; nor for the destruction that wasteth at noonday.
>
> A thousand shall fall at thy side, and ten thousand at thy right hand; but it shall not come nigh thee.

> *Only with thine eyes shalt thou behold and see the reward of the wicked. Because thou hast made the LORD, which is my refuge, even the most High, thy habitation; There shall no evil befall thee, neither shall any plague come nigh thy dwelling.*

"It continues," he said, "but I think you get the point of my offer to join us."

"Those are beautiful words, John." It was the Chief, who'd approached from behind Patmos. "But words make for poor protection against the virus."

Without turning around, Patmos smiled widely and said, "Nice of you to visit, Chief, but you misunderstand. It is not through words but only through the recognition of the suffering endured on the cross by our Lord and Savior, Jesus Christ, and through being born again into His precious blood that man has even the thinnest thread of hope for salvation." Patmos turned and faced the Chief.

"You can keep your cross. I watched enough men humiliated, tortured, and killed when I was in the Middle East. Not for just three hours either, but day after day. In complete anonymity and with no prospect of perpetual hero worship and adoration. And none of them had the luxury of knowing they'd be back in three days. So, save your death cult pitch for those who are buying."

"Is there something I can do for you, Chief?" Patmos said, no longer smiling and disgusted by the Chief's blasphemy.

"Actually, yes. You can isolate these people in separate cabins and allow us to search for any signs of infection."

A curious drone hovered momentarily overhead. We'd grown so used to their presence that none of us even glanced upwards.

Patmos ignored the Chief's request. "What's with the

hostility, J.P.?"

I'd heard the Chief's friends call him "J.P.," but there was nothing friendly in Patmos's spitting of the letters.

"No hostility, John. Just want to keep people alive and this island afloat."

"I appreciate your efforts, but your misguided compassion seems to be running contrary to the wishes of the Father. This flu is God's doing. Long ago, I warned that there will be great earthquakes, and in various places plagues and famines, and there will be terrors and great signs from heaven. These are the end times, and God has chosen this insignificant little island as the starting point for man's reckoning. Unlike you, we have no fear of this virus. We are not afraid to die. In fact, we welcome it. If it is God's will that we escape this scourge, then we will escape. If it be his will that we be infected, then, oh, happy day! The sooner will we be glorified in our Father's house. Either way, it is out of our hands, and either way, we win. We are all subject to God's will and mercy, even you, J.P."

"If it is your God's doing, that's one cruel god you worship."

"We accept that the Lord works in mysterious ways."

"You know, you throw around 'we' a lot. Why not at least educate these people about this virus and their options? Allow them to choose."

"The Lord spoke to me in a vision about your side of the island. He said, *'Come out of her, my people, so that you will not participate in her sins and receive her plagues . . . for she will be burned up with fire; for the Lord God who judges her is strong. I have no intention of disobeying my God, who has delivered me and my flock to this place in this moment.'* Be warned, Chief. *'In my vision men were scorched with fierce heat; and they blasphemed the name of God who has power over these plagues, and they did not repent so as to give Him glory.'* You take that message to *your* people. You 'educate' *them* about *their* 'options,' and you 'allow *them* to choose.'"

"What about weapons?" The Chief changed the subject.

"What about them?"

"Are there any on site?"

"To my knowledge, no, but we are all still Americans. I believe the Second Amendment was enacted exactly for times like these."

"Yeah, well, America has all but erased us from its map, and your constitutional rights aren't worth the paper they're written on. For now, for good or bad, I'm the only law that matters, and if I'm going to keep people safe, I need to confiscate as many weapons as I can."

"You're wrong."

"I am? About what?"

"God's law is the only law that matters."

The Chief stepped in so that he stood literally toe-to-toe with Patmos, "I'll tell you what, John. If you can show me in that good book of yours where god grants anyone the right to bear arms, I'll leave right now, and you and your friends can keep your guns. If not, I'm going to ask that your people surrender all of their weapons, and if we have to, we'll search every one of these goddamn cabins."

"What's in it for us?" Patmos asked.

"I've got a box full of flu shots in the trunk of my car. I'm willing to trade it for whatever guns are turned in."

Patmos's eyes widened with interest.

"I thought you were resigned to 'God's will,' John?"

"I do believe that it is God's will that brought you here with those shots."

"Hedging *your* bet, John?" Dr. Bentham asked.

Patmos smiled but didn't respond. He turned away and quickly moved among those of his followers gathered outside and sent messengers scurrying to various cabins. Within a half hour, we had added twelve handguns and several large-bladed knives to our collection.

Chapter Thirteen

"You suppose we got them all, Chief?" I asked as we carried them to the trunk of the cruiser.

"I doubt it, but we got some," he said then called, "Fare well, John."

Patmos looked but did not return the Chief's fare well.

"I've got a question, Chief," I said as we drove to return Dr. Bentham to the camp.

"What's that?"

"What's the J.P. stand for?"

"John Paul."

"Like the Popes?" I said as I choked down the irony.

"No. The Beatles. My mother was a huge fan. Not many people know it, but Patmos and I go back," the Chief said changing the subject. "Patmos wasn't always Patmos, and he wasn't always a preacher."

"Who was he then?" I asked.

"Believe it or not, he belonged to The Prophets, one of the largest and baddest motorcycle gangs in the Midwest. He ran their drug operations on the islands: pot, X, heroin, crystal meth. You name it; he supplied it. Made a killing during the summers.

"The King's home next to the airport used to be Patmos's place. He built it with drug money when he was no more than twenty-five years old. If you think it's a party heaven now, you should have seen it then, but he lost it all when the ATF nailed him. He's hated anything to do with the government ever since. I was only a deputy then. I had nothing to do with the bust, but Patmos blamed me for it."

"Why you?" Dr. Bentham asked.

The Chief tapped his badge. "Well, besides the obvious, Patmos and I are nearly the exact same age, born two hours apart. We went through twelve years of schooling together in a class of five: two boys and three girls. We were rivals of some sort from the day our mothers' brought us back to the island on the same ferry. Back then, his name wasn't Patmos. He used to be John Newman, one of the ferry family's kids, who were raised in relative luxury because of that ferry business but who wanted nothing to do with it once the old man retired. That's where that work shirt with his name patch comes from that he wears beneath his robe."

"When did he change his last name?" I asked.

"In prison. Says he had an awakening. Found Jesus Christ and right wing talk radio. Thanks to the expensive lawyers his father hired, he only served five years. I was back and forth on deployments with my reserve unit during much of that time, but when he returned to the island, he moved to that tiny piece of nearly inaccessible property owned by his family way out past the Bible camp on the tip of the peninsula. For years, nobody saw much of him except for when he came into town for supplies, but eventually, he started showing up in the park on weekends and preaching."

An interval of silence followed as we absorbed the Chief's recounting.

"There's something else," I said. "I'm pretty sure I saw Kenny back there."

"How'd he look? Did he seem sick?" The Chief asked.

"I'm not sure. He was pretty far away, but he definitely wanted nothing to do with us."

"We have to go back," Dr. Bentham said.

"Not now," the Chief said. "We'll have to check on him later."

The Chief dropped me off at the jail before getting Dr. Bentham some supper at his place and returning her to the camp. When I entered, Jalil was seated at the desk with his headphones over his ears. His laptop was open to some program for mixing beats, and an open notebook lay in front of him in which he was scratching a few words.

"What's up?" I spoke loudly, but I received no response. So, I reopened the door, slammed it shut, and got his attention.

"S'up?" Jalil greeted me and set his headphones on top of the notebook and paused the beats.

"What are you doing?" I said and nodded towards the notebook.

"I'm writing lyrics over some of these beats. Someday, I'm going to be the world's greatest Muslim rapper. Not some converted brother but genuine (He pronounced it so that it rhymed with turpentine.)."

"Can't imagine you'd have much competition."

"Go ahead. Be a smart ass, but you'll see."

"I'm just playing with you."

"It's aiight. You're the only one on this island who hasn't busted my nuts, dog."

"Speaking of busting nuts, I'd give the Chief a break if I were you. He's actually a pretty good guy, and it sounds like he saw some real shit both in Iraq and Afghanistan."

"My people aren't Iraqi or Afghani. My grandparents are Iranian, but I've never even been there, and my moms and pops haven't been back since they came to the States before I was born. And we see 'shit' every day right here in the U. S. of A. So don't give me any of your Chief's PTSD bullshit."

"Nice rhyme," I said. In order to cool Jalil's rising temper, I added, "Tell me about your girl."

A smile broke spontaneously across his face which he attempted to cover by placing his hand over his mouth, stroking his beard, and turning his head away. "She's beautiful, man."

"What's her name?"

"Monique. She's nearly as tall as me and built like a model. Dresses like one too. Her skin is smooth and caramel colored. Makes me want to lick it up!" Jalil gave me a little shove and laughed at his own lame joke before he continued his description. "She's got long black hair and the sexiest eyes. She's half-Asian; her moms is Korean."

"Do you have a picture?"

He pulled out a wallet and retrieved what looked to be a high school graduation photo. No question, she was cute, but not the goddess I expected based on Jalil's description. "You're lucky," I said.

"Now you see why I gots to get home, dog."

"I don't know, Jalil. They've got us surrounded, and you'd be putting us all in danger if you tried to escape."

"There's nothing for me on this island, dog. I didn't want to come in the first place."

"Why did you?"

"My parents. They got me a job here for the summer to keep me and Monique apart. They don't approve."

"Because she's not Muslim?"

"She is Muslim. Among my people, many marriages are still semi-arranged, and my parents have had me matched with the daughter of a friend of my father's ever since I was a baby. I hardly even know the girl, and I definitely don't love her." He lowered the volume of his voice, and his tone became really serious. "Tell me something, dog. If you were me and you wanted to get off this island and home to Detroit, how would you do it?"

I'm not going to pretend like I didn't know what Jalil was doing. I knew that his question wasn't hypothetical, and I knew that whatever plan he came up with to escape, the odds of his actually making it were infinitesimally small. I also figured that, short of locking him in the cell or killing him, we weren't going to stop him from trying, and if he got caught, well, put it this way, I remembered what Dr. Bentham told us happened to those chickens in Hong Kong and Tennessee. So I figured I may as well give him the best shot I could for all of our sakes.

I hesitated to think it through and to determine the morality of my assisting him. "First of all, you obviously have to go by water, across the lake, to the Detroit River. Do you know anything about boats?"

"I've never even been on one," Jalil said, "before the ferry ride over."

"Then, you should use a wave runner."

"They're like motorcycles for the water, right?"

"Not quite, but they aren't difficult to operate, and they're fast and very maneuverable. Break the trip up into two separate runs. Make the first run at night. The darkness should help you slip through the blockade. If you make it through, shoot for West Sister Island. You'd head northwest, keeping the lights from the Toledo Energy cooling tower to your left until you run around North Bass Island. Once around, use the cooling tower as your landmark. Head straight for it. You should run right into West Sister. It'll be about a twenty mile run which, even in rough conditions, you should be able to make in a few hours."

"Isn't West Sister where this flu shit started?"

"Yeah but you won't stay there long – just until the next afternoon. Besides, there's nothing or no one there to catch it from anymore."

"Why not do it all in one day? Detroit's only a two hour

drive by car."

"Running any watercraft isn't like driving a car on a road. There are currents and wind and wave conditions to consider. It's hard to predict exactly how long it will take, and you don't want to get caught on the water at night. Wave runners don't have running lights, and on your approach to Detroit, unless you're familiar with the channel markers and the coastline, you'll never find the mouth to the Detroit River in the dark. You'd run out of gas looking for her and be left adrift until the Coasties picked you up."

"What else?"

"There's a lighthouse keeper's cottage on West Sister. You should get some rest there. Get something to eat and gas to refuel the ski. Late the next afternoon, make the second run to the mouth of the river. Find some place to run aground where no one's around."

"Sounds easy," Jalil said.

"It's not, and there are a couple of problems," I added.

"Like?"

"There's a reason Erie is called a 'great' lake. If you get out there and a storm kicks up, you may as well be out on the ocean. The waves at this end can get pretty high. A northeast wind can kick up ten to twelve footers pretty easy and fast. You wouldn't last long on a wave runner. Plus, the water temperature this time of year is still pretty cool. If you did get dumped and separated from the wave runner, hypothermia would set in quickly. Do you even know how to swim?"

Jalil shook his head "no."

"There's more. There's a new moon tomorrow."

"Is that a good thing or a bad thing?" Jalil asked.

"Both. A bright moon would have made it easier for you to see where you're going; however, it would also have made it easier for them to see and stop you. A new moon means it's going to be dark as hell out there, and it'll be real easy for you to miss West Sister in the dark. If you do, keep going until you run aground. Hopefully, you'll have enough gas. But stay away from any marinas. They're bound to have those staked out. Then try figure out where you are. Make your way to a phone and call someone you trust to come get you, but not a family member."

"Why not?"

They're probably watching them too. By now, they've got to have a pretty good idea of who's on island and might try to get off."

Jalil had an overwhelmed look on his face, which was exactly what I was hoping for. I thought the challenges involved and the thin hopes for success might discourage him and convince him to try and ride it out on island. It didn't.

"We should do this together, dog. We could both get out of here," he said, obviously still determined to take his chances with the Lake and them rather than with the Blues and us.

I considered his proposition for a moment. "Nah, I think I'll stay here. Besides, there's really nobody missing me anyway."

Chapter Fourteen

The Chief pulled in and parked the cruiser on the street outside of the jail; it was already approaching dark. I was surprised to see that Dr. Bentham was with him. I hurried out to meet them.

"The girl scouts," was all the Chief needed to say to explain the defeated look on both of their faces.

"I had to get away for a while," Dr. Bentham said by way of explaining her absence from her post.

Collectively, we were lost in considering the horrible end to which those poor girls had arrived when a couple walked past us holding hands. The young lady had colored her mask so that she wore a constant wide-mouthed and big-toothed grin. Her boyfriend's mask had been doctored to appear as if he were locked in a Munchian *Scream*. I hadn't laughed in three days, but the incongruent silliness of their masks caused Dr. Bentham and me to laugh out loud.

The Chief just shook his head. "Where's Jamal?" he asked.

"It's Jalil. He's inside but I don't know for how long."

"What do you mean?" Dr. Bentham asked, calming her laughter.

"He's making plans to go home."

"He knows he's on an island, right? There are no busses or trains off of here?" The Chief said.

"He's thinking about using a wave runner."

"And where did he get that idea?"

I lowered my eyes to the sidewalk.

"He's a city kid," Dr. Bentham said. "What does he know about operating a wave runner or crossing a lake this size?"

"Nothing," I said.

"Do you think he'd have a chance?" Dr. Bentham asked the Chief.

"None. Even if by some miracle he made it past the blockade."

She grew increasingly agitated. "You have to stop him."

The Chief did a double take.

"Jalil's situation is no different than Tom Hobbs'," she said knowingly. "Any threat to the integrity of the blockade will force them to change their policy. Right now, it's containment. After that it's extermination."

"That's why I think it may be time to put Danny's plan into action and start supplying that cavern before the likes of Hobbs and Jalil bring down the wrath," the Chief said.

"So you're just going to let them leave?" Dr. Bentham asked, clearly disapproving of the Chief's laissez-faire strategy.

"What do you want me to do, Jenny? Lock them up? Shoot them?"

I'm pretty sure the Chief's questions were rhetorical. Both he and I were a little surprised when Dr. Bentham answered, "Whatever it takes."

"I can't do that, and don't tell me it's protocol," the Chief said in a testy manner. He looked up and away at a flock of mallards passing overhead in what little was left of daylight. "You know, I've been watching."

"For what?" I asked.

"It seems to me that except for mallards and the damn sea

gulls, which would take a nuclear apocalypse to wipe out – those shit-birds are the cockroaches of the sky – and those out on the peninsula, there isn't a bird left alive on island."

I looked around the downtown streets and sidewalks. He was right. Other than the sea gulls on and over the shoreline, there didn't appear to be any other birds perched on wires, darting overhead, or making new deadfall. The ones I did see were those of the previous day, swept or kicked to the side or off of the curbs. "Yeah, what's up with all of the gulls and the ducks?" I wondered out loud.

"I'd guess the sea gulls are somehow immune, and the mallards are the carriers," Dr. Bentham said as if she'd been keeping a secret. "The ducks most likely have the virus. They're the ones spreading it. During their migration, they mix with birds and ducks literally from all over the world. Most likely, they picked up the virus from some foreign bird, probably Asian or African in origin, and brought it here with them."

"Then, why aren't they dying?" I asked.

"Nature," she said. "The mallards are a reservoir for the virus. They contract it, but for whatever reason, they're not affected by it. The virus has been unable to replicate itself abundantly inside the cells of the ducks and maybe not at all in the gulls."

"I don't get it," I said.

"This virus has been a colossal failure."

"It seems to be working pretty effectively to me," the Chief weighed in with his layman's understanding of virology.

"You don't understand, Chief. A virus that kills its host is a failure because, unless it's able to quickly infect another host, it dies too," Dr. Bentham explained. "It goes down with the ship so-to-speak. That's why viruses mutate and jump hosts. They're looking for a new, more welcoming home. Usually, the shift is intra-species, but sometimes it jumps species. Like people, they're greedy little bastards. The perfect host is the one that will allow the virus to replicate without destroying the host and itself in the process. As for humans and the virus that causes this variation of the bird flu, we're still clearly a terrible match."

"Then it doesn't want to kill us?" I asked.

"A virus doesn't want or not want anything. It just does what it does. It's the Terminator of the invisible world. For the past one hundred thousand years or so, humans have been a new housing option. Viruses are still trying us out. Some have adjusted nicely. For example, around 90 percent of all people carry some form of the herpes virus. It rarely presents itself symptomatically, but it's there thriving as it allows us to thrive. That's a successful virus. On the other hand, take HIV or Ebola. Like the bird flu, they both shifted species. HIV jumped from monkeys to humans in search of a more hospitable host. We still don't know for sure where Ebola comes from, maybe bats. Regardless of their origins, their manifestations in people continue to kill those it inhabits. By comparison with herpes, they're both failures."

"So, the mallards have proven to be a good host for this virus."

"Exactly," Dr. Bentham said. "But some of the virus, and it takes very little to infect another, is expelled in excrement, vomit, and saliva or from a corpse like rats leaving a sinking ship. Somehow the virus got inside of Smitty. And this time, for maybe the first time in history, the virus has been reconfigured in a way that allows it to pass easily through the air from one human to another."

"But, why now? Why here?" I asked.

Dr. Bentham and the Chief exchanged a glance before she answered. "I don't believe that it's part of some plan, if that's what you're wondering, Danny. It's not god's way; it's Nature's."

I juxtaposed Dr. Bentham's explanation with Patmos's assertion that the bird flu was a plague sent by god as punishment for man's wickedness, but I drew no conclusion. Neither version brought me much comfort.

Dr. Bentham wanted nothing to do with returning to the 4-H camp just yet, so the Chief offered her his spare guest room. I winked at the Chief but he didn't find it funny.

Just then, Stan McKillips' pick-up approached from the north down Division Street. He pulled to a stop directly in front of the jail. His dirty-faced apprentice rode shotgun but never lifted his eyes from the hunting knife he was using to scrape grime out from behind his fingernails.

"What can we do for you, Stan?" The Chief bit hard on his tongue to squelch any temptation to communicate his loathing.

"People are talking about that Moslem boy. They find it kind of funny that a haji shows up on island and all of a sudden people start taking sick." Stan continuously looked past the Chief into the jail, where Jalil could be seen moving about through the large, curtain-less window.

"It's a coincidence, Stan. No more."

"Then why you keeping him in jail? If the haji wants to be an American so badly, shouldn't he be given his freedom?"

"He already is an American, and he is as free as anyone else. He's been helping me out."

"Helping? You ought to know better than that, Chief. More than anybody on island, you ought to know better than that." Stan took one more long look into the jail, shook his head in repugnance, pulled away, and turned west onto Lakeshore.

"What was all that about?"

"Don't worry about it right now," the Chief said. "I wouldn't concern myself too much about Stan. He's as lowlife as they come, but if there's no angle on making a quick buck, he doesn't stay interested in anything for long. Still, if he comes around, use the radio to call me."

"Will do," I said.

"And keep that door locked. You hear? Get some sleep. You're going to need it. Tomorrow, you're going to start preparing that cavern of yours."

"Yes, Chief."

Chapter Fifteen

Day 6, Wednesday, May 29, 201_

On waking, I found myself alone inside a sleeping bag in the office portion of the jail. Jalil was absent from the cot inside the cell where he'd slept. I heard Dr. Bentham and the Chief's garbled voices and found the two of them sitting on the single concrete step outside the door and sipping from Styrofoam cups of coffee.

I tiptoed over and snuggled against a wooden coat tree next to the door, which I opened just a crack so as to fine tune and eavesdrop in on their conversation.

"Do you really think Hobbs and the others will try to run the blockade tonight?" Dr. Bentham asked.

"I do," the Chief said. "Lifers like Hobbs love this island in a way that a mainlander like yourself could never understand. It's more than a home to them. It's who they are. They don't talk lightly about much of anything, and they never talk about leaving her. If they say they're going, trust me, they're going."

"Will Officer Burns be able to stop them?"

"No. That was just for show. There are too many private docks and too many boats for him to do much. Besides, Burnsie

Ty Roth

is from an island family himself. He isn't going to draw on these people. Actually, I wouldn't be surprised if he went with them. Can't say I'd blame him if he did."

"It won't end well," she said.

"Not much does," the Chief answered, and they stood momentarily in what I could only suppose was a quiet contemplation of the potential confrontation that was beginning to seem inevitable. "We'll just have to wait and see," the Chief finally said.

"Do you miss them?" Dr. Bentham changed the subject.

"Who's that?"

"Your family. I saw you keep a photo on your desk."

"Yeah, well there's a typewriter on there too. Don't forget I'm a Lifer myself. We're not real comfortable with change."

"I'm not buying it, Chief."

"Well, I guess I miss my little girl. Although, she was hardly even mine. The marriage was a bad idea. We met on one of those dating sites. There's not a whole lot of single women to choose from on this island. She was coming out of a bad relationship and had a daughter in need of a father. I think I fit the suit my wife had picked out for the kind of father she wanted for her child more than it was ever about her loving me. However the military and this place turned out to be more than she could handle, but I do think she was right about one thing. I would have made a hell of a daddy."

"Now that," Dr. Bentham smiled and said and raised her cup in toast, "I'm buying."

A drone buzzed overhead then sped away while the Chief took a long sip from his cup. "What about you? How have you managed to keep a ring off that finger?"

"I'm flattered that you've noticed," she said.

"Like I said, a single woman is a rare animal on this island. She's more valuable than a 14-point buck to the boys around here."

"I'm going to take that as a compliment and leave it at that," Dr. Bentham said.

"So, why no ring?"

"My therapist would tell you it's a fear of commitment combined with unreasonable expectations in a mate combined with parental dependency issues. I'd say I've been too busy doing other things: college, grad school, and the military before this gig. In the army, it was tough enough getting ahead as a woman. Being a married woman and a pathologist made promotion even more difficult. Having children would have prejudiced my superiors against me even further and limited my opportunities at work."

"Why is that?" the Chief asked.

"Their thinking was that a woman with children would be incapable of completing her necessary duties in "hot" labs, working with the deadliest pathogens. Her attention would be divided. Either she'd neglect her work, or she'd neglect her family. They saw it as a lose/lose situation. They believed that a mother would be prone to panic when handling the deadliest of viruses and bacterium and be a danger to herself and her co-workers. So, I purposefully avoided relationships as long as I was in the service. That's my explanation anyway, or it could be that I just haven't found the right guy."

"That made sense when you were enlisted, but what about now? What about kids?" The Chief asked. "I mean you're . . ."

"Not getting any younger? I know, but thanks for pointing it out."

The Chief apologized for his insensitivity. "Maybe that's why I'm divorced," he said.

"I want to be a mom. I really do. I actually have preliminary adoption papers sitting on my desk at home all filled out and waiting to be submitted. I just haven't been able to bring myself to drop them off. I'm not sure it wouldn't be selfish and more about my needs than the child's. And with my luck, the right guy would come along the day after I bring a baby home, and we both know how most guys our age love that kind of baggage. And by the time the kid finished high school, I'd be nearly sixty. I'm not sure I'd have the necessary energy during those teen years."

"For what it's worth, I think you'd make a great mom," the Chief made up for his earlier gaffe.

"Thanks. What about these boys?" Dr. Bentham said and shot a glance towards the jail behind her.

"Danny's a good kid. He'll stay with the program, but based on his conversation with Jalil yesterday, I'm not so sure about Jalil. I dropped him off this morning on the west end. He said he couldn't pray properly in the jail, but I think he was scouting for a wave runner."

"We can't let him, Chief. We can't let any of them."

"I get the plan, Jenny, and I'm with you, but I can't help thinking that Hobbs may be right. Fact is, despite our best efforts, we're failing. Folks ain't abiding and they keep right on getting sick and dying. I mean does this badge and your office give us that kind of authority? Who are we anymore to tell these people what or what not to do? We don't know the future."

"I do. I wrote the plan, remember? Our only hope is to keep everyone here and alive as long as possible.

The Chief stood and tossed the small remainder of his coffee into the gravel parking lot next to the jail.

With their conversation clearly over, I stepped out of the jail and into the morning sun.

"Where's Jalil," I asked playing stupid.

"He asked me to drive him to the stone beach near West Bay Marina. Said the jail wasn't an 'appropriate environment' for Salah."

"What's that?" I asked.

"His prayers. I got you a cup of Tomas's coffee," he said and handed it to me.

"Thanks," I said and returned the conversation to Jalil. "Did you just leave him there?"

"He said he could find his own way back."

"Do you think that was a good idea?"

"Nope," the Chief said.

I briefly contemplated his answer and my role in enabling Jalil's escape plan. "What?" I then said in a tone of mock anger. "No fritter to go with the coffee?" I asked.

"No can do. Out of dough," he answered.

At first, I thought he meant that he had no money, but then I realized that he was referring to Tomas, who was out of the necessary ingredients.

"Tomas said this is it for the coffee as well. Said he's closing up shop. He was in a bad way. His niece has the Blues."

"Paula?!"

"Yeah, I guess that's her name. I'm not sure; I hadn't really met her yet. She'd been partying at Saturday's with Andy the night he got sick. It's a shame. Did you know her?" he asked.

"Not really. She waited on me yesterday. She seemed really nice," I said.

"Either way it's time to go to work."

"Work?"

"I'm going to run Dr. Bentham out to the camp, then I've got rounds to make. I want you to get on over to your Grandpa's place. There are a few boxes of MRE's (Military Ready to Eat) in the basement of the jail and some extra flashlights, batteries, and blankets. Grab what you can and take it over to that cavern of yours. I'll get the rest later and grab some supplies from my place. We need to start preparing a Plan B."

"How will I get them there?"

"Find yourself an island car. I saw an El Camino parked up the street. Take this two-way. I'll call when I need you back," he said, handed me the radio, and left with Dr. Bentham.

After I'd created a sort of staging area at the top of the basement stairs at the jail, I went outside and found the rusted-out gold El Camino parked on Division. It's not unusual for Lifers to leave their keys in the ignition of their island cars, and it's equally common for other Lifers to borrow those cars for short errands. They'd been doing it forever that way, long before these car share programs you see in big cities created apps for it. I backed the El Camino up to the door and loaded her with as many supplies as I could fit, including a bunch of feminine products just in case.

At my grandfather's place, in order to not draw attention, I worked in the intervals between drone fly-overs. On one's approach, I'd run to and hide beneath nearby trees. I rigged a system by which I was able to lower supplies into the cave inside a bucket to which I'd tied two ropes. One rope was attached to the handle, the other I knotted and punched through a hole in the bottom of the bucket. Once the bucket touched the cave floor, I let go of the first and pulled on the second rope, which would tip the bucket over and spill its contents. I figured I would come back later, lower myself into the cave, and organize the supplies.

It was nearly noon by the time I finished unloading supplies. Knowing Daphne's voracious reading habits, on the way back to the jail, I took a chance and swung by the library on a whim. A red Vespa was parked outside. It looked identical to the one I'd seen her on in town the day before, but scooters were pretty common on the island. It could have belonged to anybody, or it could have been left there. I knocked on the front door. When no one answered, I let myself inside in the manner I'd earlier described to her.

The library hadn't changed much in the ten years I'd been off island. In fact, the layout was exactly the same. Patrons entered at the top of the long, vertical arm of the L-shaped space. To the immediate left was the circulation desk. Across from it, stood racks of newspapers and magazines. In between, four brown leather chairs for in-library reading surrounded a low, circular table. The remainder of the open space between the walls of the L's long arm was filled with free-standing shelves of hardback new releases and donated paperbacks. Four carols for the use of internet-accessible desktop computers were the only noticeable addition. Against the right side wall, past the periodicals, began the stacks with books still arranged in perfect adherence to the Dewey Decimal System.

Beginning in the 000's, I only half-read the spines of several computer science books, until my eyes were drawn to one by a man named Ludwig called *Computer Viruses*. I assumed my notice of this text was due to my heightened sensitivity to the word "viruses," sort of like after you buy a new car and you seem to see one just like it at every stoplight.

I moved deeper into the library taking intermittent peeks towards the rear of the room, where I knew the short, horizontal bar of the L contained a few tables for private study. I paused in the 100's and ran my finger down the spine of a novel by Albert Camus, titled *The Plague*, the same book from Daphne's list. The selection led me to doubt the accidental nature of the books to which my eyes were being drawn.

In the 200's among the religious texts, I was reminded of Patmos, shivered, and kept moving. The sound of a chair sliding on the tile floor caught my attention.

I paused in the social sciences to listen for further movement while my eyes alighted on a book titled *Suicide* by someone named Durkheim.

Passing disinterestedly through the 400's, devoted to languages, I saw a copy of Boccaccio's *The Decameron*, another of the books from Daphne's reading list. My hand was drawn irresistibly to the book. I removed it from the shelf. A bookmark protruded from between the pages of the "Second Day, Seventh Story," where the lines, "A kissed mouth doesn't lose its freshness, for like the moon it always renews itself" were highlighted in yellow. I returned the book to its slot in the stacks.

In the Sciences, I was stopped stone cold by a book by Richard Preston titled *Hot Zone*. It had been turned to face outward. The cover had a magnified and colorful representation of what I recognized from AP Biology to be a virus – the text was subtitled "A Terrifying True Story." I was afraid to even touch it.

I showed only cursory interest in the books on technology and completely ignored those devoted to art and recreation, but the unmistakable smell, not unpleasant but earthy, of a human presence reached me by the time I'd finished the 700's.

I had passed the outside corner of the right angle of the L, where the men's and women's rooms were located in a small alcove with a drinking fountain against the wall in between them. As I bent over to drink, I glanced behind me past my shoulder into the private study area. A blanket had been placed over one of the square tables to form a sort of tent, but I saw no other sign of life.

Against the back wall, I resumed my journey into the 800's, the literature section. My interest was sincerely piqued. My eyes zeroed in on a book titled *Pride and Prejudice and Zombies* by Grahame-Smith.

"Sucks, doesn't it?"

I nearly jumped out of my skin, momentarily having forgotten my purpose for being there. Once I'd realized it was Daphne's voice and I had regained my composure, I said, "Well, I was looking for *The Brothers Karamazov*. You know what Mr. Johnson [He was our AP Literature teacher.] always said, 'You know nothing if you don't know Dostoyevsky.'"

"Not the book, stupid. It's actually really good." Daphne sat cross-legged under the table with the blanket lifted to reveal her in a pair of gym shorts, a t-shirt, and flip-flops. "I meant it sucks that there are so many books that we'll never get to read. Sorry if I frightened you," she said and crawled out of her hiding place. "I pulled the books out as a sort of trail for you to find me. I knew you'd come. Check out this one." Daphne pulled a book from the 900's: History, Geography, and Biography.

I read the title out loud, "Daniel DeFoe's *A Journal of the Plague Year*. Nice choice," I said coyly and put it back.

"You've been keeping a secret, Danny Foe," she said. Daphne grabbed the book from off the shelf again, flipped open its thick and ornate hard cover, pointed to the bookplate and read, 'Donated by Daniel Foe, Descendent of the Author.' Fess up, Danny boy."

"Daniel Foe was my great-great-grandfather. Obviously, I never met him. He was the first Foe on the island."

"More," she demanded.

"I don't know much about them, only that my father's side of the family is English and Daniel DeFoe, the guy who wrote this book, is supposedly an ancestor of mine, but my grandfather never let fact get in the way of telling a good story. So, who knows? It's probably all bullshit."

"What happened to the 'De'?"

"According to my grandfather, the 'De' was added to make the name sound more aristocratic and, maybe, to distance himself from and to protect his family."

"Why did they need protection?"

"His people were Dissenters, kind of like the Puritans who came to America, not too fond of or obedient to the Church of England and hated by the majority of folks. Most people only know of him for *Robinson Crusoe*, but I guess his other writings pissed off a lot of people, powerful people."

"Kind of ironic that he wrote a book about the plague, huh?" Daphne said.

"You think? Hey, what's with the tent?" I asked.

"I'm staying here now," she said and started to cry.

"What's wrong?" I asked, as if the answers to that question couldn't be in the hundreds.

"I have to tell you something, but please, don't be mad at me, okay?"

"What is it?"

"Derek came with me to that house. He had nowhere else to go. I wanted to tell you when I saw you in town, but I just couldn't. I knew you'd be mad."

I did a quick visual search of the library for Derek before realizing what should have been obvious to me by then. "Oh, Daph. I'm so sorry."

"It happened so fast. He was fine two days ago. By last night, he was puking and the diarrhea and the blood. I didn't know what to do. I couldn't leave him, not even to go get help. He wouldn't let me. By this morning, he was . . ."

I hugged her close while she cried into my shoulder.

"Should you be hugging me?" she asked. "You know with the virus and everything."

"I'm the Fluke, remember? I can't catch it again."

"I forgot. But, Danny, Derek and I, we . . . we . . . Derek and I . . . we . . ."

I figured out where she was reluctantly headed. "It's okay. It doesn't mean you'll catch it," I said; although, I knew better.

"I couldn't stay there, not with . . . with . . ."

"I know. You did the right thing. I'll tell the Chief. He'll take care of Derek. You're coming with me."

"No!" She insisted. "I'm staying here. This is where I want to be as long as I . . . as long as I . . ."

The radio cackled from where I'd clipped it to my belt. "Danny. It's the Chief. Over."

"Shit! Not now," I said, still consoling Daphne in my arms.

"Danny. Chief. Over."

"Go ahead. Answer it," Daphne said and backed away.

"Yeah, Chief."

"I need you to meet me as soon as possible at the Dorm. We have a problem. Over."

"It's okay," Daphne said. "I'm good here. This is my happy place."

"Are you sure?" I asked. "I can stay, but if the Chief finds out you're here and that you've been exposed, he's going to insist you go to the camp."

"Then you'd better go."

"Okay. But I'll be back as soon as possible. Can I get you anything?"

"No. I took some food from the house. There's a drinking fountain, and I have plenty of books. I'm good, but, Danny, come back."

"I will."

"Tonight?"

"I'll try, but I can't promise. The Chief is keeping a pretty tight watch on me."

Chapter Sixteen

I met the Chief outside the dorm, but our entry was halted by a sign made from an empty case of beer. It read: "Keep Out! Dead End."

The Chief cupped his hands against the glass door and peered through them into the lobby then tore himself violently away from the door.

An unexplainable compulsion drew me towards the glass. The lobby was clogged with bodies.

"What are we going to do with them?" I asked.

"I don't know. We can't expect Captain Russo and his crew to collect them all."

"But we can't just leave them there to rot."

"Why not? It's as good a tomb as any other." For the first time, his words were laced with bitterness and defeat.

That very minute, a camp bus appeared at the end of the short walkway from the dorm to the sidewalk. When its door swung open, John Patmos descended the steps holding a six-foot long walking stick.

"What are you doing, John?" The Chief asked. "You aren't Moses and I'm no pharaoh for you to wave your magic stick at. Go home."

"I've been thinking, Chief, and it followed in my thoughts that if this flu is from God, I should stay and have no fear. Even when I turned from Him in my days of sin, he preserved me from death and danger. To flee now would be a kind of flying from Him. If he does not choose to deliver me from the infection, still I am in his hands and it is appropriate that he should do with me as should seem good to him."

I was surprised and moved by what seemed to be Patmos's genuine tenderness.

The Chief laughed.

Patmos tied a handkerchief around his mouth and nose, and with unwavering conviction regarding his consignment to God's will, he led his people into the dorm and began escorting out the few living. He prayed over the dead then removed wallets and gathered purses in search of identifications in the hope of cataloging their deaths and burials.

Against the Chief's wishes, I slipped through the front doors and was immediately rebuffed by a wall of stench and a gust of stale, hot air. To combat it, I took off my shirt and held it over my mouth and nose. Blue-colored bodies lay everywhere in the lobby, the basement, and down the halls. Most were dead but some were walking. Groans escaped from a few prostrate on the floors and contorted on the furniture. My heart nearly stopped when, stepping over what I thought to be a corpse, it grabbed me by the ankle. It was Geo. He spewed a series of unintelligible strings of words laced with bloody spittle. I wasn't sure if it mouthed wishes, curses, or an "I told you so." It didn't matter. He died with his next breath.

As I moved from floor to floor and room to room, I couldn't help but wonder if the positions in which they died mirrored the ways they'd lived. Some straight; some twisted. Some alone; some in a group. Some with mouths and/or eyes wide open; some with them closed.

When I emerged from the dorm, I saw that one of the

choppers had been sent in to take a look. It hovered and watched but seemed approving of the ghoulish undertaking it superintended.

Seeing me taking notice of the chopper, the Chief rolled his wrist to look at his watch and then showed me the time: 9:59. Seemingly apropos to nothing, he started a countdown, "Three . . . two . . . one . . . and they're off."

In the very second he said it, the attendant chopper darted away.

"How'd you know that?" I asked.

"I've been watching. Since yesterday's meeting, they've added an around-the-clock manned chopper to the drone surveillance."

"Why do you think they've done that?" I asked.

"Not sure," Chief Sarter said. "The only thing I can think of is that the drones aren't of the Predator type. They're just cameras."

"So?"

"They're not armed."

I let the significance of the Chief's observation soak in.

"But I've also noticed" the Chief said, "that every two hours on the hour, day and night, they leave. It must be some kind of shift change or refueling break, but it has been consistent for at least the past two days. It's the way the military operates. In ten minutes, it or another will be back."

"Okay," I said. "What good is knowing this?"

"There's not a point on this island that can't be reached in less than ten minutes with the right form of transportation. At some point, knowing the choppers' routine is going to be important."

"If you say so, Chief."

With the weather setting in hot, the Chief began transporting the living, in twos, to Dr. Bentham's already overtaxed care at the camp.

It was late in the afternoon by the time we'd finished and Patmos had loaded his people onto his bus to return to their camp.

Before Patmos followed his people onto the camp bus, he approached the Chief. "God is good, J.P.," he said.

"I saw *people* doing good, John. I didn't see god."

"You saw people doing good in His name and for His glory."

"I've seen them do an awful lot of evil in his name and for his glory as well, or doesn't that count?"

"It all counts, Chief. Everything counts," Patmos said and boarded the bus which drove away leaving behind a cloud of exhaust.

"Looks like a storm's coming in," the Chief said turning toward the western skyline.

The sky was royally blue and the sun shining where we were standing, but in the distance, it had turned the green and purple of a bruise. Along and on the Lake, summer storms from the west blow in fast and hard, but they are short-lived. Their sisters from the northeast, however, usually raged for three days, kicked up huge waves, and shut down the island until they were spent and had spun away.

"Let's go. We've got work to do," he said.

Chapter Seventeen

Keeping one eye peeled on the approaching storm, we made an unexpected stop at the Kelleys Island Historical Society Museum, located in what was once the United Methodist Church on Division Street, another limestone building about halfway between the jail and the 4-H camp.

"According to the sign, the museum doesn't open until June," I said when we turned into the parking lot.

"Not a problem. I've got a key to almost every building on the island. Open the glove box."

I did as told and removed a metal ring with the circumference of a hockey puck. There had to be fifty keys dangling from it, and it weighed at least five pounds.

"I don't know what half of those keys are for," the Chief said. "I inherited the ring with the job. I'm pretty sure some of the locks they open don't even exist anymore. Those keys have been passed down from chief to chief for over a hundred years. But I know that the one with the gold string attached opens the back door to the museum. Let's go."

"Why are we here?" I asked, as the Chief turned the key and nudged the door open with his shoulder.

"You'll see."

He knew exactly where he was going inside the museum. He marched directly to a display honoring the island's quarrying days. "There it is," he said.

"There what is?"

Instead of answering me, he stepped over the rope designed to prevent visitors from doing exactly what the Chief was about to do. From the wall, he detached and pulled down some kind of large, handheld tool.

"What is that?" I asked, "And why are we stealing it?"

"First off, we are not stealing it. I am an officer of the law. I am conscripting it. Secondly, it is a genuine antique hand crank drill, and it is going to allow us to cut through the limestone to create a ventilation hole in the cavern. Grab some of those longer metal rods, that sledgehammer, and those shovels. I'd bet there's less than a foot or so of stone in that backside slope. Then, it's just soil. It shouldn't be too much of a problem."

"Then you're giving up on Plan A?"

"I'm beginning to think Plan A never existed," he said cryptically.

By the time we stepped outside, the sky had turned dark, the temperature had dropped at least ten degrees, and a stiff breeze blew across the island carrying both the scent of rain and the stink of fish on its back.

We stopped at the Chief's house and garage on Pickerel Drive to get some PVC pipe to use as the ventilation tube. While the Chief scavenged, I went inside to use his bathroom.

"Chief, you've got to come here. You're not going to believe this," I called to him from the back door that opened into the smallish kitchen of his log cabin home to where he was rummaging through boxes inside of its detached garage.

"What the?" was the Chief's disbelieving reaction when he entered his home and saw the refrigerator and all of his cabinet drawers and doors swung open. The dressers and closets in his bedroom had been ransacked, the bathroom medicine cabinet emptied, and on the living room wall, a patch of paint – slightly less sun-faded than the rest and exactly 60-inches wide – mocked him.

"For Chrissakes! Those bastards!" The Chief swore.

"I guess you should have let Stan have Mrs. Barnes's television, huh, Chief?" It took every ounce of facial muscular control for me not to smile.

He looked at me. He looked at the wall. He stormed out through the kitchen and into the cruiser, which he'd already loaded with the PVC pipe and a few odds and ends from his garage. The horn blew angrily and I hurried out before he left me to walk. Before I could even reach the cruiser, a white-blue streak of lightning flashed accompanied by a nearly-simultaneous clap of thunder. "It's the Thunderbird," I said, as I settled into the passenger seat and drew the seatbelt across my chest.

"The what?"

"The Thunderbird. There's one etched into Inscription Rock," I said, having just remembered my grandfather's love of summer thunder storms and the legend he'd told me of the Thunderbird.

"It's a real thing?" the Chief asked.

"According to my grandfather, when the Erie Peoples lived in this part of the Lake, they worshipped giant birds called Thunderbirds."

"Is that right?" the Chief said. His tone affected indifference, but I could tell he was interested.

"They were giant birds with wings the size of airplane wings, and they had sharp, dagger-like claws."

"Were they friendly?" the Chief asked.

"Yes and no," I answered. "They were supposedly both life-giving and life-taking. The Eries believed that the return of the Thunderbirds in spring is what brought life back to the Lake.

Migrating animals and birds returned home, and the plants and flowers began to bloom. But they also brought huge storms with them. Their voice made the sound of thunder, and lightning flashed from their eyes. They could destroy with the wind, cause flood and drought, or burn with lightning."

"What about plague? Did these Thunderbirds bring that with them too?"

"No. I believe we did that."

We sat in silence for a moment before another thunder clap inspired the Chief to turn the ignition. "Okay, kemosahbe. We've got work to do, and this storm is going to allow us to do it. The lightning's going to force the chopper and the drones out of the sky, which will give us a half hour or so to supply the cavern without being watched."

By the time we arrived on my grandparents' property, the rain was falling in huge droplets. The Chief backed up the cruiser as close to the hole in the cavern roof as possible. "Have you ever been down there?" He asked.

I told him no.

"Then I think it's time."

After retrieving a black, hooded poncho from the trunk, he tied one end of a long length of rope to his bumper and the other end in a loop around my waist. He handed me a dual-function, lantern-style flashlight, which I stuffed down the front of my shirt, and the Chief lowered me the ten-or-so feet into the cavern. I descended fine, but I thought it might be a tight squeeze for the Chief.

When I could no longer brace myself against the side of the hole and I hung entirely from the rope, I removed and lit my flashlight and aimed it into the space below to reveal a cavern the size of a large living room. The light reflected off bluish celestite crystals that grew and extended in conical shapes. Some were only inches long; others were several feet. They grew from the floor, walls, and ceiling.

I touched down on the cavern floor among the supplies I had dumped there earlier in the day. In the near dead center of the cavern, I converted the flashlight to its lantern mode, held it in front of my face, and did a slow 360 degree turn. It felt as if I stood inside a prism. Mesmerized by the array of colors reflected off of the crystals, a sense of calm washed over and through me. I don't mean to get all new agey, but I'd never felt like that before. I grew completely oblivious to the horror film that was playing out up on the surface, and for a moment, I forgot my purpose for being inside the cavern in the first place.

"Are you okay?" The Chief yelled from the top of the tunnel and snapped me out of my reverie. "How's it look?"

"Awesome. It looks awesome."

Sporadically, a flash of lighting would backlight the Chief's head in the opening above, where he looked to be a million miles away.

"How many could fit down there comfortably?"

"Comfortably? I don't know. Five, maybe six."

"Is it dry?"

"Yes."

"How's the temperature?"

"Perfect."

"Great. I'm going to start lowering you some supplies. Try to organize the space. We need to hurry and get out of here before the chopper and drones are back in the air."

First, he lowered the tools we'd stolen from the museum, then he emptied his trunk of blankets, bucket after bucket of bottles of water, canned goods, energy bars, toilet paper, wet wipes, flashlights, batteries, and garbage bags. I didn't know and I didn't care where he had gotten the supplies from.

A half hour later, we were finished. Through the opening in the Earth, I could see the passing clouds turning whiter and exposing occasional patches of bluing sky.

"Wrap the rope around you, and I'll pull you out," the Chief called down.

I did as told, heard the cruiser's engine start, felt the rope grow taut, then myself gently lifted off the cavern floor until I was rising like a container inside a pneumatic tube.

I was just about to get in the passenger's side door when I saw an elderly gentleman – barefoot and dressed in white, linen, pinstriped pajamas – shuffling down Bookerman Rd. towards the just-beginning-to-set sun and the Kellstone Quarry, which was less than a quarter mile west of where we stood and, as recently as when I lived on the island, had been Kelleys' largest employer. In recent years, due to the construction bust and the subsequent reduced demand for building materials, such as stone, cement, and concrete products, it steadily reduced its number of employees and the amount of limestone mined until it completely ceased operations.

"For Chrissakes," the Chief said, before he called out, "Cleats! Cleats, what are you doing?"

Cleats made no acknowledgement of the Chief's call.

"Chief," I said. "I think he's got the flu. He's on a zombie walk."

The Chief took a few steps in Cleats' direction before he came to sudden standstill, placed one hand on his hip, and ran the other around the back of his head, where he rubbed his neck before – maybe out of training, maybe out of necessity – he placed it over the butt of his revolver.

I joined the Chief near the base of the onetime driveway from where I could clearly see the telltale signs: the bluish skin, the wheezing, the faraway stare, the futile cough, and the bloodstained chin and shirt front.

When the Chief called again, Cleats stopped and turned his head in our direction. "Where you going, Cleats? We need to get you to the camp."

"No," Cleats said in a raspy, barely audible, but firm voice, and continued his walking.

"No? What do you mean, 'no'? You're sick."

"Not sick. Dead," Cleats said in staccato fashion.

"Where're you going?"

Cleats stopped once more and looked the Chief in the eyes. "Quarry," he said and resumed his solitary journey.

"Get in the car," the Chief ordered me. We backed up, quickly caught up with Cleats, and followed him. The Chief continued to plead with Cleats to stop, but there's no reasoning with a dead man. We stayed on his heels for the entire death march and watched as he edged his way towards the ledge, which rose at least a hundred feet over the quarry floor. Clearly, Cleats knew exactly where he was, for, without hesitation, sound or ceremony, he stepped off the cliff and disappeared into the massive manmade hole.

I climbed out of the cruiser and walked to the ledge with the Chief. Together, we leaned over and looked for Cleats' flu-ravaged body, which lay sprawled, broken, and bleeding on top of the peak of the limestone cairn that rose from over the fast-accumulating bodies of the flu's victims.

"It's coming undone," the Chief said.

"What's that?'

"People. The island. Society. Everything. I saw it in the war: in the soldiers, in the prison camps, on the streets. We all make the mistake of clinging to the idea that someone, some organization – more powerful and smarter than ourselves – has it all under control, that common decency and life as we've known it is sacred and absolute and will continue as it always has, but it won't. It can't. Everything has an end."

"But that was war."

"What do you think this is? Everything's at war with everything else. For all I know, right now, inside of me, my white blood cells are battling legions of this bird flu virus and most likely losing." The surveillance chopper returned and passed over our heads. "Us versus them," the Chief continued and pointed to the chopper. "Patmos and his kind versus Captain Russo and his versus Hobbs and his, everyone on this island fighting for its few remaining resources. It's all war, Danny."

"That's not true. You, Burnsie, Dr. Bentham, and me are working together. Captain Russo talked about coming together."

"But it isn't working. Look at what happened to those Booze Cruisers and the rest of those kids in the dorm, and we haven't even checked on the birders in the hotel or the boaters in the transient docks downtown. And what about Patmos and his followers? They're on the other side of the island right now probably thanking their god for this plague, congratulating each other for being among those 'saved,' and enjoying what they believe to be god's wrath being let loose on the rest of us sinners. And," he pointed south towards the mainland, "they want us dead. It's all too much. Where's the 'working together' in all of that?"

"But this is just one tiny place during a crazy time," I argued.

"Is it?"

"Well, yeah," I answered in a less-than-convincing tone.

"I think Mr. Hobbs may be right. It has always been and always will be every man for himself. Survival-of-the-fittest. It's in man's nature, just beneath the surface, waiting for something like this plague to expose it, and it can't be schooled or churched out."

"But, we have to try. Right? I mean to rise above all of that. You and Dr. Bentham both said that showing them that we could survive was our only chance."

"Danny, I'm afraid that Mr. Hobbs may also have been right when he said that any chance we had ended the moment

Officer Dooley returned from West Sister."

Chapter Eighteen

The Chief did a U-turn on Bookerman and headed east toward the center of the island. He wanted to check on Dr. Bentham and the sick at the camp. At the stop sign where Bookerman met Division Street, we were forced to wait for a one-ton pick-up truck heading north, whose blinker indicated its intention to cross our face and turn left onto Bookerman and towards the quarry. It was an old quarry truck. The driver wore a black ball cap pulled down low and a black t-shirt. He had dark eyebrows and a five o'clock shadow approaching six. It was the same guy I'd seen plowing dead birds and bugs on the morning Daphne surprised me in the park outside of the port-o-potty. When he passed the Chief's window, he looked our way and let loose a self-satisfied grin that revealed gnarly, yellowish teeth inside a mouth as red as a cat's and that sent a chill racing up my spine and formed gooseflesh on my skin.

When it had passed, I turned to see its tailgate suddenly drop open to reveal a day's worth of harvested corpses piled one on top of the other. One, lying on its back with arms and legs akimbo and with its head flopped backwards and eyes wide open, seemed to be flashing a knowing smile in our direction, but I quickly attributed it to gravity pulling at the corners of his mouth and dismissed it as my own overactive imagination.

"Who was that driving?" I asked the Chief, figuring he knew just about everyone on the island.

"I have no clue. Never seen him before. Must be one of Captain Russo's guys."

When we turned onto Division, a surveillance chopper swooped in from the south and temporarily escorted us. As we drove, we passed more-than-a-few vehicles, both island cars and trucks and personal vehicles, driverless and parked in the middle of the street, which had turned the road into a slalom course. "What's up with these cars?" I asked. "They can't just park in the road."

"They're not parked," the Chief explained. "They're out of gas. The marina has the only public pumps on island. Its supply is delivered on Saturdays. The ferry hasn't run since last Friday, remember? The marina's tanks haven't been filled in going on two weeks now. They're probably empty as well. People are leaving their vehicles wherever they run out of gas. There's a pump behind the jail for village vehicles. I've been using that, but it won't last much longer. I'm sure folks are poaching from it already."

"Chief," I said as we approached the school/library at the corner of Division and Ward Road. "Can you drop me off at the library? I'll catch up to you and Dr. Bentham later."

For just a moment, the Chief looked at me suspiciously, then said, "Sure. Why not? If we end up down in that hole, it could be for some time. Might be a good idea to pick up something to read."

The Chief dropped me off in front of the glass library doors. "I'll beep the horn when I'm back. I won't be long. No more than a half hour. The sun will be setting soon."

I let myself in again and retraced the route I'd taken earlier in the day. My eyes then fingers were drawn to the spines of each book I had examined on that visit. I pulled Camus down from its shelf and carried it with me.

The sound of the toilet in the Women's room flushing betrayed Daphne's whereabouts, but she didn't promptly emerge. Instead, she coughed in violent and prolonged fits, and I knew she was in the early stages. It wouldn't be long. I grabbed hold of the shelving to prevent myself from crumpling to the library floor in grief, but I grew determined to pull myself together and to make things appear as normal as possible for Daphne's sake.

"It's only me," I called out so as not to frighten her when she exited the bathroom and saw someone inside of her sanctuary.

She came out wrapped in a blanket and carrying a chair leg in a clubbing position in one hand and a scissors in stabbing position in the other. "I thought you might be one of the zombies," she said. "One walked right up to the door and tried to get in."

"They're not really 'zombies.' They're sick and delirious."

"I know that, but it'd be a lot more interesting if they were."

"You really think so?"

"Well, yeah. I never got into the whole vampire thing, but I can't resist a good zombie story."

"If you'd seen what I have the past couple of days, I think you'd change your mind."

"You're probably right," Daphne said. "You know, I think they walk because as long as they're walking, they know they're not dead."

"Or read?" I said.

"Ouch," she said and noticed me holding Camus. "I pulled them all, you know. Just a little so you'd notice them. And, except for that computer one, which I only used to get your attention, I've read them all. I want you to take them with you when you go."

"Why? I have little better chance of living through this than anyone else. What good will they do me?"

"That's not true, Danny. You're the type that survives. It's like at school, you didn't belong to any particular group. Everybody liked you and you liked everybody else. You're the kind that lives to tell everyone else's story. You're more narrator than character."

Not surprisingly, I was stung and offended by her characterization, and my pouty-faced expression gave it away.

"Don't be hurt, stupid. The world and literature need the storytellers like you or else the crazies on one side or the other would win permanently and would control the narrative. Then, we'd really be screwed."

Her complexion was pale and her eyes watery. "You don't have to face this alone, you know," I said.

"I'm not going to that camp, Danny. Please, don't try and make me. Besides, I've been brushing up on my *Zombies Survival Guide*, and I'm used to being alone. Even at home, it has been just me and my mom." The mention of her mom caused her voice to break a little. She turned her head away to wipe her nose on the blanket. "I can't imagine how much she's worried about me." She pulled herself together. "But as long as you have a book, you're never alone, right? And I have lots of books."

"But you can't live here forever."

She cast her eyes to the floor, and I remembered that she didn't have to. The Blues were already advancing through her system. "Nobody can live anywhere forever," she said. "Besides, I don't plan to," Daphne said in a cryptic manner that gave me pause to consider her meaning and cause for concern. She set the scissors on the circulation desk, grabbed me by the hand, and led me along the stacks where she took down all of the books she had pulled one by one and handed them to me to carry.

Her mood seemed to brighten. "Do you really not remember what today is?" she asked.

"Of course I do, but it doesn't seem to matter much considering."

"But it's your birthday. These books are my presents to you."

"You could have picked a few with happier subject material," I said.

"I did," she said and handed me a book called *Dandelion Wine* by Ray Bradbury.

"What's this?"

"It's my all-time favorite," she said.

"Why? What's so great about it?"

"Nothing. Everything. You wouldn't remember, but I was reading it the summer you moved to Port Clinton, and I've read it every summer since. I want you to read it now – this summer and every summer after – and when you do, promise you'll think of me."

"I don't . . ." I began to object.

"Just promise me and read it. You'll understand."

"Okay, I promise," I said and added it to my stack. Just then the Chief arrived and lay on his horn.

"You've got to go," Daphne said.

"I don't have to. I could stay."

"I don't want you to," she said and placed her hands on my arms and gently spun me toward the door.

After the door closed behind me with a thud, I turned back toward the library. I watched as Daphne approached as if she were rising from deep waters. She closed her eyes, tilted her face upwards, and pressed her lips against the glass. With my arms cradling the stack of books between us, I leaned in and kissed the glass where her lips touched the other side. After a moment, I opened my eyes only to watch Daphne disappear, stepping slowly backwards into the depths of the darkening library.

Chapter Nineteen

"What was all that about?" the Chief asked after I'd slid into the front seat of the cruiser.

"Just saying goodbye," I said.

"To the library?" he asked confusedly.

"To the past," I said and left it at that, and the Chief let it go.

"Burns is on the radio," he said. "There's a problem at the jail. We've got to hurry."

"The jail? Jalil's at the jail."

The Chief didn't respond to my tongue-twisting statement of the obvious; instead, he flashed me a "no shit, Sherlock" look and blindsided me by asking, "Whose scooter back there?"

"What scooter?" I asked.

"Uh-huh," he said disbelievingly. But in a true islander's fashion, he didn't pry.

In the shadow of the water tower, from the intersection of Division and Chappel Streets, and still a good hundred yards from downtown, the Chief stopped the cruiser. We could see a mob milling outside of the jail. Predictably, it was being goaded by Stan McKillips and was mostly made up of Lifers and a few others I didn't recognize. More than a few were brandishing baseball bats and gardening tools as weapons.

"For Chrissakes," the Chief muttered.

As we reached the fringe of the crowd, the Chief turned on the flashers and blasted the siren in short bursts. Neither managed to disperse the crowd or to dissuade it from its desire to vent its fears and frustrations on the most easily-identifiable scapegoat on the island: Jalil.

Positioned between the mob and the jail, Officer Burns absorbed its growing malevolence.

The Chief threw the cruiser into reverse, drove back to and across Chappel and down Addison to Lakeshore, where he turned right and eventually stopped in front of the park. We spilled from the cruiser and sprinted through the park and the alley that ran behind the jail and the town hall and the Island Hardware Store, the two buildings south of the jail. However, designed to limit the means of coming and going and constructed in an age long before modern fire codes, there was no rear entry into the jail.

"How are we going to get to him?" I asked.

The Chief, for a change, had no ready answer.

Suddenly inspired, I kicked off my tennis shoes, stripped down to my boxers and t-shirt, and messed up my hair.

"For Chrissakes, Danny. What are you doing?"

"I've got an idea. By now, most of these people have seen an infected person, right? It's what they're most scared of and the one thing that will get their attention. Punch me in the nose."

"What?" The Chief asked.

"Punch me in the nose. Make it bleed."

My plan must have crystallized in the Chief's mind, for before I had time to reconsider or to flinch, he threw a quick right jab square into my nose. Immediately, the blood flowed and my eyes watered. As soon as I picked myself up off the gravel and my head had cleared, I smeared the blood around my mouth and chin, and I blew the rest onto the front of my white t-shirt.

"Thanks," I said sarcastically.

"You realize they may just beat you to death."

"I thought of that, but I think they'll be afraid of the splatter. Let's just hope we got enough of their guns."

"It only takes one," the Chief said.

"I was trying to be optimistic."

"Sorry."

As I came around the side of the jail, I went into an imitation zombie walk, held my breath until my lips turned blue, put on a thousand-mile stare, and headed into the crowd, which was so intent on spitting its anger towards Jalil, they failed to notice me until I had stumbled in amongst them. I drew in a breath and crumpled to the street.

"The Blues! He's got the Blues!" A woman screamed.

The crowd immediately scattered like water bugs on linoleum in the night when surprised by an overhead kitchen light. Momentarily, I basked in the success of my performance until I realized that Officer Burns was standing over me with his gun drawn and pointed directly at my head.

"I'm not sick," I whispered to him while lying motionless and flat on my belly.

I remained frozen and staring at the blacktop until I heard the Chief's voice. "Burnsie! It's okay. He's not infected. He's with me."

"Then what's with the blood and the walk?" Officer Burns asked, hesitant to lower his weapon.

"It was the only way we could come up with to clear the mob and save your ass."

We found Jalil calmly praying behind the Visqueen inside the locked cell. Without opening his eyes and before realizing it was the good guys, he greeted us with "Allah Akbar [God is the greatest.]."

"That may very well be true," the Chief said, pulling back the Visqueen, "and if we don't get you out of here right now, you may have a chance to tell him in person in the next ten minutes."

"I am not afraid to die," Jalil said, but his tone lacked conviction.

"Well, I am," the Chief answered.

Burnsie guarded the front door while I quickly dressed and cleaned up. Thankfully, the Chief's punch hadn't broken my nose.

"You two need to pack up your personal items. You can't stay here any longer," the Chief told Jalil and me. "Only the stuff you can't do without.

As I watched Jalil pack his Koran, pictures of his girl and family, his headphones, laptop, and notebook full of lyrics, I glanced at my pile of belongings and didn't see anything that I couldn't "do without." It was kind of pathetic. I'd brought no photographs, no love letters, no favorite books or CD's, no trophies or trinkets of sentimental value. I grabbed my backpack for the books Daphne gifted me, but I decided to leave the rest.

The Chief and Burnsie disappeared in a hurry down the stairs to the basement, where the Chief had locked up the confiscated weapons. We heard them destroying the rifles and shotguns. When they returned, Burnsie carried a large duffel bag full of the remaining handguns and ammunition.

"Take this," the Chief said and handed me his service revolver. "Tuck it inside your belt."

I took the gun and held it flat in my palm without grasping the handle or slipping my finger around the trigger. "Chief, I really don't want this," I said. The revolver still rested unwelcome on my now extended palm.

"Take it, Danny. You're the only one immune to the flu. Maybe, the only one who will keep a clear head. It has a full clip."

"I can't shoot those people," I said.

"I don't expect you to," the Chief said, staring hard into my eyes, and I understood that the bullets were to be saved for us.

I did as the Chief had asked and walked towards the large glass front window, where movement on the street in the fast-receding twilight stole my attention away from the revolver and the possibility of its future use. The crowd was gathering again.

"Chief," I said, calling him to the window.

"Half of them are probably already infected and don't even know they're passing it on to the other half," the Chief said when he drew near and took a look for himself.

The squealing tires of Patmos' bus taking the corner of Lakeshore and Division at much too high a rate of speed drew our and the crowds' attention. It pinballed back and forth up the street bouncing off parked or stalled vehicles and sending the mob scattering once more. The church bus came to a brief stop directly in front of the jail. I watched as Kenny McKillips was dumped like garbage out of its rear doors. He was clearly infected, in the final stages of the disease, and too weak to even pick himself up off of the street. The bus roared away.

This time the mob re-formed almost immediately. Unlike my earlier infiltration into its ranks, which precipitated an immediate panic, Kenny's caused hardly a splash. A distinctive switch in strategy had taken place within the collective mind of the mob, and instead of running away from the threat, it intended to deal with it directly and immediately. Its response was a perfect, if perverted, example of the manner in which white blood cells are programmed to attack an alien virus. The members of the mob picked up sticks, stones, bricks, anything that could be used as a missile, and they bombarded the defenseless Kenny from what they hoped was a safe distance.

A chopper arrived and hovered over the scene of the stoning, but it did nothing.

I looked to the Chief. "Let's go," he said.

We all headed to the door, but instead of hurrying to Kenny's rescue, the Chief turned towards the rear of the jail.

"Chief?" I asked and brought the group to a standstill.

"There's nothing we can do for him. He's dead either way. This is our only chance to get this one," he indicated Jalil with a glance, "out of here, or he will be the next stone catcher."

We formed a train with the Chief as engine and Officer Burns as caboose. We squatted as low as we could and slipped out the door in a sort of duck walk. Once around the corner of the jail building, we shuffled with our backs pressed against the outside wall facing the north side parking lot, then half-ran down the back alley, and through the park, where the nearly-set sun was throwing the long shadows of the trees. Jalil and I jumped into the backseat of the cruiser, still parked on Lakeshore, while the Chief and Officer Burns slid into the front.

In order to avoid Division Street and the mob, the Chief performed a U-turn then circled around the massive block, until the cruiser sputtered and ran out of gas near the corner of Division and Chappel and just outside the gate of the barbed-wire-topped fence that surrounded the stone-covered base of the water tower.

"Damn it!" The Chief barked then oddly leaned over the steering wheel and turned his head in order to look up through the windshield. He'd had an epiphany.

"What's up, Chief?" Officer Burns asked for all of us.

"Up is exactly right. We need to make Jalil here disappear for a few hours," the Chief said. "We're going to spend the night on the tower. I guarantee no one will look for us up there."

The Kelleys Island water tower rose above even the tallest of island trees and was at least four times higher than any other structure on the relatively flat island, which accounted for it being the home for the cell phone antennae that, when it was installed when I was a boy, brought out a crowd of islanders unsure if that new link was for the better or the worse for the island and its way of life. Either way, it provided islanders with easy and regular contact with the mainland for the first time.

I wasn't particularly crazy about the idea, but Officer Burns hated it. "Not me, Chief. I'm afraid of heights. There's no way you're getting my ass up there. I'd rather take my chances with the virus and these crazies down here."

"It's your call, Burnsie, if you're sure."

"I'm positive, Chief."

The Chief reached across the seat and firmly shook Officer Burns' hand. "You've been a good deputy, son."

"Thanks, Chief. I'll see you next season."

"Maybe," the Chief said. Officer Burns left the vehicle and disappeared in the dark in the direction of downtown.

"Me too," Jalil said. "I'm not going up there."

"Are you kidding?!" the Chief said. "You saw those people. They wanted to tear you apart. If you stay down here, they damn well will."

"I'm not staying down here either," Jalil insisted. "I'm leaving. I have to get home. I found a wave runner tied up to a private dock on the west end. I didn't see anyone around who might be planning on using it. I'm going to borrow it"

I'm not entirely sure of what his motives were for allowing him to go. It could be that the Chief was just fine with whatever misplaced retribution the people downtown wanted to inflict on Jalil. On the other hand, it could be that the Chief sincerely wanted to help him make it home. Whatever his motivation, he gave Jalil directions to his own home on Pickerel Drive and told him where he could find a wet suit and a watersports life vest hanging in his garage.

"Jalil," I said. "You have to know this is crazy. You'll never make it."

"What I know is that Allah is good and that in Him I trust.

It is not for me to outthink Him or to question His plan. I also know that one day I'll go to paradise with great joy, but I hope it is not today. If it is the will of Allah to save me, He will. Today, I want to live, and I want to go home to my girl and my family. Allah Akbar, Dannyfoe."

"Allah Akbar," I repeated, then Jalil slipped from out of the cruiser, closed the door soundlessly, looked all around, and slipped away into the night in the direction of the Chief's home.

I never saw him or Officer Burns again.

"What about us?" I asked the Chief.

He pointed up toward the top of the tower.

"But why?" I asked. "We don't need to hide without Jalil."

"We're not hiding. We're scouting. If Hobbs goes through with his plan, it will change everything. We need to know in order to plan our next move."

"How will we see them? It's pitch black."

The Chief pulled from his pants pocket what looked like a pirate's miniature spy glass.

"What's that?" I asked.

"This is a Predator Series 6X Night Vision Combination Monocular/Rifle Scope. It's worth around six grand. That's more than I make in two months."

"Then how did you afford to buy it?"

"Didn't. Some boys from the Border Patrol visited the island a few weeks back in one of their fancy new boats. Those bastards don't know what to do with all the money Homeland Defense funnels their way. Anyhow, they got all drunk up on the clock, and one of them left this on a table at Gulliver's. The King passed it my way. I figured I'd give it back after the BP guy had sweat it out a while. With this, from the water tower, we'll be able to see whatever goes down in a 360 degree sweep."

I wasn't exactly crazy about climbing the water tower, but it did make sense. Standing at its bottom preparing to climb with my back pack crammed with books and strapped tightly to me,

I craned my neck to get a good look at the water tank looming over me. At ten o'clock, the night was especially dark beneath the new moon. The Chief and I had ten minutes to climb the nearly vertical ladder, encased in a sort of cage-tubing, to the service landing, before we'd most certainly be spotted by a chopper returning to its patrol.

By the time we reached the eight story-high landing, I was completely spent. I don't think I could've climbed any faster or higher. What had seemed a relatively windless evening on the ground proved different at that elevated height. A steady breeze quickly evaporated the perspiration produced by the climb and caused goose flesh to rise on my skin.

The platform was made of the same thick metal grating as the tube we'd climbed up inside of. Its see-through design was a bit unnerving. To counter an emerging sense of acrophobia, I rolled over on my back and found myself staring into a million pinpricks of emerging lights. For a few moments, I rested, stared into the stars, and lifted myself out of the unraveling that was occurring several hundred feet below me. The view made clear my and man's infinitesimally small place within the vastness of the immeasurable universe, and I laughed.

"What are you laughing about?" the Chief asked as he moved about the platform adjusting the scope. The view from there extended well into the mainland toward the south and clear to Canada toward the north, beyond the Bass Islands to the west and far out into the open waters of the Lake to the east. He actually seemed to be enjoying himself.

"It really doesn't matter, does it?" I said.

"What's that?"

"Our lives. What's happening here. In the big picture, I mean. Everyone on this planet, hell, the planet itself is disposable. We're no more-or-less than mayflies."

"More-or-less," the Chief confirmed my dark conclusion.

"I was hoping you'd cheer me up," I said.

"And I was hoping for a quiet week, but here we are."

For the next two hours, the Chief continually checked his watch. We took turns circumnavigating the water tank, pausing at each of the four cardinal compass points, and scanning the lake through the night vision scope as the pall of night settled over the dying island like a shroud. There was literally no movement and no noise rising from the island below. Even the wind had died. In every way imaginable, Kelleys Island Village was becoming a ghost town. Every so often a drone buzzed beneath us or a chopper whirred past us, but it always kept its nose downturned and its spotlight on the ground. We kept our profiles low and always kept the water tower tank between us and the chopper to evade whatever night vision or thermal imaging capabilities they possessed.

"There they go," the Chief said. "It's midnight." With ten minutes until the chopper's return, we both stood up and directed our attention toward the southeast and the ferry dock, where Hobbs' plan was to begin by setting the ferry loose. Through my naked eyes, I was unable to make out much of anything beyond outlines of the park below us and buildings downtown.

The Chief looked a bit like a pirate on watch in the ship's crow's nest as he peered intently through the night vision scope. "The ferry is on its way," he said.

"Can you see any of our boats?"

"Not yet," he said as he slowly rotated to take in as much of the island's southern coastline as possible. "It looks like they may be taking the bait."

"What's happening?"

"A Coast Guard chopper has intercepted the Janus and is hovering over her. It's lowering someone onto the deck."

The Chief continued to watch as I impatiently demanded play-by-play.

He performed another sweep with the scope.

"I can see a few boats making their way out."

"How many?"

"Ten? Twelve? Not enough." He turned, "A few more to the west."

"Any wave runners?" I asked, thinking of Jalil.

"I can't tell."

He moved to the other side of the tower. "A couple more putting out from the ramp at the state park," he said then redirected his attention back to the ferry. "Damn!"

"What?!"

"It stopped. Whoever they lowered on deck stopped the ferry. That doesn't make sense," the Chief voiced his thoughts. "They had to have known it was empty, or they wouldn't have approached it so aggressively, and they would have sent soldiers along to board her."

"How could they have known?" I asked.

"I don't know. Oh shit!" the Chief said as he looked farther out into the South Passage then quickly back-and-forth from the easternmost to the westernmost points of the island.

"What?!"

"There's got to be fifty ships out there or more." He ran around to the north side of the tower and surveyed the waters there. "And as many on the Canadian side. That's at least twice as many as before."

"But why? Why are there more tonight?"

"Like I said, they had to have known about the plan."

"How?" I asked again.

"I'm not sure. Listening devices maybe."

Suddenly, the entire island was haloed by high-powered, shipboard spotlights that shined onto the near shore lake waters in search of the escapees.

The Chief lowered the scope. "I can't see anything into those lights."

"What's happening?" I demanded to know.

"Shut up and listen!" The Chief's patience had grown thin and his fear for Hobbs' blockade runners fat.

It took a few seconds to block out the typical sounds of night and sea, but eventually sporadic but recurring pops could be heard.

I looked to the Chief for an explanation.

"Gunfire."

We continued to listen until, as suddenly as they had been turned on, the spotlights were all at once extinguished. The entire skirmish lasted fewer than two minutes. It was a slaughter.

"Can I?" I indicated the scope with a nod. The Chief sat down on the platform and buried his face in his hands.

I looked into the green, miasmic world of night vision and surveyed the waters near the shore. All around the island, the remains of the islanders' flotilla were scattered and drifting. Some of the vessels were on fire; most of them were smoking and at various stages of sinking, and all had dead bodies strewn about the deck, including women and children. Still others showed no signs of damage; they looked as if their crews had abandoned ship or had been plucked from off deck. These were being boarded and searched by soldiers in full biohazard suits. I searched the waters for swimmers but saw none.

I leaned back against the water tank and slunk down next to the Chief.

"Why didn't they listen? You told them they didn't have a chance." I said.

"I think they knew that. They never really believed they would escape."

"Then why try?"

"Control."

"Control? Over what?"

"The how and the when, if not the why," the Chief said. "In the end, that's all any of us have – if we choose to exercise it."

We sat until we heard the roar of the surveillance chopper returning.

"What now?" I asked.

"Stay on your toes. It's going to be a long night of running around this tank and out of the chopper's sight. I'd rather they didn't know what we know. We'll wait until morning and climb down during the six a.m. shift change. It looks like the shit's really going to hit the fan tomorrow."

"Sounds like a plan, Chief. Not a very good one, but it's a plan."

I think he started to laugh, but it came out as a series of coughs.

"Chief, are you okay?"

"I'm fine," he said."

Down below, what few lights had been on were suddenly and simultaneously extinguished. "What's up, Chief?" I asked.

"It looks like their first response to the escape attempt. They've shut down the electricity to the island."

We heard a few gasoline generators spark to life and saw a few scattered lamps reignite, but with the lack of gasoline on the island, they wouldn't last long.

BOOK THREE

"He knew that the tale he had to tell could not be one of final victory. It could be only the record of what had to be done, and what assuredly would have to be done again in the never-ending fight against terror and its relentless onslaughts."
Albert Camus,
The Plague, Part 5

Chapter One

*Day 7, Thursday, May 30, 201_*

Morning broke hot and sweaty as if overnight Nature herself had come down with the Blues. Everything was different and climbing towards a fevered pitch. We hustled down from the tower, left the cruiser, and sprinted as the crow flies through backyards and empty lots rather than using the roads to the Chief's house. My run was made especially uncomfortable by the Chief's revolver that I still carried tucked into the back side of my waist band.

The Chief woke Dr. Bentham for whom the cries of misery at the camp had made sleeping there impossible. The Chief dug up a box of clothes from somewhere in his bedroom that his wife had left behind when she'd moved off island. After she'd cleaned up and changed clothes, Dr. Bentham and I scrambled and shared the last of the Chief's eggs along with some dry toast while he showered, shaved, and changed into a clean uniform.

Dr. Bentham insisted on walking the relatively short distance to the 4-H camp to begin another day of futility. The streets and sidewalks were nearly absent of mayfly and bird carcasses as the Chief and I walked into town. The bird population was simply dying out, and with no electricity to power the lights that attract them, the mayflies were bypassing the island and continuing on to the mainland. The only activity in the sky was the constant surveillance by the pesky drones and menacing helicopters.

Not knowing if we'd return to the Chief's place, I took along my book bag. As stupid as it sounds, it was as if caring for Daphne's books had given me a purpose. As the Chief and I walked toward the intersection of Division and Lakeshore, a number of defectors hurried past us on bicycles "borrowed" from one of the rental shops. They carried with them as many of their possessions as they could manage.

"Where you going?" The Chief called as they passed.

"Patmos" was the abbreviated reply.

The Chief's plan was for us to head down to the public docks in order to check on the few transient boaters who'd been trapped on island with the rest of us then to walk the half-mile out to the Kelleys Island Hotel on the west end of Lakeshore Drive and do the same with the unfortunate guests and birders who'd been holed up there for nearly a week. That changed, however, when we realized that they had already come to us.

Many of the remaining healthy were gathered at the southwest corner of Lakeshore and Division across from Saturday's and The Village Pump. In normal summers, that corner was used as a small public parking lot of a single row of ten slots; however, a flash flea market had opened in those spaces with a half dozen vendors all selling an assortment of items and home remedies to ward off or cure the Blues. One hawked necklaces and bracelets strung with garlic bulbs to protect the wearer from the virus. Another peddled a self-brewed potion inside dark-colored, glass bottles, which "guaranteed" to cure the contagion. Several amulets made of crystals and magnets, said to repel the virus, were being sold. One offered hand-held, battery-operated mini-fans with

"Kelleys Island" printed on the sides, whose usage he demonstrated by holding one constantly in front of his mouth and nose as if to blow away any attacking virus.

Not a single vendor wore a mouth covering of any kind. "Bad for business," one told us.

It was as if after three measly days of isolation, the entire island, excepting Patmos' people, had independently and simultaneously decided to ignore the quarantine and risk infection in favor of life, or death, as usual. The fatalists arrived downtown on foot, in golf carts, on bicycles, and in the few remaining cars with gasoline. In response, several merchants opened up shop, wheeled merchandise on racks onto the sidewalk, and cheekily advertised, "Going out of Business" sales with signs exclaiming, "Everything Must Go!" The restaurants and bars were quick to follow suit. Doors opened, charcoal grills were fired, and outdoor patios were prepared for diners. The occasional choppers overhead showed no signs of disapproval.

It was as if those gathering believed that a collective and conscious turning of a cold shoulder to the virus could somehow cause it to go away, like the new student who had the audacity to sit at the cool kids' table. However, what they failed to consider was that, unlike that new student, the new virus had no thoughts or feelings at all, nor was it interested in their affection, attention, or lack thereof. It simply didn't care or not care. It just was. It was an unthinking Xerox machine doing what viruses have always done: invading a host, replicating itself, and spreading deeper into that host's cell population. It was a boorish party crasher who, once inside an individual's or species' home, opened the door for its similarly obnoxious family members and refused to leave until the party was no party at all.

When we saw King Charles arrive downtown in a van full of what remained of his cast from the Real World Kelleys Island and throwing open Gulliver's doors to patrons, the Chief made a beeline in his direction.

"Charles," he scolded. "Are you crazy? You should know better."

"Know better? Know better than who, Chief? These folks who would rather risk the Blues than sit lonely in their rooms and the hulls of their boats, who want to eat and drink and talk and dance rather than wait to die, or better than you, who wants them to quit living like you have – and I don't mean just since this virus arrived – and wallow in self-pity in fear of losing a life that isn't worth living in the first place? Exactly which one should I 'know better than'?"

The Chief ignored the King's brutal analysis of the situation and his life. "I can't be held responsible for this. You agreed to ration and deliver food supplies and not to sell alcohol."

"First off, no one is holding you responsible. Secondly, that was before they shut off the electricity. If we don't eat and drink it, the food and beer will go bad and to waste. None of us asked for it, Chief, but face it – our lives have been put in fast forward and shrunk to a few days or maybe even hours. According to that doctor-lady, if the Blues don't kill us, the government will, so what's the point of resistance to the flu or temptation?"

"It's protocol," the Chief said.

"You've lived according to someone else's protocol your entire life, J.P. Please, tell me you're not going to die by it too."

King Charles's words struck the Chief like bullets to the chest. He slowly backed away. I followed for a few steps, but he said, "No, Danny," and turned and walked straight up Division towards the jail.

"Let him go, son," the King said. "He needed to hear it. Would you like some breakfast? Everything's on the house. And if you want a drink, nobody's checking I.D.'s today. Take a bite out of the little of life that's left, kid."

I accepted the King's offer and spent much of that day in Gulliver's. I gorged myself on eggs, sausage, bacon, and pancakes. When morning turned to noon, I fed from a buffet table holding every sort of food that could be cooked on gas appliances or grilled in a barbecue pit. I started out drinking iceless screwdrivers then switched to lukewarm bottled beer. Patrons literally threw money around like confetti, and I emptied my wallet one bill at a time, slipping them into the cleavage of the former Gulliver's Girls, who danced Coyote Ugly style on top of the bar until the batteries died inside somebody's old boom box.

Men and women, men and men, women and women paired up and made out in the bar like there was no tomorrow. In the men's room, I opened a stall to find some middle-aged woman bent over the toilet with her shorts puddled around her high-heeled wedges as one of the college-aged bartenders screwed her from behind. It was either one big festival of self-inflicted temporary amnesia or one tiny moment of life distilled to its most intense sensual pleasures.

At some point in the early afternoon, I wandered out into the street in time to see a fully-loaded bus from Patmos's camp roll into town. A voice over its loud speaker claimed the world was ending, but redemption was still available through the cross – whatever that meant. One of the partiers flashed a hastily-drawn, handmade sign towards the bus which read, "Prevent bird flu – choke your chicken!" More than a few beer bottles were thrown, full moons bared, and breasts flashed at the bus. It parked in the middle of the intersection of Lakeshore and Division, smack in the heart of downtown.

Inside his work shirt and a pair of flared jeans over his sandals, Patmos came bounding down the steps of the bus, stood on top of a park bench, and began to preach. He was forced to nearly shout in order to be heard over the persistent whomp-whomp-whomp of two helicopters' blades overhead: *"In the days to come, the island will be purged of the cowardly,* unbelieving, murderers, sexually immoral, idolaters, and all liars." Folks began to gather. "It will have no need of the sun or of the moon to shine in it, for the glory of God will illuminate it. The Lamb is its light. And those who are saved shall walk in its light . . . and its gates shall not be shut at all by day. But there shall be no means to enter anything that defies, or causes an abomination or a lie, but only those who are written in the Lamb's Book of Life."

"Amen," a voice rang out from the growing crowd.

"He who overcomes, I will make him a pillar in the temple of My God, and he will not go out from it anymore; and I will write on him the name of My God, and the name of the city of My God, the new Jerusalem, which comes down out of heaven from My God. There is balm in Gilead, immunization in New Jerusalem, and there is salvation."

Suddenly, a targeted sonic blast, a monotonous, high-pitched tone that grew increasingly intense and caused all gathered to cover their ears in a fruitless attempt to shield their ear drums from the invisible assault, burst upon those gathered in the park. Pained and disoriented, the crowd dissipated. From the army helicopters, soldiers in a full biohazard suits stood at the opened doors and directed fan-shaped sonic weapons down upon the people who ran screaming out of the park.

I touched my finger to my ear, held it before my eyes, and saw blood. I watched others drop to their knees in excruciating pain and with similar crimson streaks running down the sides of their faces. Others curled into full fetal position with both hands cupped to their ears. Still others were bent over expelling waves of nausea from the depths of their innards. The desired chaos ruled and the flu spread.

I crawled beneath a picnic table and did my best to protect my ears and sanity. Chaos was everywhere around me. I was completely deaf to anything but the continuous ultrasonic blast. Tears spilled from around my vibrating eyeballs as I wept openly and without shame. I think I even prayed to Patmos's god for the debilitating tone to stop my heart and end my misery.

In the ongoing Pandemonium, Patmos futilely attempted to shepherd his scattering flock. He ran hither and yon waving his arms and trying to gather his erstwhile faithful, but he may as well have been trying to lasso mayflies. At one point, he stopped amid the bedlam and held his Bible in both hands above his head in the direction of the continually circling helicopters. He spun in slow turns trying to shield his followers from the sound waves or maybe trying to deflect them with his Bible back at the helicopters. I turned away and didn't see Patmos again.

I'm not sure if it was because of the pain, the shock, the alcohol, or a combination of all three, but I passed out beneath the picnic table.

Chapter Two

"C'mon, Danny. Wake up." A voice dripped unwelcome into my unconsciousness.

I must have mumbled something about Daphne.

"Daphne? Who's Daphne? Come on. You're dreaming," the Chief said.

The choppers were gone. I wiped the drool from the side of my face and squinted to see the Chief standing over me dressed in civilian clothes. In khaki cargo shorts, a "Pump This!" t-shirt from The Village Pump's sidewalk sale, gold-rimmed aviator sunglasses, and a pair of top siders, he could have passed for a typical weekend boater. Whatever existential crisis King Charles had prompted in him, it had either been settled or tabled because the Chief was clearly back to his old, on-task self.

I sat up, crawled out from under the picnic table, and slowed my head's spinning by sitting on its bench and placing my feet solidly on the ground. I rubbed my eyes, pushed the cotton around in my mouth with my tongue, then squinted in order to better make out the Chief against the late afternoon sun. "You going undercover now or what?" I asked.

"We have work to do, and I'd rather not be such an obvious target of interest to the eyes in the sky."

"Work? What kind of work?" I performed a quick scan of the once again empty downtown area, "What about . . ."

"These people?" The Chief finished my question. "We can't save them from themselves, and that cavern isn't large enough to save them all. What we can do, maybe, is save ourselves. At least, we should try. Unless, of course, you'd rather stay here."

"No. Trust me, Chief. This isn't for me. The bird flu may not be able to kill me, but any more glasses of the King's cheap-ass beer will, and I don't even want to talk about the viruses being spread inside those restrooms."

"Let's go," the Chief said. "We need to shut down the 4-H camp and collect Dr. Bentham, but I don't think it's a good idea to travel together. I'll meet you at the head of the East Quarry Trail across from the camp in a half-hour. Try not to be seen," he said and pointed to the sky once again.

"No problem," I said.

With my book bag over my shoulders, I took off north cutting through the alley, backyards, fields, and woods that I hadn't traveled since I was a boy. I avoided open spaces whenever a drone or chopper was near and ran in short bursts from cover to cover.

I arrived at the trail head first. From across the street, I heard howls of discomfort, cries for help, and humorless laughter coming from the tents, which had more than doubled in number since the previous day. Apparently, people had begun not only to abide by but to cooperate enthusiastically with the Chief's order to quarantine the infected at the camp, and they were gladly surrendering their sickened loved ones.

The Chief arrived shortly after, and together we crossed Ward Road and let ourselves into Dr. Bentham's command post.

"They pull in and all but push the sick out the car door," Dr. Bentham greeted us with a complaint rather than a hello. "And the Sanderson brothers are nowhere to be found. They just left me!" Dr. Bentham said and blew past us out the door.

"They both have families," the Chief answered by way of explanation as we trailed her back out.

"I can't put up these tents by myself, and I'm out of restraints, ibuprofen, and clean towels and sheets. Every time one of them dies, I have to burn all of their linen. Do you have any idea what it's like here? They're all dying. Nothing is working. At this rate, we'll all be dead by the end of the week!"

"Jenny," the Chief tried to calm her borderline hysterics.

"This is harder than I thought. I mean, I thought I could do this. I thought I could handle it, but there is so much death. And the children call out for their mothers. I don't think I can take much more. I'm an administrator not a fucking hospice nurse."

"Jenny, it's okay," the Chief said. "We did all we could. It's time to shut this down. It was a good idea, but it's not working. From now on, people are just going to have to fend for themselves, including us. There's no other way."

"What about the infected?" Dr. Bentham directed her eyes towards the tents and cabins.

"Do any of them have a chance?"

She bowed her head and she shook it "no."

"Then we'll do the merciful thing."

The Chief went inside the Director's cabin then reemerged wearing a surgical mask and rubber gloves and carrying a pillow.

"What? Wait," I said. "What are you doing? You're not going to . . . Some of them aren't walking yet. They might recover."

The Chief charged past me.

I appealed to Dr. Bentham. "You're not going to let him just. . . ."

"Chief!" she called in her most authoritative voice and seemingly in response to my plea. "Wear your sunglasses. The eyes are especially vulnerable to the virus." She turned away, went back inside the office, and shut the door behind her.

"I can't believe this!" I said. "You can't just murder them."

The Chief stopped his progress towards the tents. "What's *your* plan, Danny? We can't just release them, and we can't take care of them. We have no doctors, no nurses, no medicine. You tell me: what's the right thing to do? Because I'd really like to know. If you've got a better idea, let's hear it. Because if by some miracle we survive this, there's nothing about what I'm about to do that won't haunt me for the rest of my life and, if Patmos is correct, even longer. So pay attention, and one day, when you give witness to it, be sure to get the facts straight."

With that, he turned and methodically moved from tent to tent. I watched from the porch as he made his meticulous orbit. In many of the tents, the flu had already done the Chief's work. Most of the suffocations happened noiselessly. In a couple of the tents, I heard pained but cordial greetings from the infected, which quickly turned into muffled pleadings for their lives. As the Chief emerged from each tent or cabin, the pillow's case grew increasingly saturated with the bloody red sputum of its victims, and the Chief's face looked less and less human.

It took a little more than half an hour.

When he finished, the Chief walked directly to the fire barrel, which Dr. Bentham and the Sanderson brothers had been using to incinerate all cloth touched by the infected. He stripped down to his boxers and top siders and dropped the pillow and the rest of his clothes, including the sunglasses, into the fire, then he stood beneath an outdoor shower for what must have been ten minutes with his face buried in his hands and his shoulders heaving for much of that time.

Dr. Bentham appeared from the cabin-office carrying two white, hotel-style towels and a green, extra-large 4-H camp t-shirt left over from seasons past. For a moment, she stood on the small porch and watched the Chief shower before she draped the towels and t-shirt over the porch railing, sat down on the top step, and averted her eyes, both from me and the Chief.

A nosy chopper had taken notice of the increased activity and settled over the camp. Once he'd composed himself, the Chief shared his observation that the drones and choppers seemed to be suspicious and intolerant of any groupings that seemed to be purposeful or directed; however, they were more permissive of those who moved in singles, and they had no problem with aimless and brainless mobs because they were effective breeding grounds for spreading the contagion and expediting the natural extinction process. However, if, like at the Chief's community meeting at the ball field or Patmos's revival meeting in Memorial Park, a group showed signs of organization or the potential for resistance, they were immediately put to rout by the choppers.

So rather than walking together and immediately to my grandfather's place, we departed singly and in different directions with a plan to reunite at the cavern as soon as we each could arrive without drawing the attention of the drones or choppers. I was the last to leave the camp. It took all of my resolve not to head for the library and take my chances by staying with Daphne. In order to remove all temptation, I headed in the opposite direction, through the woods, and along North Pond Trail. After delaying at the pond to make sure I hadn't been spotted and wasn't being followed, I cut through the graveyard, moving from headstone to headstone, until, crouching and pausing at the waist-high, black wrought iron fence that separated the cemetery from Division Street, I once more made sure I hadn't caught attention from above. After crossing the street, I paused in the woods behind the VFW hall. Its back door had been kicked in, and its kitchen ransacked. From there, I headed south. My progress was slow. As often as possible, I moved from tree to tree. When I reached the

Kellstone quarry, I followed the quarry's eastern edge until I reached Bookerman Road and could cross near my grandfather's house. In total it took me over an hour to travel a distance that would have taken me less than fifteen minutes when I was a boy blazing new shortcuts around the island.

At my grandfather's house, I waited beneath the tree line at the fringe of the backyard. A chopper appeared and momentarily loitered overhead. I was afraid that with their night vision and thermal imaging capabilities I would actually be more visible in the dark that was fast descending than in the current twilight. I had no way of knowing for sure. It may have been paranoia, but I was convinced that the chopper and the drones were looking specifically for the three of us. By then, they would have had complete profiles and histories of everyone trapped on island. They would know of my grandfather's property, but they couldn't have known of the cavern, and I had to make sure they didn't discover its existence. I hoped they would remain patient following the previous night's breakout attempt, but I had a feeling that their tolerance had worn thin. As evidence, I noted that all of the choppers patrolling the skies over Kelleys were no longer Coast Guard affiliated but Army, and the sonic devices that had been mounted in the side bay doors had been replaced by machine gunners.

"Danny?" Dr. Bentham's voice startled me. She had beaten me there and was hiding crouched deeper into the woods and hugging her own backpack to her chest.

"You made it," I stupidly stated the obvious.

"I only knew one way, but I was careful."

"After their next pass, let's make a run for the house," I said. "If a chopper or drone flies in low, we'll be exposed. It's getting dark. We'll be less visible to the choppers' night vision and thermal imaging in there as long as we stay away from the windows. We can wait for the Chief inside. We need to limit our trips to the cavern opening."

"Are you sure holing up inside is a good idea?" she asked.

"I'm not sure of anything anymore, but at least we'll be able to rest for a while without worrying about being seen."

A chopper flew past us toward the downtown.

"Let's go," I said, held out my hand, and pulled Dr. Bentham to her feet. We hurried across the yard and up the three wooden back steps that led into the kitchen. The house had been broken into a long time ago, probably by some squatter or some partiers who missed the last ferry and found themselves stuck on the island overnight and in need of a place to crash or party. The stale smell of must and mold rudely greeted us. Mouse droppings were scattered about the kitchen floor and counters.

Out of habit, I slid open the kitchen junk drawer, where my grandfather had kept opened packs of gum and lifesavers. It was always full of the other stuff that my grandfather didn't want to throw away but for which he had no permanent place: loose pens and pencils, phone books, rubber bands, decks of cards, etc. In the back against the back wall of the drawer, something white and flat captured my eye. I freed it with a moistened fingertip and slid it to the front. It was a wallet-sized photograph lying face down. For a moment, I just stared at its blank back side. Flipping it over, I saw a photo I had never before seen: a formal family photo like one of those that department stores used to take. The four of us were posed. My father and brother stood on the left. My dad had his hand resting on my brother's shoulder. On the right, my mother sat on top of carpet-covered box and held me in her lap. I was just a baby.

"Hey," Dr. Bentham said. "What'd you find?"

"Nothing," I said and slipped the photograph into my pocket. "Let's go into the dining room. There aren't so many windows."

Spider webs hung pretty much everywhere. Beer cans littered

the floor of the carpet, splotched with charred cigarette burns, but it was better than the hard tile floor in the kitchen. We sat and leaned against opposite, internal walls and listened to the roar of a chopper grow louder until it was directly over the house, then it began to wane in identical degrees as it continued in the direction opposite to its approach. I felt like Tom Cruise in that *War of the Worlds* movie hiding from alien spacecraft inside that abandoned home.

I must have dozed off, for when I woke up, it was fully dark. From the backyard, I heard the Chief calling, "Danny?! Danny?! He was on all fours in a pair of jeans, tennis shoes, and a black t-shirt feeling around in the dark for the plywood covering of the cavern. Stan McKillip's pick-up idled in the driveway with its headlights off.

"Chief," I called and hurried down the back steps with Dr. Bentham hard on my heels.

"We have to hurry!" The Chief said. "The chopper will be back soon. Find the opening. I'll get the ladder."

"What ladder?" I asked.

"It's in the back of the truck. I borrowed it from Stan. I owed the bastard one."

Before dropping to my hands and knees, I glanced at the truck in which a twelve foot extension ladder was sticking out from its bed alongside a 60-inch screen TV. "What's with the TV, Chief? It won't fit through the opening, and there's no electricity. Remember?"

"Moral victory," he said. "Now find that opening. Fast!"

I did as told. We dropped the ladder into the cavern, and while the Chief ditched Stan's truck in the wooded lot, throwing a large canvas over the hood to hide the engine's dissipating heat from any thermal imaging devices, Dr. Bentham and I climbed down into the cavern. I found the flashlight/lantern and lit it while she held the ladder steady for the Chief, who slid the plywood back into place before descending. "We made it," he said triumphantly when he reached the cavern floor.

"It's like being inside a diamond," Dr. Bentham said to no one in particular.

"About time you joined us, Chief," I said.

For just a second, I thought he might hug me; instead, he ignored my comment, looked up, and said, "We're going to have to rig something over that hole in the ceiling. Can't have light shooting out of here every time it's opened, and we'll need to get going on drilling that ventilation hole first thing in the morning. From there it's just a matter of driving one of those rods we took from the museum through the soil then replacing it with the PVC pipe."

He was all business. I smiled.

Suddenly dirt sprinkled down from the cavern ceiling, and we could feel something heavy on the surface above us.

"The lantern!" The Chief said.

Dr. Bentham doused it and handed it to Chief Sarter. He converted it to its flashlight function but muffled the beam with his cupped hand. For a moment, he pointed it up into his own face turning his expression diabolically red and orange and black, like kids do to make monster faces and tell ghost stories. It may have been fatigue or an optical illusion caused by the poor lighting and shadows, but the Chief's eyes were bloodshot and watery, and dark circles seemed to be forming around them. He put a finger to his lips to shush us then looked directly at me then the ladder to indicate that I should be the one to climb up and discover what was happening on the surface. The Chief's build, like a power forward's, restricted the speed of his movement.

Once I was on the ladder, the Chief turned off the flashlight. I had to rely completely on feel to find the rungs for hand and footholds. At the top, I slowly, silently inched back the plywood cover to expose a sliver of space for me to peer through. My eyes were immediately assaulted by light and swirling dirt, my ears by the deafening whirr of a Black Hawk helicopter that had landed directly on top of the entrance to the cavern with its runners straddling the opening. About fifteen yards away, in the light of the chopper's spotlights, I saw a group of soldiers, wearing full biohazard suits, mustered in front of a second Black Hawk.

Four of the soldiers, all wearing headlamps and with flashlights attached to their weapons, entered my grandfather's home through the back screen door. The others performed a quick sweep of the surrounding woods, where, although I couldn't see, I'm sure they found the truck. A few seconds later, the soldiers returned from inside the house and reconvened between the two Black Hawks. Through their plastic face shields, I could see the soldiers speaking into the mouthpieces of their wireless headsets. However, the noise of the Black Hawks' engines and blades made it impossible for me to hear what they were saying. An officer made a circular motion with his hand over his head. While the other soldiers crouched, ran, then piled into the Black Hawks, one removed a can of orange spray paint from his utility belt and hurried to the back door then front door, where he painted a series of symbols on each before boarding a chopper, which immediately lifted off and headed west.

I slid the board back completely over the hole, ducked my head inside, and descended.

"They're gone," I called down, and the Chief lit the lantern to light the remainder of my way.

I sat on a boulder and stared at the cavern floor.

"What happened? What's going on?" The Chief asked.

"They found the truck," I said. "I think they know we're around here somewhere, but I don't think they've figured out where – yet."

"Damn it!" The Chief said then guessed that the soldiers

were most likely black ops Special Forces.

"What do you think they're up to?" I asked.

The Chief deferred to Dr. Bentham who had the most knowledge of their plan.

"I wasn't in on the details of military operations," she said, "but the plan allowed for the deployment of boots on the ground should it be deemed necessary."

"Necessary for what?" The Chief asked.

She didn't answer, but I'm pretty sure images of the Chief's actions at the camp earlier in the day were playing inside each of our minds.

"Nothing personal," Dr. Bentham said. "Just what has to be done."

"What are we going to do?" I asked.

"Well, I guess, we could just settle in and hope they don't find the opening," the Chief said, "or we could initiate Plan C."

"Plan C?" Dr. Bentham asked. "What's that? We never discussed a Plan C. Danny, do you have any idea what he's talking about."

"I do not," I said.

"So what is it, Chief?" She asked.

"I could tell you . . ." the Chief started the familiar joke.

"Yeah, whatever," Dr. Bentham said. "Why go out there? There's no more you can do, no one you can save. You're safe down here. We have everything we need to survive for weeks if not months. Why risk getting caught? And killed?" She added.

"So, you're not coming?" I asked her.

"No, Danny," it was the Chief who answered with surprising vehemence. "She's not coming. We need someone to get this place organized." The Chief turned to Dr. Bentham. "Could you do that, Jenny?" He asked with an unfamiliar tenderness in his voice – unfamiliar to me at least.

"Sure. Why not? Just please don't bring anybody back with you."

The Chief went and busied himself among the supplies he'd brought from his garage. He pulled out two olive, drab wool army blankets, a pair of camouflage hunting pants, and a matching jacket. "These are going to be hotter than hell, but they'll have a hard time spotting me," he said. He then threw me one of the blankets and a hooded camouflage rain poncho. "Here, put this poncho over yourself."

I did as I was told. The poncho draped to below my knees and promised to keep me pretty well hidden. 'What's the blanket for? It's still gotta be ninety degrees up there," I said.

"Let's hope it's hotter, as close to 98.6 as it can get," he answered.

"Why's that?" Dr. Bentham asked. "You'll have a heat stroke."

"The closer the ambient temperature is to our body temperatures, the less differential there is between our bodies and our surroundings, and the less distinguishable will be our heat signatures that their thermals can pick up. They may even mistake us for deer," the Chief explained. "We have to move slowly to avoid overheating and raising our body temps."

"And why the blankets?" I asked.

"Whenever we hear a drone or chopper approaching, we'll pull the blankets over our heads. They'll hide our glow for a little while. It's what the Taliban fighters did to hide from our guys. The blankets will only buy us a few seconds, but we shouldn't need much more than that to give them time to pass. So keep your ears open."

Chapter Three

I lifted the cover slowly and only part way so as to take a look around. Confident that no one was nearby or watching from above, I shimmied myself out of the hole, headed immediately for the wood line, and squatted like a baseball catcher inside my poncho. After covering the plywood with brush and branches, the Chief joined me.

We heard a string of pops. I looked to the Chief for explanation.

"Gunfire," he said.

As if the shooter was moving executioner-style down a line of victims, the sound of the shots came from the southwest end Lifer enclave that the Chief and I had searched a few days back. The special ops squad must have cleaned out that neighborhood quickly since the Chief and I had inadvertently made their job much easier by our confiscation of weapons. The Black Hawks soon rose from amidst the treetops and headed toward the northwest quadrant. Almost immediately, one came down. My guess was it landed at Chief Russo's helipad. The other looked to come down in the meadow where Lakeshore Drive becomes Titus Road. From those locations, they could continue their sweep of the homes along the northwest lakeshore.

"Here's the plan," the Chief drew my attention back to our situation. "Now that they're going door-to-door, at least we'll know where the choppers are at all times. The lights on the choppers will give away their positions and tell us when to move. When they're down, we go. When they're up, we duck and cover, but don't forget about the drones. Got it?"

"Got it."

"We're going to move east towards Division always staying off road and as much as possible under the tree canopy. There's no hurry; we've got all night. We'll move from tree to tree. One at a time if we have to. From there, we're going to move fast down Division to the jail. We can hole up, rest, and gather some supplies before we hightail it to and climb the water tower."

"What supplies? And why the water tower again?" I asked.

"Plan C," was all the explanation I received.

The outside of every house we passed had already been marked with orange paint by the soldiers from the Black Hawks. It looked like some street gang had gone through tagging its territory, but I recognized the technique – if not the actual meaning of the symbols – from television news reports after various natural disasters in which search and rescue workers for FEMA made the same markings to indicate that a house had already been searched, when, and by whom, or to indicate that a dead body was inside. The markings seemed somehow more impersonal than the crosses the Chief had drawn for a similar purpose.

Staying beneath the tree canopy as much as possible, we advanced meticulously along Bookerman. Whenever we heard a drone, we stopped and threw the blankets over ourselves. Along the way, we spotted two former walkers with bullet holes in the side of their heads. It took us nearly an hour-and-a-half to travel a distance that should have taken five minutes. Before beginning our sprint to the jail, we sat and rested inside an old dilapidated barn behind a house on the corner of Division and Bookerman. From that position, we'd advanced far enough into the interior to see two more Black Hawks working in tandem on the eastern half of the island.

Panting heavily, the Chief fell to one knee and vomited profusely.

"Are you okay, Chief?" I asked.

"Compared to what?" was his cryptic answer. "If you're asking if I'm going to die of the Blues, the answer is no."

I left it go at that.

From where I stood, through the barn door, I could see the south side of the two-story school building. On the other side of which was the library and Daphne. Just then the two Black Hawks from my grandfather's appeared low on the northern horizon and once again put down. This time near the state park. They were beginning their final sweep of the western half, which would take them on a north to south route down Division Street to the downtown area. Because of the paucity of homes along Division Street, it wouldn't take them long to finish their mission of extermination.

I took off in a sprint toward the library and the Black Hawks.

"Danny! No!" I heard the Chief complain, but I had to see.

I ran through the wide open three-way crossing, where Bookerman T-bones with Division, and across the expansive front lawn of the school building. I stopped at the front steps and glass double doors. There were no markings from the soldiers yet. Vaguely, I heard the sound of gunfire toward the north as I hurried around to the library entrance. Again, no markings.

Under the cover of a small awning, I pounded on the doors and called, "Daphne! Daphne! It's me." When I popped the door open, its progress was stopped by a padlocked chain, which usually lay unused in the vestibule. I could only open a space of a couple of inches.

I let go of the door handle, cupped my hands against the glass and peered into the library, which was being partially lit by the exit sign over the door that was still operating on emergency battery power.

"Daphne!" I called. "It's me, Danny."

Another rifle shot rang out. This time closer.

I looked again. Deep inside, I detected movement. Daphne, barefoot and wearing a white shortie nightgown, bloodstained in front, stepped out into the aisle and stood looking in my direction.

"Daphne! Open the door! Let me in!" I shook and rattled the door.

I peeked over my shoulder to see if any of the soldiers were nearing the library. A team of four turned east into the Sweet Valley subdivision, which consisted of no more than five or six homes and wouldn't require them more than five minutes to search. I turned my attention back inside the library and watched Daphne walk past the free standing shelves in the middle of the aisle and towards the door until she was standing no more than four feet from me.

Her hair was matted. Her eyes were misty and circled by dark rings. Her skin pale and nearly translucent so that the blue of her veins showed through.

"They're coming," I said.

She didn't answer. She just stared.

She was so close I could have reached out and grabbed her if not for the layer of glass between us.

"The soldiers. They're coming."

I think she said "good," but her words were garbled.

"No. No, it's not."

Daphne's pained expression communicated her misery and her resolve.

"We don't have time. You have to come with me. Now!" I pulled the door and rattled the chain again like a madman.

She walked forward but was forced to stop in order to cough up a large quantity of blood. When she recovered, she slipped *The Last Man* through the opening allowed by the chain and immediately backed away. "It's you," she said, then slowly backpedaled into the depths of the library.

"Daphne!" I yelled and shook the door violently. I repeatedly broke the seal, but I could do nothing about the chain.

I hesitated, pressed my cheek against the glass and closed my eyes. When I opened them, in the glass's reflection, I saw soldiers exiting the Sweet Valley subdivision.

Self-preservation insisted that I move. Instead of retracing my previous path, I ran towards and around the rear of the building, pressed my back against the brick to reduce my visibility, and slid along its length past the gymnasium until I reached the southern face of the school. From there, I could see the Chief, who had repositioned himself behind the south side, front corner of the barn, which shielded him from the view of the approaching soldiers. He held up his hand toward me with his palm out, as if he were a crossing guard, to indicate "stay put."

I heard the first Black Hawk then the second approach and land in the north parking lot in front of the library. Theoretically, the school could have been harboring a large number of people. It would require all eight soldiers to conduct a classroom by classroom search, which would give us the time we needed to escape.

The Chief, with his right hand still communicating "stop," began to make that "come hither" motion with his left index finger. I interpreted his mixed signals to mean, "Come forward, but slowly."

When I reached the front of the building, I slid under an

exterior, fire escape. The Chief again gave me the stop sign. He then pointed down Division towards the jail. I assumed the soldiers had entered the school. Starting with five fingers, he counted down to a closed fist zero. Simultaneously, we took off in a full sprint. We were slowed due to our less-than-ideal-for-running camo outfits, the necessity of weaving around the stalled vehicles, and a general lack of conditioning, but we didn't stop running until we reached the jail, where we slipped inside and closed the door shut behind us just in time to hear the four Black Hawks converge on the downtown.

Down to what felt like our last breaths, we both doubled over, leaned our butts against the door, and gasped for oxygen.

"For Chrissakes, Danny. That was close. What was all that about back there?"

"I needed a book," I said and showed him *The Last Man.*

"That must be one hell of a book," he said. Still bent at the waist and unhappy with my answer, the Chief rolled his head to look into my eyes. He must have decided to give me a pass on my evasiveness in the face of larger impending concerns.

I stood full upright. When I did, I saw something that trumped the Chief's concern for my reading habits. I nudged him. "Chief."

He was still too depleted of breath to respond.

"Chief," I repeated and nudged him once more.

"For . . . Chrissakes . . . Danny," he managed to spit out between inhalations. "What . . . is . . . it?"

"I think, it's Officer Burns."

"What?"

The Chief stood up and finally shared my vision of the glazed silhouette of a body swaying gently, two feet off of the ground, inside the cell. Chief Sarter walked over to his desk and fished out a tiny flashlight from one of the drawers. He then approached the closed cell door, cupped the bulb end of the flashlight inside his hands to muffle its glow, turned it on, and directed the light toward the figure. He illuminated the flashlight for only a second, but in that instant, behind the blood-spattered Visqueen curtain, we saw Officer Burns hanging from his belt. Backing away, the Chief slipped on the cell keys which lay on the floor in front of the desk, where Burns must have thrown them after locking himself inside.

"Aw for Chrissakes, Burnsie," the Chief said.

Chapter Four

In near-total darkness and as noiselessly as possible, we rolled up Officer Burns' body inside the Visqueen and lay him on the floor of the cell. We then retreated as far away from the body as we could – the natural repulsion felt by the living towards the dead – and sat down against the wall behind the Chief's desk and beneath the large front window, where he still struggled to catch his breath after all of the exertion.

"Were you two close?" I asked.

"Me and Burnsie?"

"Yeah."

"Not really. He only worked part-time and seasonal. Good guy though and a good cop."

"It just gets easier, doesn't it?"

"What's that?" The Chief asked and muffled a hacking cough into the crook of his arm.

"The killing. The watching people die. It's just like anything else: the more you do it; the easier it gets. Like cleaning fish, I guess. The first time I watched my grandfather gut and fillet a walleye, I cried like a baby. But I eventually got used to it. I'd hold the knife while he held and guided my hands and the knife through the process. Now, those are some of my favorite memories."

"I suppose people can get used to just about anything if they do it enough. But those things, the killing and watching people die, cost you a little of yourself each time you see it."

"Is that what happened to you?"

"In the war you mean?"

"Yeah."

"You could say that. I saw some things, and I did some things I never thought I'd see or do. Things that would make what happened at Abu Ghraib and Guantanamo look like playtime at a day care center. I've been those soldiers out there," he said and nodded his head backwards toward the window. "I've been part of clandestine operations and cover-ups. We're really good at it."

"You don't believe we can survive in the cavern, do you?" I asked. "If you did, we wouldn't have taken the chance of being here right now."

The Chief hesitated, rolled his head, and rubbed his neck while he weighed his response. "Not really. No."

"Then why all of the planning and stockpiling of supplies and the talk of drilling holes?"

"I guess because you were so excited about it, and it gave you a purpose and a reason to hope."

"What about Dr. Bentham? Does she believe it can work?"

"I don't know for sure. You'd have to talk with her. But, I doubt it. She knows the score. She's ex-military too. I think that's why she and I get along so well when I couldn't get along with my own wife. Dr. Bentham knows how these things usually turn out."

I could smell the sweat running from the Chief's pores inside the stifling air of the jail. He had the smell of fever.

"Then what's the point?"

"If you're looking for 'points,' son, you're playing the wrong game."

"You know what I mean. Why shouldn't we just walk out there right now and surrender? Why prolong our misery."

"Because all of our lives, we surrender to so many things – to parents, to churches, to teachers, to officers, to courts, to the government, to rules, to reason and common sense. I'm tired of surrendering, Danny, and if my life has been reduced to no more than the choice between dying with some shred of dignity or trying to prolong my miserable excuse for a life, well, there's a sort of freedom in having that choice, and I refuse to give that up. And, I'm going to give you a chance." He then actually said, "Excuse me," and crawled to the toilet inside the cell and puked what little remained inside of him. "Maybe we should just quit all the gabbing and rest for a while," he said once he'd returned. "We'll need all the energy we can get to make it to the water tower."

Fifteen minutes later, the Chief was nudging me out of a restless sleep.

"They're here," the Chief whispered."

"Who's here?"

"The special ops guys. They're crawling all over the place. Look across the street."

I slowly rose to my knees, turned around, and looked across Division, where through the windows of the general store and the clothing boutique next door to it, I could see headlamps moving about inside. In addition, the four Black Hawks were hovering over the buildings and shining massive spotlights onto the downtown streets, alleys, and the park. The search teams from both sides had met up to perform their final sweep through the downtown buildings and docks. Their lights were making the outside as bright as mid-day and, dangerously for us, illuminating the inside of the jail as well.

The Chief turned around and slowly elevated his eyes over the window ledge.

"What are we going to do?" I asked.

"I don't know," he said as he slunk back down beside me. "Think," the Chief ordered himself.

I slipped the Chief's gun out from my waistband and held it out before me.

"Put that away," he said. "Be serious."

We resumed our mental search for a way to avoid detection.

"The spray paint!" I said. "We can mark the jail ourselves. Maybe, in the dark, they'll buy it and pass us by."

"Good idea, but it's in the cruiser, which we left on Chappel."

I thought for minute. "The hardware store is right next door isn't it?" I asked.

"It is," the Chief said, immediately getting my drift. "Paint supplies, paint supplies," he repeated to himself trying to visualize the arrangement of merchandise inside the store. "Back right corner!" He finally said. "The paint is in the back right corner."

"But how will we get in? It's got to be locked."

The Chief crawled to his desk and pulled his key ring from out of the drawer." I emptied the cruiser this afternoon when I realized it was going to run out of gas soon." He sorted through the keys until he settled on the one he knew to be to the hardware store and slid it off of the ring. "But getting in without being seen is the bigger problem," the Chief said.

"We can create a diversion," I suggested, "like before."

"If you play zombie this time, they'll shoot you in the head."

"You must have a flare gun or confiscated fireworks or something," I said.

"No good. It can't be anything that requires us to instigate it, or they will know we're alive and around here somewhere. It has to be natural or at least seem to be so."

I swear, the Chief no sooner finished saying "natural," than we heard a barrage of tiny taps against the window above us.

We looked at one another, then, in unison, rose up to investigate. Drawn by the spotlights on the Black Hawks, a massive swarm of mayflies had descended on downtown from the south in biblical proportions. I shit you not. They were so thick that we couldn't even see the buildings across the street. The choppers immediately cut their lights and pulled up and away from the invading hordes of mayflies. They had to be concerned with sucking so many insects into their engines. Once more, the streets were pitch black. We'd also be invisible to any drones. The soldiers were hunkered down somewhere. I could only hope I wouldn't run smack into them.

Before the Chief could insist on his being the one to go, I grabbed the key from between his fingers, threw my poncho back over my head, and tore for the door.

"Be fast," he called after me.

Out of the jail, I turned left and headed for the door to the hardware store no more than twenty yards away and up on an elevated porch. Moving through the mayfly invasion was equivalent to walking into a blizzard or sandstorm. I slipped and slid like I was walking across an icy pond, fell a few times, and walked straight into a sidewalk bench obscured by the combination of darkness and insects. I ducked my head and used my arm to shield my face as much as possible without losing sight of my direction, but the noxious bugs continually struck my eyeballs, filtered into the space between the poncho hood and my neckline, and I gagged on and swallowed more of them than I wish to remember. Put it this way, if I thought they smelled bad, they tasted a thousand times worse.

I reached the porch, which was caked in mayflies, quickly let myself into the store and caused the entry bell on the door to ring. There was no time to worry if the soldiers heard and would be drawn to the clanging. I moved immediately for the paint supplies where the Chief promised they'd be in the back of the store. In the dark, I couldn't be absolutely sure I grabbed a can of orange paint or red, but there was no time to be picky. I headed directly back outside and into the mayfly maelstrom. Though still steady, the storm of insects was already beginning to let up. Familiarized with the route, I was able to advance much more quickly on the return trip. I shook the can and popped the top as I ran. When I reached the jail door, I quickly sprayed an "X" and some nonsense hieroglyphics around it and ducked back inside, where I removed my poncho and the Chief helped brush the literally hundreds of mayflies out of my hair and off of my body.

The Chief locked the door behind me, and we returned to our position beneath the window. Within minutes the bugs were either settled or gone, and the downtown dark except for the bobbing of headlamps and the flashlights attached to the barrels of the soldiers' M4-carbines. A pair stopped on the sidewalk directly behind us, separated only by the stone and window of the jail. They shined their lights through the glass directly over our heads and past us and performed a visual sweep of the interior.

They were so close to where we sat that, despite his protective face shield, we heard one weary soldier say, "Hey, dude. Look. Someone's already marked this place. There's nobody here. Let's get out of here."

We didn't move a muscle for nearly fifteen more minutes. When we finally did, there were no signs of the Black Hawks or the soldiers anywhere. We assumed that the drones were still in the air, so we agreed to use our duck and cover strategy to reach the water tower.

"Bring the paint," the Chief said.

Before we left, he grabbed a roll of duct tape and the night vision scope from the same drawer in which he had stowed the key ring, and he stripped the white bedsheet from the bunk inside the cell – stepping over Officer Burns in order to reach it – and he brought that with him too. At exactly two a.m., we stepped out of the jail and headed north. There were no choppers to be seen or drones to be heard. A large mass of clouds had ridden in on the jet stream and were making an already dark night even darker. The first fifty yards or so of our walk were still slick with mayflies, but the footing got better as we neared the tower. We were only forced to stop once when we eventually heard a drone approach, so the entire walk took less than five minutes. Feeling exposed but with no way to reduce our heat signature while on the ladder, we climbed as fast as we could to the platform that ringed the water tank like an Elizabethan collar. Once we'd arrived, a drone occasionally zipped past the tower, but they were always at a lower altitude than our own and with their cameras pointed down.

We settled in on the north side of the tank, and I felt a level of relative safety. Even in the darkness, I could see that the Chief looked like Hell, and he was going to get a lot worse fast. Other than a light breeze that was causing a few cables from the cell tower to snap against the water tank, it was absolutely soundless up there. The Chief disappeared around to the opposite side of the tank with the bed sheet and spray paint. I deduced it had something to do with Plan C, but I knew better than bothering to ask him. I was lying on my back, once again looking to the stars, when I heard a low murmur of voices rising from beneath us. I rolled over onto my stomach and looked past the edge of the grating towards the ball field, which lay just beyond a line of trees to the east. A mix of still uninfected folks had been herded there.

"Chief," I called, and he came quickly. I'm sure he sensed the concern in my voice.

Taking turns with the scope, we watched them – I'd guess maybe fifty or sixty at most. Some sat slump-shouldered on the ground, resigned to what they'd accepted as their fate. A few of them milled about the park. Others lay flat on the grass, basketball court, or on the bleachers. There were no soldiers, nothing keeping them contained except the broken-down snow fence, the drones keeping watch overhead, their own resignation to defeat, and the knowledge that, like the song says, there was "nowhere to run to and nowhere to hide," even if they'd wanted to. The Chief preferred not to look and rolled over onto his back and closed his eyes. His cough had become more regular, and he had to fight hard to stifle it.

"Can I?" I asked and nodded toward the scope nestled in his hands, which rested in a prayer position on his chest.

Scoping the space below, I saw the King deposed and holding depleted court on a bench in the third base side dugout. I saw old man Sutherland, who may or may not have tried to smother his own wife, just beginning the zombie walk. I saw Mrs. Beck, who abandoned her husband and child, sitting utterly alone on a swing in the playground. I saw many of Patmos's sheep scattered throughout the outfield grass grazing shepherd-less.

I raised the scope toward the south and looked to the mainland. Though mostly-darkened, the Marblehead Peninsula seemed no more than an arm's reach away. It was absurd to think that life out there continued as before and that things would soon return to normal, even though inside the evacuation zone nothing was normal, and life was ending all around me. I thought, "How could so much have changed in such little time?"

"Lay your blanket beneath you just in case, and get some rest," the Chief said, sensing my restlessness.

I did as I was told. "What about Plan C, Chief?" I asked.

"In the morning, son. In the morning," he said.

Chapter Five

Day 8, Friday, May 31, 201_

I awoke to the "Beep! Beep! Beep!" of an alarm sounding from a wristwatch placed next to my ear. In a panic, I pressed all of the buttons around the watch's face until the damn thing stopped its beeping. "Chief? Is this your watch? Chief?" It was still dark. I sat up and looked around, but the Chief was nowhere to be found. I crawled around the entire circumference of the platform, but still, I couldn't find the Chief.

I returned to where I'd left the watch. It read 5:58 a.m. A few feet away, I noticed the night vision scope. It seemed purposefully placed. I scooped it up and scooched over to the ledge of the platform, where I peered through the eyepiece and directed the scope towards the ball field. Initially, all seemed still, but soon a figure's upright stance and waving arms drew my attention. I centered the figure inside the round lens of the scope and adjusted the settings to zoom in on the Chief. Sometime in the night, he had climbed down and joined those corralled in the park. I set the scope down and reached around underneath the poncho and to the back of the waistline in my jeans. The Chief's gun was gone. When I looked back down, the Chief was holding it up in his left, non-shooting hand and smiling. He pointed up towards the opposite, south-facing side, of the water tank.

I literally crawled around and there it was: Plan C. Printed in large, bright orange letters and duct taped to the side of the water tank facing the mainland was the white bedsheet. It read "WE'RE ALIVE!"

I smiled and returned my gaze to the park and the Chief below.

With the fingers of his right hand, the Chief deliberately formed letters like a gangbanger flashing gang signs and spelled: U L – I – V – E. He then switched the gun from his left to his right hand.

"No, Chief!" I whispered.

I stood up and took off my poncho, hoping that my white t-shirt would make me more visible to him in the half-light of morning. I waved my arm above my head from side to side as a sign of goodbye, then I hurriedly lifted the scope to my eye once more.

The Chief gave me a military salute then walked out of the lens's view.

I didn't try to follow him with the scope.

Knowing they'd be converging on the water tower once they discovered the Chief's message in the daylight, I hurried down the ladder. It struck me that the Chief's sign was firstly, intended as a distraction to allow me to scurry unnoticed back to the cavern while they busied themselves with removing the bedsheet from the water tower, and secondly, it was a longshot, but maybe someone, somewhere, somehow had a camera pointed at the island from the mainland, and they would have time to get a view of the Chief's sign before it was taken down. If so, Dr. Bentham and I would only have to survive in the cavern long enough for questions to be asked, investigations to begin, and for search parties to commence. As for those corralled in the park, the sign would most likely expedite their ends. I'm not sure if the Chief's plan fulfilled Dr. Bentham's belief in the greatest good for the greatest number, but it was definitely the greatest good for Danny Foe.

Halfway down the ladder, I heard a single gunshot, and I knew the Chief was dead. I guess in some small way, he had maintained what little control he had over the situation and exercised one last freedom of choice.

For just a minute, to rest and scout out my escape course, I squatted beneath the water tower. Other than a breeze blowing through and rustling the leaves of nearby trees, there were no sounds and nothing moved. I felt like Shelley's last man. A profound sense of aloneness washed over me like I hadn't felt since the deaths of my parents. Perhaps, on second thought, I was more like Adam, the first man, separated from his father and alone in the Garden prior to Eve's creation. I imagined all of the manmade structures removed and thought how idyllic that island must have once been when the native peoples had lived on island. I wondered what life must have been like in that state closer to nature. Stripped of all of our social constructions, institutions, and leisure time distractions, what is man? Is he good, like I think Captain Russo believed? Is he evil, like Patmos insisted? Or, was he neither? Are such labels like good and evil simplistic, romantic notions that have allowed us to deny that we are actually no further evolved socially than the dispassionate bird flu virus that had systematically and single-mindedly decimated its island hosts and, in so doing, was on the verge of its own extinction? I didn't know the answer then, and I still don't today.

My return to my grandfather's property was a simple repeat of the route and strategy employed on the trip downtown: a mad dash up Division Street, followed by the methodical movement, tree to tree, down Bookerman. On the way, I passed the dead bodies of the former walkers, which the Chief and I had encountered the previous day, still lying where they'd been executed. At the time, the lack of the Army's concern for the unsanitary nature of leaving corpses to rot all over the island gnawed at me in some quiet way but not enough for me to conjecture as to the reason for their careless disregard for fundamental decency – a reason that was soon to be made clear.

What did surprise me was that I found Dr. Bentham sitting exposed on the back steps to the house with her head buried in her hands and totally visible from above.

"Dr. Bentham! What are you doing?!"

"I've been waiting for you," she said. "Where's Chief Sarter?"

Instead of giving voice to it, I looked down at the top of my shoes and communicated his death just as effectively.

"The flu?" She asked.

I nodded "yes" and didn't bother to tell her the rest. "Why are you sitting out in the open? They'll spot you and find the cavern."

"Look up, Danny. Listen and think," she said and paused. "Now tell me, when was the last time you saw a chopper or drone?"

The thought sparked a realization that I hadn't heard or seen a single one since I'd risen. Their surveillance had become so constant that I had simply assumed their presence.

"I guess a couple of hours," I finally answered.

"That's correct. Ever since I called them off."

"Called them? What're you talking about?"

Dr. Bentham dropped her hands from her head, looked dejectedly towards me, then reached across to the step on which she sat. She retrieved then held up what looked like an early model cell phone with a stubby antennae extended from the top.

"There hasn't been cell service for days," I said.

"It's a satellite phone, Danny."

The full realization of her betrayal slowly dawned on me. "I don't get it. Why would you call them?" I asked, and my words inspired a lightning bolt of epiphany. "Wait," I said. "You're the one who warned them. You're the reason they knew about Mr. Hobbs and the others – Jalil –running the blockade."

Dr. Bentham's lack of denial was as good as a confession.

"Do you realize how many people were killed because of you?" I asked as a week's worth of anger and frustration and suffering and degradation all boiled to the surface. "I do because I watched them get shot out of the water."

"Danny, I understand you're angry and you're hurt and feel betrayed, but those people were going to die anyway. It would have been a lot easier had they just stayed and let the virus run its course. Maybe we could have convinced them to allow the uninfected to live, but once Hobbs tried to escape, it left them no choice but to expedite the process."

"How could you?" I asked.

"How could I not? It was my job to monitor events and to report to my superiors."

"But, when? When did you make these calls?" I asked, still trying to make sense of her revelation.

"Usually, when I was left alone at the camp. I was a plant from the very beginning. I volunteered for the job. If I hadn't, somebody else would have. What I said at the meeting I believed with all my heart and it still holds true. If the death of every person on this island, including my own, is the price for stopping the spread of the bird flu virus into the general population, it achieves the greatest good for the greatest number of people. Every one of these people who have died on this island is a hero. They're all martyrs to the cause of extending the survival of human society into future. There are a lot of worse reasons for which people die every day."

"But no one will ever know that. Where's the justice in that?" As I spoke them, I recognized the naivety of my words.

"Only children and fools expect justice, Danny. And you're neither of those."

While I stood dumbstruck and tried to absorb all that Dr. Bentham had shared, a sort of curtain call played inside of my head. First, the Gulliver's Girls, the Booze Cruisers, the Patmosians, even the chopper pilots and the special ops guys took the stage, linked hands, and took a shared bow. They were followed by the bit players: Officer Dooley, Andy, Geo, Mr. Hobbs, Mrs. Barnes, the Sanderson brothers, and the McKillips. Then the actors in minor roles joined the cast on the stage in my mind: Officer Burns, the King, Captain Russo, Daphne. Finally, the stars of the show, Jalil, Patmos, and the Chief appeared and jogged upstage, bowing, waving, and blowing kisses, while Dr. Bentham and I remained the only two seated in the audience, clapping.

"Danny?" Dr. Bentham said.

"What happens next?" I asked, snapped out of my fantasy.

"I wait."

"For what? Some kind of pick up?"

"No, Danny. My evacuation is not part of the plan. The fact that I've survived this long without infection has been a miracle in itself, which I'm going to take as an endorsement from God or Nature or Fate or whatever, that I did the right thing. The call I just made initiated the end game."

"What exactly is that?"

"The complete annihilation of life on this island."

"What about the Bass Islands? Were they infected?"

"Some birds but no people. The virus never made it there. Those islands have been evacuated. The people from them will never see their homes and businesses again. The islands will be a forbidden zone for the next fifty years."

"What's next here?" I asked.

"Once I dialed the number, three aircraft scrambled from Wright-Patterson Air Force Base in Dayton. An attack aircraft should be arriving soon over West Sister, where it will drop a Neutron Bomb, which will kill any remaining bird life and hopefully any of the remaining virus. It releases a controlled amount of radiation over a relatively small area. The other two planes are C-130 Hercules, each carrying a Massive Ordnance Air Blast bomb – known as the MOAB or as the 'Mother of All Bombs.' They will drop their payloads here. The MOAB is the most powerful non-nuclear bomb we have. Its blast emits a shock wave, about six-feet off of the ground that stretches a mile in each direction. It will incinerate anything and everything in its path, again including any of the remaining virus."

I was speechless.

"Danny, listen. I shouldn't tell you this, but I made that call fewer than five minutes ago. Those C-130's are huge planes; their estimated flight time to the islands is one hour. That gives you fifty-five minutes. Your immunity wasn't part of the plan. Like I told you, you're a fluke. The risk of your spreading the infection is almost nil. I want you to try."

"Try what?"

"To escape. To live. Please."

"What about the blockade?"

"The minute I made the call, the blockade was withdrawn for the safety of the ships. They should all be heading to port by now. Fifty-five minutes is not much time, but it's a chance. You know this island and you know boats. I suggest you get your ass in one as fast as you can and hightail it east. But, Danny, you have to promise me that everything that you saw and did here will remain a secret. Nothing good can come from sharing the truth of what happened here. You must understand that, and you must keep it to yourself."

I didn't respond; instead, I ran to the uncovered cavern and descended in record time. I found my backpack and began to fill it with the temporary badge given me by the Chief, with the family photo, and with Daphne's book selections. Two days earlier, when we abandoned the jail, I'd had no valuables to pack. Now I could barely zip my bag.

The delay in gathering my things only took a short time, but those were precious minutes. When I reached the surface, Dr. Bentham had already pulled Stan McKillips' truck from out of the woods. She stood by the opened driver's side door and chastised me like my sister-in-law did on mornings on which I was slow to drag myself from bed to catch the school bus.

She hugged me, then stepped out of the way. "Now, go!" She said.

Chapter Six

I headed immediately towards West Bay Marina. In just a couple of minutes and with my tennis shoes, cargo shorts, and backpack stored in the watertight front storage compartment of a wave runner, I stripped down to my boxers, slipped on a life vest, and headed out onto the water.

It was a rare day, one in which the Lake lay down like glass; however, the relatively cool water of late spring contrasted sharply with the heat and humidity of the air to give rise to a thick haze. The conditions were conducive to high speeds but dangerously lacking in visibility. I would be traveling more-or-less blindly, like a jet flying through a cloud bank. Thankfully, due to the quarantine and blockade, the Lake was empty of fishing or pleasure boats, other wave runners, ferries, or freighters. The very good news was that my getaway would be obscured to the view of others, The very bad news was I could be running head on into any blockade vessel that may have lingered or been delayed in its withdrawal, and I had no way of knowing it.

I'd spent my entire life on Lake Erie. I knew that haze can form in minutes and disappear just as quickly. Should it lift, the chances were good that I would be spotted from sea or air. Even if the haze persisted, it was a real probability that I'd be picked up by the monitoring systems on the surveillance aircraft, which would surely be arriving to observe the bombing operations; however, that was the chance I had to take.

Having fished near the reefs off of Middle Island, I knew that the less than one square mile of island was a little more than six miles away and due north of Kelleys just beyond the border in Canadian waters, so instead of heading north then east around Kelleys and into the open waters of the Lake as Dr. Bentham advised, I checked the odometer on the ski, stood up, bent my knees so that my legs would act as shock absorbers, and rode full throttle at speeds approaching sixty miles per hour over calm waters and on a beeline for Middle Island.

In its history, Middle Island had been a layover for slaves headed into Canada on the Underground Railroad and later was home to a resort hotel, which served as a way station for the rum runners who hopped across the American islands during Prohibition. Later, however, Middle Island had been purchased by the Canadian government and established as a nature preserve, much like West Sister, and as one of the only completely uninhabited islands of any substantial size in all of Lake Erie.

The haze cooperated and refused to clear. When six miles had clicked off of my odometer, I released the accelerator and idled forward. Soon after, the tree line of Middle Island appeared. As I neared the shore, I saw the bodies of thousands of birds bobbing in the water around me. I was welcomed ashore by an overwhelming silence. I beached the ski on a sand and gravel beach at the base of a spit on the island's west end. With my backpack, I scrambled into the nearby trees. Within minutes, I felt the ground vibrate and knew that the bomb had been set off on West Sister, ground zero for the bird flu and now, ironically, America's first known deployment of nuclear weapons for anything other than testing purposes. The typical westerly winds were absent and the air still, so I had no rational concerns regarding fallout, but the next half hour was torture as I watched and listened for the arrival of the C-130's. The stench of rotting birds all around me and the thought of those corralled at the ball field and Dr. Bentham, alone on Kelleys and waiting her annihilation, left me nauseated.

It may have been because of the high altitude at which the planes flew and from which the GPS-guided bombs were dropped combined with the haze rising from the surface of the water, but I never heard or saw the C-130's. Rather, all of a sudden, I saw a blurred flash to the south followed by the immediate rise and melding together of two mushroom-shaped clouds. I felt the Earth shake as on the previous explosion, and within minutes, I felt the warm, dying breath of the blast wash against my skin.

I should have felt something more. Sadness? Regret? Nostalgia? Thankfulness?

I didn't.

Giving all possible reconnaissance planes time to do their flyovers and post operation video recordings and all of the blockade ships plenty of more time to return to port, I sat under a copse of blue ash trees for hours with insects crawling and buzzing around me and an occasional sighting of a black water snake for company.

Flying in V-formation, a group of thirteen mallards, returning from their southern migration, crossed the finish line into home Canadian air space. I stood and screamed, "Fuck you!" But, indifferent to my childish rage, they continued on their journey.

At dusk, I set back out onto the Lake. Heading toward land inside of the evacuation zone was an impossibility. Those areas were bound to be heavily patrolled by the National Guard or federal troops. My only choice was to try to make it beyond the evacuation zone, so I headed into the waters east of Kelleys. I had traveled no more than a quarter-mile off shore when I ran smack into a swarm of mayflies rising from their watery beds. Once more I was forced to spit them out of my mouth and pluck them from my hair and off my body.

For better and worse, the haze had been burned off and blown away. Better, because I could see where I was headed and there were no ships in sight. Unquestionably for the worse, because after a day of the windless doldrums, a northeasterly breeze was slowly coming around and producing one to two foot rollers. At the least, it guaranteed a wet and bumpy ride. At the worst, the rising waves were a harbinger of a Nor'easter, a typically three-day blow with winds that howled down the St. Laurence Seaway and kicked up the deep waters off the coasts of Buffalo, NY, Erie, PA, and Cleveland and bullied them into the much shallower waters of the Western Basin. This phenomenon created ocean-like waves as the water sloshed back-and-forth like water in a bowl being tipped to one side then the other, and I was about to insert myself into the middle of this sloshing.

I considered going back, but to what? And how far back? To Middle Island? If this was a nor'easter, after three days on that no man's land, I'd be badly undernourished and severely dehydrated or sick from drinking contaminated water, or I'd be hypothermic from being overexposed and underdressed in cool temperatures and colder rains. As a result, when the weather cleared, I'd most likely be too weak to operate the wave runner. To Kelleys? It didn't exist anymore. To my brother's house in Port Clinton? He had been evacuated to who knows where? Besides, my welcome had already been worn out. I had to go forward, so I unzipped my life vest, slipped it off, and set it afloat on the water. There was no "back" to return to.

As a result of my running wide open from Kelleys to Middle Island, the wave runner was under three-fourths of a tank of gas. My plan was to stay as far away from shore as possible in American waters, then once beyond the thirty-mile evacuation zone, I would try to put in. From there, I had no clue what I would do. I was certain that all of my identifying information: driver's license, social security number, birth records, etc. would have been entered into local, state, and federal databases as a precaution. I would be flagged instantly if I ever used them or my real name, but that was for a future hour's worry. My most pressing concern was that the evacuation perimeter would be at the outer limits of the remaining fuel, especially in heavy seas, and I was still susceptible to being intercepted by Coast Guard patrols. I consoled myself with the knowledge that at least I had a plan, not a good plan, but a plan nonetheless. The Chief would have been proud.

I skirted past the northeastern peninsular arm of Kelleys and tried not to look at the destruction done by the massive, fuel-saturated air blasts that had leveled much of its once pristine woods, but I failed. I couldn't see a single manmade structure, including the water tower on which I'd spent the previous evening. It was impossible to believe that anything was left alive – not even the smallest and most resilient of viruses. If any had survived, there were certainly no living hosts – human, animal, or avian, which they could invade and colonize. Other than the minor glitch that I was alive and leaving the island with knowledge of the truth of the events that had taken place over the past eight days, I had to concede that their plan had fallen just short of being a complete success.

To preserve fuel, I tried to run at a slow and constant speed, but battling the wind and what had become white-capped four to six footers, made any constancy nearly impossible. Adding to my misery, thunderstorms had accompanied the northeast winds. By late afternoon, lightning flashed all around me. I was wet, cold, tired, and more scared than I had ever been. Every ounce of energy, strength, and focus was required just to stay on the wave runner. I actually found myself envying the Chief and the others. At least their suffering was over and their fears behind them.

In the darkness beneath low-ceilinged clouds, I lost all sense of time. With no visible landmarks, I lost all sense of place as well. During the night, the wave runner ran out of gas, and I fell to the mercy of the waves that continued to grow higher and to batter the wave runner and me on it. I had no idea in which direction I was being pushed or if I'd been merely bobbing up and down in one spot. I felt like a sock in a washing machine. Three times, a wave washed me off of the wave runner. On each occasion, I managed to climb back on board, but the hours of being buffeted by the waves and white-knuckling the handlebars had sapped most of my strength.

Chapter Seven

Day 9, Saturday, June 1, 201_

By morning, which was only discernible by the black night's blurring into gray, I was shivering uncontrollably, a sure sign of a drop in my body's core temperature and of the onset of hypothermia. I desired sleep with the same sense of urgency that I wanted to walk when the Blues was at its peak. I wished for a set of the Chief's handcuffs to keep me on the wave runner so that I could sleep without falling overboard. As it was, to fall asleep was to drown.

My thoughts grew addled, and on several occasions I found myself talking out loud in words increasingly difficult to form to people who weren't there. I was fifteen minutes deep into a conversation with the Masur twins when all of a sudden a massive beam of light illuminated me from behind. I remembered the spotlights from the blockade vessels that lit up the blockade runners before gunning them down. With a surprising degree of indifference, I waited for the bullets to shred my flesh; however, no guns were fired. I turned my head around and read A. Schopenhauer in white letters on the port bow of a massive coal freighter. I had drifted directly into one of the most heavily traveled shipping channels in the Great Lakes. I would learn later that the A. Schopenhauer had been en route from a power station in Nanticoke, Ontario, to the coal docks inside the Sandusky Bay, when the thirty-mile wide evacuation zone had been established. It remained idled just outside the perimeter as it waited for amended instructions.

Deckhands draped a cargo net over the side, but it took a few minutes for me to register that the ship, the spotlight, the voices, and the whistles were not figments of my imagination and that the net was intended for my rescue and not my capture.

My transfer from wave runner to the cargo net was tricky, especially in my exhausted condition. I had no way to maneuver the wave runner, and the positioning of the freighter was extremely limited by its massive size, All she could do was to remain as solidly in place as possible and let the wave runner drift towards her.

After retrieving my backpack from the storage bin and strapping it tightly to my torso, I carefully repositioned myself on the wave runner so that my back was turned to the handlebars and I was poised to jump. The draft of the freighter drew the wave runner towards its hull. The transfer required me literally to leap into the cargo netting and to enmesh my arms and legs so as to be capable of being pulled on board. As the wave runner drew near to the side, several dangers grew increasingly obvious. One, a badly-timed leap could leave me grabbing for air should the wave runner dip into the trough of a wave as the tanker rode the crest. Two, should the wave runner draw too close to the tanker before I was ready and/or able to jump, the wave runner could be sucked beneath the steel hull and crushed beneath her with me on it. Three, in my weakened state, I could simply fail to latch securely onto the cargo net, slip into the water, and be lost in the waves. I'm sure there were other dangers posed by nature, physics, and the limitations of my condition, but I didn't have time to contemplate all of them.

Once, twice, three times, I wasted opportunities to jump as the freighter and the wave runner passed one another like elevator cars headed in opposite directions inside a fourteen story building. Due to my dithering, I reached a point at which I'd drawn so close to the ship that the upper reaches of the bowed hull were actually directly over my head, and I had to lean back to see the faces of the deckhands leaning over the rail and looking down on me. I was down to my last chance before being sucked beneath the freighter. I needed to time my leap so that I could grab hold of the netting as the imagined elevator cars intersected on the seventh floor.

I jumped so that I was airborne when the cargo netting was still above my head. I managed to entangle one arm at a position of approximately three-fourths of the net's length. I was spun around immediately and hard into the hull. If not for the backpack cushioning the impact, I doubt if I would have managed to maintain my hold. Clinging with the one arm, I quickly enmeshed the other and then both feet so that I hung in cruciform position from the cargo net against the side of the freighter. From that awkward vantage point, I watched and heard the wave runner being crushed beneath the freighter. In the next instant, I was rapidly rising as the deckhands heaved and hoed until I was pulled head first and backwards over the rail.

"Do you know how lucky you are, son?" A thin-lipped, middle-aged man with salt-and-pepper stubble underlining a face weathered and burnt to the consistency of rawhide asked as he sat on a stool pulled up next to where I lay in the crews' quarters.

I rolled over and vomited into a steel bucket that had been placed next to the bunk inside the crews' quarters.

I was tired of waking up to horrible news and new adventures. "Just once again," I thought, "I'd like to wake up to a familiar voice and in my own bed to face a day of boring and predictable normalcy." What I said, however, was "Do you know how lucky you are?"

He blinked a few times and rubbed his beard. I think he was confused by my seeming lack of utter and profuse gratitude, but I could tell he was not insulted. In fact, I felt as if he were relieved, as if he were glad to avoid having to listen to me gush.

"Are you the captain," I asked somewhat confused. Unlike the ferry captains that I'd seen and who had always worn white captain's shirts with epaulets, this guy was dressed like a construction worker in jeans, a flannel shirt, and steel-toed boots.

"I am," he said. "Disappointed?"

I shook my head, "No."

"I'll be short," he said. "The next move is yours. Is there anyone you want to call?"

I shook my head, "No."

"Does anyone know you're out here?"

I shook my head, "No."

"Do you suppose that there is anyone out looking for ya?"

I shook my head, "No," again.

"I can call the Coast Guard, and they can come and pull you off the deck."

I shook my head emphatically.

"Didn't think so. Here's the deal. If you'd like, you're welcome to stay on board through this trip – if and when we finish her – but you'll have to work to earn your bunk and board. No pay. I'm guessing you're not wanting to surrender a name or fill out any tax forms anyway."

I nodded, "Yes."

"We're not a talkative crew. Won't ask any questions and don't much care to answer any. It's nothing personal; it's just the way it is. If we liked company, we wouldn't be out here in the first place." With that, he turned and walked towards the hatch. "You know what you are, son?"

"Yes, sir, I do. I am a fluke."

"Welcome aboard."

Epilogue

Through some connections of Captain Heiler of the A. Schopenhauer, I obtained a phony passport, and a social security number. I was provided a new identity, probably some dead guy's, but except for a few official purposes, I never used the name, passport, or social security number in all of my years on the water. Instead, everyone I ever sailed with just called me Fluke.

Daphne, Dr. Bentham, Chief Sarter – they've all been dead now for over eighty years, while I've been bouncing from one Great Lake port to another. It hardly seems fair. I can hardly believe it has been that long. I'd be lying if I said I thought about them much during the time I was on the Lakes. Maybe, at first, I did, but I soon realized it wasn't doing me or them or anybody else any good. There was no one with whom I could sit and reminisce or anyone to whom I could tell my story. What good are unshared memories? Are they even real or no better than half-remembered dreams?

On runs into and out of the Sandusky coal docks, where the channel slides past the southeast coast of Kelleys, I'd always be drawn to the rail from where I'd watch her as we'd pass, and I'd recollect conversations and events from that week all those years ago, but that was pretty much it.

I never kept up with the news, and I've completely ignored books that claim to purport history or that wear the false cloak of nonfiction. They are all manipulated – twisted or completely fabricated from thin air – in order to serve the narrative that serves the purposes of those who write and champion them. If you want the truth of history, you'll have to reach higher, dig deeper, and search farther, sometimes, even to the very last man.

That's the story of Island No. 6. Ignore it if you want. Believe it if you can.

Afterword

"Without question, another people/bird pandemic will surface again. If our country's preparations work, we'll have moved science forward in much-needed ways. 'First, we'll have cell-based technology that will allow us the capacity to produce vaccines in sufficient sized and within the constraints of time," said HHS secretary Michael Leavitt. 'Second, we will have made substantial progress in expanding our annual flu capacity. Third, we will have better state and local preparedness for any medical emergency. Fourth, we'll have an international network of diseases surveillance that will serve this country and others. And last, we'll have peace of mind knowing we're ready.'

Let's hope that we will indeed be ready . . ."

From *The Bird Flu Pandemic* by
Jeffrey Greene with Karen Moline

.

Made in the USA
Monee, IL
11 June 2020